S0-ADQ-267

"WHAT AM I GOING TO DO, JOHNNY?"

"Ashley Millard's wedding is ruined. I'm ruined. Carla's ruined. She'll kill me."

He tried to soothe me. "It's not your fault, Brenda. Carla will understand."

"It is my fault. I never should have given the hats to the Lady in Pink. I packed them all up and watched her walk out the door. I should have knocked the gun out of her hand. It was just a little gun. Wait till Carla hears my news."

I tried to call Carla. A man answered. I didn't recognize his voice. "Who are you?" I asked.

"Crime Scene Unit, ma'am. Are you a friend of the victim?"

When a crime scene unit guy said "victim" I knew he wasn't talking misdemeanor. I looked at Johnny and burst into tears.

Other Brenda Midnight Mysteries by
Barbara Jaye Wilson
Coming Soon from Avon Books

ACCESSORY TO MURDER

Avon Books are available at special quantity discounts for bulk purchases for sales promotions, premiums, fund raising or educational use. Special books, or book excerpts, can also be created to fit specific needs.

For details write or telephone the office of the Director of Special Markets, Avon Books, Dept. FP, 1350 Avenue of the Americas, New York, New York 10019, 1-800-238-0658.

DEATH BRIMS OVER

BARBARA JAYE WILSON

AVON BOOKS ◆ NEW YORK

This is a work of fiction. Names, characters, places, and incidents either are the product of the author's imagination or are used fictitiously. Any resemblance to actual events, locales, organizations, or persons, living or dead, is entirely coincidental and beyond the intent of either the author or the publisher.

AVON BOOKS
A division of
The Hearst Corporation
1350 Avenue of the Americas
New York, New York 10019

Copyright © 1997 by Barbara Jaye Wilson
Published by arrangement with the author
Visit our website at **http://AvonBooks.com**
Library of Congress Catalog Card Number: 96-97086
ISBN: 0-380-78820-9

All rights reserved, which includes the right to reproduce this book or portions thereof in any form whatsoever except as provided by the U.S. Copyright Law. For information address Curtis Brown, Ltd., Ten Astor Place, New York, New York 10003.

First Avon Books Printing: April 1997

AVON TRADEMARK REG. U.S. PAT. OFF. AND IN OTHER COUNTRIES, MARCA REGISTRADA, HECHO EN U.S.A.

Printed in the U.S.A.

RA   10 9 8 7 6 5 4 3 2

If you purchased this book without a cover, you should be aware that this book is stolen property. It was reported as ''unsold and destroyed'' to the publisher, and neither the author nor the publisher has received any payment for this ''stripped book.''

Dedicated to my mother,
Bertha Florence Hobbs Wilson

ACKNOWLEDGMENTS

For inspiration, information, advice, and encouragement—thanks and a tip of my hat to Bob Zimmerman, Bob Moore, Steven Martin Cohen, Peter Stathatos, Barbara Wheeler, Jay B. Wilson Jr., Ann Albrizio, Casey Bush, Laura Blake, Lyssa Keusch, Gene Daly, and X-Dot Potato.

If you know how New York's streets are laid out, you'd think West Fourth Street would run parallel to the other numbered streets. But in Greenwich Village nothing is ever quite as it should be; laws of physics and cartography get broken and West Fourth Street deviates so far off the grid pattern that in places it flips around and intersects the other numbered streets. Attracted by the photogenic century-old town houses and charming sidewalk cafés, location scouts have turned it into one of the most filmed streets in the city. Every couple of weeks the cops block off the street to traffic, production crews overrun the neighborhood, and equipment trucks and location trailers hog the few parking places. Tourists and gawkers jam up the sidewalks.

This is bad for business. At least my business. My customers are hardly the kind to elbow their way through a mob to get to my little hat shop, Midnight Millinery. It's located in the ground floor storefront of a three-story red-brick building on West Fourth Street between Bank and West Twelfth Streets.

I'm Brenda Midnight and no, the shop was not named after me; I'm named after it. When I first rented the place five years ago, all that remained of the former tenant, a deli fronting a numbers-running operation, was a sign painted on the window in dramatic swash letters outlined with real gold leaf: *Open 'til Midnight*. Due to a recent divorce, I found myself waffling between last names. Brenda Midnight sounded good to me so I took a razor blade to the words "Open 'til." My divorce lawyer handled the official name change stuff.

After a quick paint job—white with the slightest touch of pink—to cover up decades of deli dirt, I moved in my collection of wooden hat blocks, a professional steam iron, and two old but reliable sewing machines. The little money left over after paying deposit and exorbitant rent flew right out of my pocket when I spotted an antique vanity with a large oval beveled mirror at the flea market down on Canal Street and couldn't resist. I knew the vanity would add a touch of class to Midnight Millinery. Seated at it, my customers could try on hats in style. The vanity pretty much left me broke. To save money I moved into the store, promising myself I'd get a real apartment just as soon as I got on my feet. That was five years ago and I'm still sleeping underneath my hat-blocking table. I figure I can only occupy so much space at one time anyway.

This summer, rather than moving into an apartment, I invested in a brand-new 17,000 BTU energy-saving air conditioner. It was powerful enough to keep the shop pleasant during the smelly, sweltering New York summer even when I used hot steam to make my fall line of hats. Air conditioner or not, here it was almost the end of August and I was way behind on my fall line. I'd never get the shop filled with hats by the beginning of September. It was all Carla's fault. She'd talked me into doing the hats for Ashley Millard's big splashy wedding.

Carla Haley and I met years ago in a How to Run Your Own Business seminar at FIT. Carla was studying dress design and I was studying millinery. We were both recent transplants to New York with similar dreams of making it big. That was about all we had in common. Aesthetically, we clashed. She laughed at my gravity-defying hats, calling them too plain, too severe. I claimed her frilly, fussy wedding dresses were all surface decoration with no guts. Even so, we became great friends and stayed great friends by promising never ever to work together, even though her apartment, which doubled as her studio, was around the corner and across the street from Midnight Millinery.

That all changed when Carla somehow landed the Ashley Millard wedding job. She had pleaded with me. "Please take the gig, Brenda. I can't trust anyone else to get the millinery part right." She invited me over and fed me a warm slice of gooey homemade pecan pie drenched with whipped cream to butter me up.

"No, no, no, a thousand times no," I'd said.

I wanted nothing to do with an extravagant affair like the Ashley Millard wedding. It didn't matter that it would be covered in the society pages; I didn't care about the money, the power, or the reception at the Plaza. I knew it would be one big headache.

"Please, Brenda," Carla had said, slicing off another hunk of pie, "it really means a lot to me." Then she mentioned how much the Millards were willing to pay, and I took the job. I had no choice. The bridal veil alone would pay rent and Con Edison for two months. Besides the veil, the job included headpieces for the entire bridal party of seven bridesmaids, maid of honor, flower girl, mother of the bride, and mother of the groom, and little hatlettes for the female catering staff. If that wasn't enough, several ladies who'd been invited to the wedding had come in wanting custom hats.

That's why I found myself surrounded by soft pastel-colored fabrics instead of deep-toned, full-bodied, fuzzy fall textiles. The weird thing was, as I worked with the frothy stuff I started thinking that some of it was maybe sort of okay, especially the half yard or so of beaded ivory lace Carla had given me to cover the veil's headpiece. It matched the bodice of the bridal gown. Whoever designed this lace exercised good taste and restraint in placing the beads, scattering only a few about. I liked the effect. I got the idea to design a holiday line based on the lace, dyed a rich bright red. It would be Midnight Millinery's first dressy line. I called Carla to ask where the lace came from and how much it cost. She didn't answer, so I left a message on her answering machine and went back to hand hemming the edge of the veil—a seemingly endless task.

As I tied off the final hem thread, the bells on the door jangled and in marched a mid-fortyish henna-haired woman. Gigantic round sunglasses camouflaged the top half of her face. Her hot pink lipsticked lips perfectly matched her out-of-date too short too tight hot pink suit, which perfectly matched her out-of-date too high hot pink spike heels. She looked like trouble, the kind of customer who'd blame me if a hat didn't make her every bit as beautiful as she thought she was.

She approached me, heels clicking on the hardwood floor.

"Hello," I said, wishing she'd go away.

Without so much as a hello back, she said, "You're doing the Ashley Millard wedding." The way she snapped, it sounded more like an accusation than an inquiry. She drummed ridiculously long hot pink polished fingernails on the countertop.

I figured this Lady in Pink must be another one of Ashley's mother's friends who wanted something special whipped up at the last minute to wear to the wedding. With only forty-eight hours to go, she was out of luck. I couldn't work miracles. I hoped she'd be satisfied with a stock item.

"I'm afraid it's too late for a special order," I said, "but I'll be happy to show you some perfectly lovely . . ." I exaggerated the midwestern drawl I'd left behind years before as a counterpoint to her brisk manner of speech.

"A special order wasn't what I had in mind." She reached into her hot pink patent leather handbag, pulled out a gun, and aimed it straight at me. "Pack up all the hats for the Ashley Millard wedding."

Lightning fast my entire universe closed down until there was nothing in it but me, the Lady in Pink, her gun, and fear—lots of fear, heaps and gobs of fear, incapacitating fear. I heard the beat of my heart, felt the blood surge through my veins.

Like everyone who runs a small retail store anywhere in New York City—even in a low-crime area like the West Village—I had, tucked into the back of my brain, a half-formed plan of what to do in a stickup. My plan was simple: Quickly hand over the cash, duck under the counter, and hope the perpetrator left peacefully. Remembering the plan was one thing; implementing it, quite another. All I could think of was the deadline. I said something stupid. "But, the wedding's only . . ."

She took four steps toward me. "I want those hats."

As guns go, hers was rather small. But then I'm a small person, size four, so it didn't take me long to come around to her way of thinking. Hands shaking, I put all the hats for Ashley Millard's wedding into two shiny black hatboxes. Then I watched helplessly as the Lady in Pink walked out the door with my profits and reputation.

2

I did what I always did when I didn't know what to do. I called my ex-boyfriend, Johnny Verlane. He may not have been much as a boyfriend, but he made a great ex. Many times he'd come through to help me out of one jam or another.

We'd tried to live together a couple of years ago but fought like cats and dogs about how the apartment should look. Since it was his place, he usually won. Our final battle raged on for three days over an orange-and-yellow shag rug. He wanted it, I didn't, and both of us were stubborn. I'd already given in on the issue of the see-through plastic shower curtain and wasn't about to budge on the rug. At the end of the three days, I admitted defeat and moved my few belongings back to Midnight Millinery.

From the looks of Johnny you'd never guess he had an ugly rug like that plopped down in the middle of his living room. Physically, he was the essence of cool. A craggy face kept him just the other side of handsome. Close to six feet tall and thin, his thick dark hair fell forward over his brow, emphasizing high cheekbones and smoky gray eyes.

Most of the time Johnny was an unemployed actor. His last role was the lead in the *Tod Trueman, Urban Detective* cop show. It never made it beyond the pilot. Still, he said it'd been a worthwhile experience. His agent, Lemmy Crenshaw, called in a few favors and Johnny got to spend a week in a squad car with a couple of real cops. They taught him how to walk like a cop, talk like a cop, and think like a cop, all potentially useful skills.

Johnny picked up his phone on the first ring.

"I've been robbed at gunpoint by a lady dressed in all pink," I said.

"My god, are you all right?"

"A little shook up is all."

"Damn it, Brenda, I've told you a million times not to keep cash around the shop. How much did she get?"

"She wasn't after money. She took all the hats for the Ashley Millard wedding. Strutted out of here swinging two hatboxes filled with hundreds of hours of work."

"Weird. Why would anybody want a bunch of wedding hats?"

"I don't know."

"I'll be over in a few minutes. Meanwhile, try to stay calm."

Stay calm? Johnny must have been kidding. How could I stay calm with the hats due this afternoon and the wedding less than two days away? How could I stay calm knowing I'd have to tell Carla that I'd blown the biggest and most prestigious job she'd ever had? I wouldn't blame her if she never spoke to me again. Because of me, Carla would have to face Ashley Millard and tell her there were no hats for her bridesmaids, no veil for her.

The spoiled daughter of Simone and Walker Millard of the very, very successful Millard Art Gallery down in Soho, Ashley wasn't exactly a friendly, understanding sort. She'd probably sue both of us. She sure had the background for it. Ashley was an associate attorney at Bateman & Crews, one of those big-time law firms that billed about five hundred dollars a minute.

I'd met Ashley only once, the time she sacrificed her lunch hour to come in for a veil fitting. In a snit, she slammed the hat frame on her head and stared at herself in the vanity mirror. She frowned. "I'm a very busy person. I don't see why I had to come in. Mother could have handled this."

I told her that unless she wanted to send her mother down the aisle in her place, she should sit still for the fitting. I adjusted the frame so the shape flattered her face, a challenge because she wouldn't stop scowling.

"Can't you hurry the hell up?" she'd asked, a real nasty edge to her voice.

She was the perfect foul-tempered bride for her arrogant, bombastic artist husband-to-be, Gil Davison. He was a big deal on the New York art scene. His assemblage paintings, which he cranked out at the rate of one every month or so, were handled by none other than the Millard Art Gallery—Ashley's parents. In my opinion, Gil's work stunk, a rehash of tired concepts. But the critics adored him and collectors lined up, eager to spend five hundred thousand apiece for the things.

Pulling off a job as big as the Ashley Millard wedding would have been my ticket to the big time. Screwing it up meant I'd never sell another hat in this town again.

It didn't take Johnny long to get to the shop. He lived two blocks away in a four-story walk-up on Bleecker Street.

"What am I going to do, Johnny? Ashley Millard's wedding is ruined and it's all my fault. I'm ruined. Carla's ruined. She'll kill me."

He tried to soothe me. "It's not your fault, Brenda. Carla will understand."

"It is my fault. I should never have given the hats to the Lady in Pink. I packed them all up and watched her walk out the door. I should have knocked the gun out of her hand. It was just a little gun."

"No, Brenda"—Johnny shook his head—"you did the right thing. No one in their right mind would expect you to have done anything more."

"Carla won't *be* in her right mind. You don't know the kind of pressure she's been under. She's had to work around the clock for weeks to finish all the dresses in time. She even gave up teaching some of her sewing classes until this wedding is out of the way, and you know how much she enjoys them. She's an absolute wreck. Wait until she hears my news.''

"You're overreacting, Brenda."

"No, I'm not."

"Did you call the cops yet? They might be able to track down the Lady in Pink and get the hats back in time."

"I want to check with Carla first. Because it's the Millards and they're such a big deal, I don't know how she'll want to handle it. Maybe they'll want to keep it quiet."

"You'd better call Carla, then. If you do want the cops in on it, the faster they get here, the more likely they'll be to catch the Lady in Pink."

I'd hoped to put that chore off indefinitely, but Johnny was right. I had to tell Carla. I dialed her number. Again I got her answering machine. "That's strange," I said. "She's still not there. I tried her earlier this morning and she wasn't there either. She should be working."

"Maybe she finished all the dresses and went out."

"She would have called me."

Johnny and I sat around for a half hour with me trying to reach Carla every five minutes or so. Johnny couldn't get over the fact that the Lady in Pink hadn't taken any money. "You say she specifically demanded the Ashley Millard wedding hats?"

"That's right."

Johnny got into his role of Tod Trueman, urban detective. "I think," he said, "to solve this case we have to put ourselves in the perpetrator's shoes . . ."

"Ouch," I said. "They were hot pink spikes."

Johnny continued, ". . . and think why she wanted them. Could she sell them?"

"I don't know. That doesn't make sense. Why not take money? Maybe she's got a daughter who's about to be married. Or maybe she wanted to ruin Ashley's wedding."

"Why would anyone want to ruin a wedding?"

"Oh, Johnny, you're so naive. There could be a million reasons why someone would want to ruin a wedding—jealousy, revenge, a former lover. Not all marriages are as simple as yours was.''

Johnny's marriage to a blue-haired punk rock singer had been a forty-five-second city hall civil ceremony that ended in divorce three months later when his wife left him for her band's drummer.

I tried Carla again. This time a man answered. ''Hello,'' he said.

I didn't recognize his voice. What the hell was going on? ''Who are you?'' I asked.

''Crime Scene Unit, ma'am. Are you a friend of the victim?''

3

I felt raw and exposed, like someone had yanked a couple of vital organs from my body and left my skin turned inside out. Then again, I tried to convince myself, maybe it wasn't so bad. I probably was overreacting, letting my imagination run hog wild, making a catastrophe out of nothing. After all, "victim" could mean just about anything. These days every jerk on the block wanted to be a victim, pin the blame and settle out of court for a six-figure payoff. But Carla wasn't another jerk on the block. Maybe she'd witnessed a stickup at the corner deli while picking up her morning coffee and bran muffin. Or had her fanny pack snatched on the way home from the newsstand. It was probably nothing, nothing at all.

I didn't fall for it. None of the spins I put on the word "victim" were good enough to convince me everything was okay. No way around it, when a Crime Scene Unit guy said "victim" he wasn't talking misdemeanor. Something awful had happened to Carla. I looked at Johnny and burst into tears.

A few things registered on the way to Carla's: a blast of searing heat, a pigeon splashing in a curbside puddle of murky water, three cop cars double-parked in front of Carla's building, and Johnny grabbing my hand asking if I was sure I wanted to go inside.

"Of course I want to go inside," I said.

A man I'd never seen before sat at the doorman's desk. He cringed as the red-faced building superintendent yelled at him. The super, a hot-tempered man who ran a tight building, punctuated each word with a bang of his fist. As soon as he saw Johnny and me, he shut up. I think he recognized me as a friend of Carla's because he started shaking his head even before I opened my mouth.

"Carla Haley," I said. "I'm here to see Carla."

He continued to shake his head but didn't say anything. I ran past him and pushed the button for the elevator.

"No," said the man at the doorman's desk. "You can't go up there."

"What the hell difference does it make now?" said the super. "Let em go up."

On Carla's floor, a vase of fresh pink and orange gladiolus on a stand across from the elevator made me feel better. How could anything terribly bad happen in a building with gladiolus in the hallway? I ran around the corner to Carla's apartment, anxious to see her so we could laugh about how I'd taken one stupid little thing a cop had said about a victim, blown it up all out of proportion, and assumed the worst.

It was not to be.

Yellow crime scene tape stretched across the hallway in front of the apartment. A uniformed cop stood guard. Carla's door was open a crack but I couldn't see in. I tried to push past the cop.

He put his arm across the doorway to block me. "You can't go in there," he said.

"Why not? What's going on?"

"Are you a friend of the victim?"

There was that word again.

I felt a tap on my shoulder. It was Carla's across-the-hall neighbor, Elizabeth. She held on to a wiggly little long-haired dog who was trying desperately to get free. I didn't know too much about Elizabeth except that, against the rules of the condo, she boarded dogs in her apartment.

"This is Jackhammer," she said. "He wants in there too, to see what all the fuss is about." The tighter she hugged, the more the dog struggled.

"What's going on?"

"Carla's been shot," she said.

"Is she going to be all right?"

"No. I'm afraid not."

I cried. Johnny pulled me close and made me feel safe. The cop in front of Carla's door said he was sorry about my friend and that he knew how tough it must be and could he please have my name and address because the detectives would surely want to talk to me later.

"Can I see her?" I asked.

"No," he said. "Believe me, it's for your own good."

"He's right," said Elizabeth.

"You saw her?" I asked.

"Yes. On my way out with Jackhammer this morning. I stuck my head in Carla's apartment to see if she wanted anything from the deli. I knew how busy she'd been lately with that wedding and thought I could help out. She asked for an iced coffee with extra cream. Jackhammer and I couldn't have been gone more than half an hour. When I got back, that's when I found her. Damn. If Jackhammer and I hadn't walked so far, maybe . . . well, who knows." She shook her head. "No. You don't want to see her."

Yes I did. No matter what anyone said, I wanted into Carla's apartment to see for myself. No amount of talking was ever going to convince me otherwise. "Johnny, can't you talk to the cops or something? I want in there."

"I'll see what I can do," he said, but he didn't look very hopeful.

I hung back with Elizabeth and Jackhammer and watched Johnny talk to the cop at the door. The whole time Johnny talked, the cop never stopped shaking his head no. So much for the polite approach.

Jackhammer licked my hand, opening up another possibility. "Nice doggie." I scratched the long reddish hair on top of his head. "You're quite a squirmer, aren't you?"

"That he is," said Elizabeth. "I'd put him back in my apartment, but I'm afraid with all the commotion outside he'll bark and bug the neighbors. I'm in enough trouble around here already because of the dogs. Somebody's always complaining about one thing or another." Rolling her eyes, she jerked her chin toward the door next to Carla's. I remembered Carla telling me about her pain-in-the-ass next-door neighbor. Randolph, I think, was his name.

If the dog did what I thought he would, my plan would work. "Mind if I hold Jackhammer?"

"Not at all." Elizabeth handed the dog to me. "Just be careful that he doesn't . . ."

I put Jackhammer down on the floor, gave him a pat on the butt, and sent him on his way. Two quick yaps and he tore off like a rocket. He shot across the hall, raced between the cop's legs. In a flash he was inside Carla's apartment. When the cop at the door chased after him, I seized the opportunity.

Jackhammer and I, the uniformed cop, and two other cops in suits pretty much filled the small apartment. "What the hell was that?" asked one of the cops when Jackhammer ripped by.

"Neighbor's dog," said the uniformed cop.

"Get it out of here, for chrissakes. Her too. This is a crime scene."

The cop thrust Jackhammer into my hands and pushed me out of the apartment, but not before I saw Carla sprawled out on the floor on top of Ashley Millard's red-stained wedding dress. The red came from Carla.

4

The two cops who came by to question me acted like they'd never seen a hat shop before.

"What do you do here?" asked Detective Turner, the older gray-haired one. He examined a big-bowed yellow beret left over from last spring.

"I'm a milliner," I said. "I design and make hats."

"Any money in that?"

"Not a whole heck of a lot," I answered.

The other detective, Detective McKinley, a tall thin black guy in a good-fitting natural-colored linen suit, eyed the mattress under my blocking table. "You live here too?" he asked.

"Sometimes I work late." I hedged, afraid to admit to a police detective that I lived illegally in a storefront. Or that I'd illegally sublet my basement out to Pete's Café next door to use for their wine cellar. Or that Pete and I had illegally knocked a hole in the basement wall so he could access the basement without going through Midnight Millinery. Not that it was his jurisdiction or anything but still, a cop's a cop and living in a store was against the law.

"Hmmm," he said.

Thankful he didn't pursue my living arrangements any further, I got down to the real subject.

"Here," I said, handing Detective McKinley my sketchbook. "I drew a picture of the Lady in Pink. I thought it might help you."

He looked at the picture.

"Who is the Lady in Pink?" asked Turner.

"I don't know who she is. That's for you to find out. All I know about her is that she barged in here this morning, head to toe in pink, stole Ashley's hats, and then killed Carla. Or maybe she killed Carla first. Yes, that makes more sense. She killed Carla and then she came over here and robbed me."

Detective McKinley looked at the ceiling and sighed. "Did you report the robbery?"

"No. I was going to but I wanted to check with Carla first. It was really her job; I was just a subcontractor. She was going to be the one stuck with telling Ashley the bad news. I couldn't get in touch with Carla, and then—"

"Who's Ashley?" asked Turner.

I told them about how Carla and I had been working on the Ashley Millard wedding job.

"So," said McKinley, "you think this Lady in Pink killed Carla?"

"Of course. Who else could it be?"

McKinley handed the sketchbook to Turner. "Why don't you tell us a little about Carla Haley."

"What do you mean?"

Turner looked at me like he thought I was stupid. "Like, for instance, who might want to see her dead?"

"No one. That is, no one besides the Lady in Pink."

"Why would your so-called Lady in Pink want to kill her?" asked McKinley.

"I don't know. I guess she must have wanted to ruin Ashley Millard's wedding?"

"Ruin a wedding?" Turner sounded skeptical. "Come on now, why would anyone want to ruin a wedding?"

"Yeah," said McKinley. "You sure it didn't have something to do with Carla Haley's drug involvement? Or her prostitution activities?"

"Her what?" It was the most outrageously absurd thing

I'd ever heard. Carla? Drugs? Prostitution? Unthinkable. Too shocked to respond intelligibly, all I could say was, "No, no, no."

"Well," said Turner, "according to our sources, Carla Haley was a heavy-duty user who hooked to pay for her habit. She may even have been involved in dealing certain controlled substances like crack cocaine."

"Who told you that?"

"We can't say," said Turner.

It started small, my giggle. When I looked at the poker faces on Turner and McKinley, my giggle got bigger and bigger until finally I let it rip. I laughed hysterically. I couldn't breathe; tears ran down my cheeks. I knew it was inappropriate, but it was so blasted funny, the idea that Carla was any of those things. Funny that is, until I remembered that Carla was dead. Then I quit laughing.

Trying to recover my dignity, I dabbed my eyes with the sleeve of my blouse and said, "I don't know who told you those things, but it is absolutely not true. You didn't find any drugs in her apartment, did you?"

"No," said McKinley.

"Doesn't mean a goddamned thing," said Turner. "The way we figure it"—he looked at McKinley, who nodded in agreement—"is that she was killed in a tussle over the drugs with another dealer or a customer. The killer snatched all the drugs."

If I understood right, they were telling me that drugs in the apartment or no drugs in the apartment—either way meant that Carla was involved in drugs. "That's crazy," I said. "No, not drugs. Not Carla."

I told them how Carla had moved here years ago from South Carolina. "She worked double shifts as a waitress to put herself through fashion design school."

"That may be the story she told you," said McKinley, "but in my experience there's waitresses and there's waitresses, if you catch my drift."

"What about the Lady in Pink?" I asked. "Isn't it a little weird that around the same time Carla was murdered,

I get robbed and the only things taken were the Ashley Millard wedding hats that I had been designing while Carla was working on the Ashley Millard wedding dresses?''

Turner looked at McKinley. ''I don't think it's weird, do you?''

McKinley looked at Turner and shook his head. ''In this city? Hell no. It's all random. There's a robbery here, a murder there; the only connection is that somebody wanted something that somebody else had. And in this case it's all different somebodies.''

It was no use. Nothing I could say was going to change their minds. If Turner and McKinley said it was drugs and prostitution, it was drugs and prostitution. At least until I could prove otherwise.

5

On the worst day of my life I had to call the last person in the world I wanted to call, Ashley Millard, to tell her the last thing in the world she wanted to hear a day and a half before her wedding, that her bridal veil and hats had been stolen and her bloody bridal gown was in an evidence bag at the Sixth Precinct.

It took me awhile to get up the nerve to call. When I did, Ashley's secretary at Bateman & Crews refused to put my call through.

"I'm sorry," she said, "but Ms. Millard is not to be disturbed this morning. If you care to leave a message, I'll be happy to see that she receives it."

"It's an emergency, about her wedding. Surely she'll talk to me."

"Ms. Millard wants all calls about her wedding referred to her mother. I can give you the phone number at the Millard Gallery if you like."

I scribbled the number on the back of a piece of pattern-drafting paper.

I wanted to talk to Simone Millard even less than I wanted to talk to her daughter. To tell the truth, I was a little intimidated by the Millard Gallery.

Though not a pioneer, the Millard Gallery had been early on the Soho scene. They moved into their West Broadway loft a year or so after the first galleries had settled into former mattress factories. The Millard Gallery arrived after the first art bar opened but before clothing boutiques pushed thousand-dollar leather jackets to tourists, and years before cheesy souvenir and knickknack stores invaded the neighborhood.

My friend and frequent wholesale client Margo ran an exclusive boutique on Wooster Street called Einstein's Revenge. When I first agreed to do Ashley's wedding, Margo filled me in on the Millards. It seemed that Ashley's father, Walker Millard, had been a solid B-list painter himself before marrying his art dealer, Simone. Together they started the Millard Gallery. Walker had the sensitive eye for scouting out new artists; Simone ran the business end. It was a winning combination. Even now, after Soho had become too trendy for its own good and the art market had strangled on excess, the Millard Gallery still raked in the money, much of it from the art of Gil Davison, Ashley's husband-to-be.

Reluctantly I dialed the gallery's number, reminding myself it was for Carla.

I had no better luck with the snotty-sounding man who answered the gallery phone than with Ashley's secretary at her law firm. "I'm afraid," he said, "neither of the Millards is taking calls."

"This is important," I said. "Tell them I'm the milliner who's been making their daughter's veil. There's a problem—"

He cut me off. "If there's a problem, I'm sure you'll be able to work it out without bothering the Millards." The next thing I heard was a dial tone.

I hated to ask Johnny for two favors in one day but these were extraordinary circumstances. He agreed to walk down to Soho with me. Together, we'd get one of the Millards to listen to us.

While I waited outside Johnny's building, an out-of-control van came barreling across Bleecker Street, ran a red light, and smashed into parked cars for half a block before jolting to a stop in front of a coffee-and-pastry shop. The whole episode made me feel fragile, like any second something totally unexpected could happen, and I'd be nothing more than a smear on the sidewalk.

Johnny interrupted my gruesome thoughts. "Sorry to keep you waiting. Just as I was leaving, my agent called and guess what? He thinks there's a good chance Tod Trueman will be reprised. He's working on a six-episode deal."

"That's great, Johnny. I'm really happy for you."

"The only problem is that I have to learn to drive. The budget's low, not enough money to get a double to drive for me. Know anybody who knows how to drive?"

Like many born-and-bred New Yorkers, Johnny had never learned to drive. While I was still in the Midwest, peeling out of burger joints, he'd been riding the subway. I hated driving, though, and as soon as I got to New York, I let my license expire. Carla, however, was another story. She loved to drive.

"Carla had a license," I said. "She always said someday she'd get a little yellow pickup truck to tool around town in."

Johnny put his arm around me. "I'm sorry, Brenda. You must feel awful and here I go babbling on and on like nothing's happened."

"It's okay. I haven't let it hit me yet. Right now, the only thing I can think about is telling the Millards."

On the way down to Soho I told Johnny about the visit I'd had from Detectives Turner and McKinley. "The bottom line is they think Carla was a druggie, either a dealer or a user, and a hooker to boot."

"That's absurd," said Johnny. "Didn't you tell them about the Lady in Pink?"

"Sure. They didn't think too much of my theory, though."

West Broadway was deserted. Traditionally, the movers and shakers of the downtown art scene abandoned the city in the summer, leaving it to the tourists. This late in August, though, even the tourists stayed away. Most of the summer shows were down and the galleries were preparing for the big fall openings.

The Millard Gallery was no exception. The odor of fresh wall paint greeted us as we got off the elevator. A thin, sharp-featured man dressed in all black, hustled over to us, a frown on his face. "You must leave the premises," he said, sounding peeved. "The gallery's closed today. You should have picked up a schedule down in the lobby. The dates and hours are clearly indicated."

"We didn't come here to look at art," I said. "It's very important that I see Simone Millard or, if she's not available, Walker Millard. It's about their daughter's wedding."

"Hmmp," he said, looking down his nose at me. "I suppose you're the one who called earlier? The one with the problem."

I nodded.

"Let me repeat myself," he said, pronouncing his words slowly and precisely, "if there's a problem, you fix it. That's what you're being paid for."

"Believe me," I said, "if there were anything in the world I could do to fix this problem I would."

Johnny slipped into his Tod Trueman persona and took over. "It's become a police matter now," he said. "So if you know what's good for you, you'll tell Mrs. Millard that Brenda Midnight and Johnny Verlane are here to see her."

"Police?"

"Yes. It's a police matter."

"Hmmp," the man said. He seemed to be in a perpetual snit. "Wait here." With his nose up in the air he walked the full length of the gallery to the offices in the back.

While he was gone Johnny and I looked around. Not that there was anything to see except a two-thousand-square-foot expanse of newly painted white walls and a super shiny golden brown floor, interrupted only by a row of ornate columns every twelve feet or so.

"What I could do with this space," said Johnny.

"I just bet you could." And it would be a nightmare.

The cranky man stuck his head out of the office area and motioned for us to come back.

"Mrs. Millard has agreed to see you," he said, sounding surprised by this turn of events.

"Thank you," said Johnny.

Compared with the spacious white gallery, Simone Millard's office seemed small and cavelike. Of course, with a couple million dollars worth of art hanging on the walls, it was a fancy cave. She sat behind a bare chrome-and-glass table in a black leather Barcelona chair that was probably the real thing. Simone was precisely groomed and fairly attractive, with shoulder-length sleek shiny blond hair.

I started to introduce myself. "I'm—"

Gold bangle bracelets clanged together as Simone brushed her hand in the air, signaling for me to stop talking.

"What's this about a police matter? Something to do with my daughter's wedding?"

I took a deep breath and gave her the summary version. Johnny helped, filling in the parts I couldn't bring myself to talk about. Throughout, Simone remained composed, hands folded in front of her, fingers interlaced. When I finished she stood up and glared at me. "You're telling me," she said, her voice rising in volume with each word, "that with little more than one day to go before my daughter's wedding, that goddamned dressmaker bled all over the goddamned bridal gown and someone stole the goddamned veil? Is that what you're telling me?"

I started to tell her that Carla was a designer, not a dressmaker, but Johnny pulled me out before I could say anything.

After leaving Simone Millard to call her attorney or whatever it was she screamed at us as we were running out of her office, Johnny took me to my favorite dark grungy neighborhood dive, Angie's, and ordered me a grilled cheese. As usual, Sinatra was on the jukebox, singing about New York.

"I can't believe that Simone Millard," I said.

"What did you expect," asked Johnny, "that she'd be happy?"

"I expected her to at least be civil and to show some sympathy. Instead she called Carla 'that goddamned dressmaker.' All she could think about was herself. What was all that screeching at the end about calling her attorney? She didn't mean Ashley, did she?"

"Probably not. I wouldn't worry about it if I were you. People like Simone Millard always call their attorneys. They get upset, they call their attorney, he charges them five hundred dollars, and they feel better."

"As far as I'm concerned, I've fulfilled my obligation to the Millards. They can rot in hell for all I care." I pushed the paper plate with my half-finished grilled cheese sandwich to Johnny's side of the table. "You want this? I can't finish."

"You've got to eat something, Brenda. You'll feel a lot better."

I took a bite. "Nothing's going to make me feel better until I find that Lady in Pink and make Turner and McKinley take back the bad things they said about Carla."

6

In my dreams everything was all right. Carla and I finished the Ashley Millard job in time, the clients were delighted, and our work got high praise in the society pages. But when I woke up the next morning, reality intruded. I lay in bed for what seemed like hours, paralyzed with overwhelming grief.

Over and over the words "Carla's dead; Carla's been murdered" ran through my head with a vision of her sprawled out on Ashley's dress. After a few choked-back attempts I managed to say "Carla's dead" out loud, but the meaning was abstract.

Later that morning Johnny dropped by with black coffee, giant-size blueberry muffins from the bakery on Hudson Street, and the newspapers.

He pried open the lid on the coffee cup and handed it to me. "How are you feeling?"

"About how you'd expect." I sipped the coffee. "Let me see the papers."

"I don't know, Brenda. Maybe you should wait until you've got something in your stomach."

I grabbed the papers out of his hand. "Waiting's not going to change a goddamned thing." One glance at the headlines and my grief moved into the background, edged out of my consciousness by the flat-out rage that took over.

Because Carla had been killed in the Village, where murder was still not a daily occurrence, it made all the papers.

Because of the tie-in to Ashley Millard's big-deal wedding, it got the front page of the *Post*, which blared in zillion-point type: DEATH BY DESIGN: VILLAGE DESIGNER BLEEDS ON SOCIETY GAL'S WEDDING GOWN. The story inside referred to Carla as a "sometime call girl" and reported that "police indicated drugs may have been involved in the grisly murder." Aside from these lies, the story added nothing I didn't already know, except that Detective Turner's first name was Spencer and that he'd been on the force for twenty years. There was no mention of the robbery at Midnight Millinery or any possible link.

"This is garbage." I wadded up the *Post,* threw it and the other papers off my worktable, and kicked them across the floor. "Those blasted cops are too pigheaded to see the obvious connection between the Lady in Pink robbing me and Carla's murder."

Johnny tried to soothe me. "Don't go by what the papers say. For all you know, Turner and McKinley may be following up on your Lady in Pink story. There's no law that says they have to reveal everything to the press or, for that matter, to you." Looking thoughtful, he sipped his coffee, then continued. "A common investigative technique is to hold back on some detail that only the cops and the killer know about."

"No," I said, "Turner and McKinley are convinced it's drugs. I never expected them to pursue the Lady in Pink angle, but I don't see why they had to go ruin Carla's reputation."

Ever since Johnny got the Tod Trueman role, he tended to defend the police. "You and I know that drugs had nothing to do with Carla's death," he said. "On the other hand, Turner and McKinley must have had some reason to think she was mixed up with drugs. Maybe they found something in her apartment."

"Stop making excuses for the cops. They found no drugs in her apartment because there were no drugs in her apartment. To them, with their warped logic, that meant the drugs were stolen by the murderer. The whole thing's ridiculous. When I find the Lady in Pink myself and present her, hot pink spike heels and all, to Turner and McKinley, I'll make them eat their words.''

"It could be dangerous, Brenda. For whatever reason, someone *did* kill Carla. That's playing for keeps. I think you should leave the police work to the police.''

"If I leave the police work to the police, Carla's murderer will never be caught. As for the danger, well, I kind of thought maybe you'd help me. How hard can it be to find the Lady in Pink? All we have to do is find out who, of all the people who'd want to ruin Ashley's wedding, would go so far as to commit murder. Then we'll know who the Lady in Pink is.''

"I don't know, Brenda. . . .''

"Please. Tod Trueman would help.''

"All right, all right, you win. I'll make you a deal. Before we go off poking around into Ashley Millard's business, let me ask some questions at the precinct and see what I can find out. While I'm doing that, you can finish up your fall line.''

"You've got to be kidding. How can I think about my fall line now? My best friend's been murdered, the cops say she's a drug-dealing hooker, and you think I can sit back and make hats. What kind of person do you think I am?''

"I think if you don't get going on your fall line, Midnight Millinery will be belly-up by Christmas. You'll be a person without a millinery store, which in your case, means without a home. You'll have to come live with me and the rug you hate so much. That's what I think. So, make some hats, Brenda. It's what Carla would have wanted.''

Actually, Carla would have wanted to finish up the Millard wedding job, wallow in the good publicity, slip into a fabulous dress, and go to her favorite Flatiron district restaurant to celebrate. She'd have ordered a fine Bordeaux, an arugula salad, and grilled salmon. She'd have invited Johnny and me to join her and would have laughed when the waiter told her red wine didn't go with fish. That's what Carla would have wanted.

In the end I gave in and promised Johnny I'd work on my fall line for a couple of days to give him the chance to snoop around the precinct. I figured I could use the time to plan the best way to find out who were considered Ashley's friends and enemies.

I went through all the design motions. I dragged out my head block, stared at it. I unrolled my pattern paper, rolled it up again. I sharpened my pencils and opened my sketch-book, plowed through my trunk of fabric samples. Nothing clicked. The dressy holiday line I'd thought about was completely out of the question. It seemed a lifetime ago that I'd considered getting some lace like Ashley's and dying it red. Now all I could see was the lace stained red with Carla's blood.

My plans on how to find out about Ashley were no more successful than my fall line. In a perfect world I'd confront her directly, and she'd tell me who wanted to ruin her wedding, which would lead me directly to the Lady in Pink, who'd make a teary confession to the police and spend the rest of her miserable life folding stained sheets in the prison laundry. In the real world, where I was stuck, I doubted things would go so well. If Ashley talked to me at all, she'd lie, and if I somehow found the Lady in Pink, she would not turn herself in, would not confess, and if ever accused at all, would get off due to a stupid technicality.

With my work getting nowhere, I was happy to be interrupted when Carla's sister Bernice roared into town. She claimed her family didn't "do funerals," whisked Carla's body out of the morgue, had it cremated, and shipped the ashes back to South Carolina, where she planned to bury them illegally under the cover of night beneath the weeping willow tree that Carla had climbed as a child.

I met Bernice at Carla's apartment. She'd taken a cab straight from the crematorium. Thoroughly pumped up over a shouting match she'd got into with the cab driver, she ranted, "Where in the hell did that cab driver get off thinking I'd pay him to get stuck in traffic for half an hour? What the hell is wrong with you people in this stinking, lousy city anyway?"

Questions to which I had no answers, not that she seemed to notice.

Never in a million years would I have guessed that this fat, brash, crude woman was in any way related to the soft-spoken, delicate, and reserved Carla. Skintight white capri-length leggings and a rhinestone-encrusted turquoise T-shirt exposed all the lumps and bumps of her chunky body. She wore her bleached blond, ratted, and sprayed hair piled on top of her head in a beehive shape last seen when white lipstick was all the rage. Round smudges of rouge highlighted her puffy cheeks; caked black liner defined red-rimmed eyes.

Bernice had never seen Carla's apartment. "You mean to tell me my baby sister lived *and* worked in this hellhole?" She marched through the one-room studio apartment dragging her forefinger along the top of surfaces to check for dust. "My husband, Billy, and I, we never could understand why Carla left home to live in this depraved city when she could have married that nice boy Bobby next door and had a slew of babies. Bobby's a big success. Got himself a fried chicken franchise out on the highway. It's a damned shame. My kids, god bless 'em, have no cousins, hardly ever saw their aunt Carla. Now they never will." When Bernice ran out of dusty surfaces to inspect, she wandered into the kitchen.

I followed her. "I guess it's nothing like South Carolina, but . . ." I wanted to explain all that New York meant to Carla. I wanted Bernice to know that Carla had been happy here, that she'd thrilled to the beat of the city. I wanted to tell Bernice that Carla had hated the smell of fried chicken.

Bernice didn't listen to a thing I said. She opened all the kitchen drawers and cabinets, then slammed them shut. She peered into the sink. "I can't believe it. There's not even a goddamned garbage disposal." She pulled a flowered handkerchief out of her handbag and sobbed into it. When she could speak again she took an envelope out of her bag and handed it to me. "It's Carla's will. Read it."

Carla's last will and testament was short and simple. She left everything to Bernice and me. I didn't know what to say. "Are you sure? I had no idea. . . ."

"Listen up," said Bernice. "We're going to make this short and sweet. As executor of my sister's will, I can tell you right now that this is legit. She left everything to you and me, fifty-fifty split, including this sorry excuse for a home. What is it anyway, one of those co-ops?"

"It's a condominium."

"Same thing."

It wasn't, but I knew it was no good arguing the point with Bernice.

"Well, except for a few keepsakes, you know, family pictures and the like, I'm washing my hands of the whole mess. You can have this shithole and all the crap in it."

"You can't be serious," I said.

"I couldn't be more serious," she said.

"We'll talk about it later, when you feel a little better."

"There won't be any later. I've got a flight out of this godforsaken city at six o'clock tonight and I mean to have things settled by then. What do I need with three hundred square feet of New York real estate to worry about? I'd be out of my mind to take on another headache. I've got enough problems back home what with Billy Junior getting booted out of school and all, and the septic tank needing repair. I have no use for New York Stinking City. My god, the taxes must be sky-high, not to mention Carla's mortgage. I tell you it's nothing but trouble. I want you to take it off my hands."

"But," I tried to explain, "Carla had paid off most of her mortgage. She always said she didn't like to owe anybody anything, so she made double payments, even triple, whenever possible."

"That's another thing I have to bring up," said Bernice. "Where did my sister get that kind of money? Those damned cops were trying to tell me Carla messed around with drugs and sold her body, but I didn't believe them for a minute, not even a perverse New York minute.''

"Carla made good money," I said. "Her sewing classes assured her a steady income even when she didn't have a big design job. Except for an occasional splurge, almost everything she made went to pay off the apartment."

Bernice sighed. "I can't tell you what a relief it is to hear you say that. Why are the police saying such garbage?"

I looked Bernice straight in the eyes, and for the first time I could see the family resemblance. "I don't know," I said, "but I sure do intend to find out."

"Good," said Bernice. "So everything's settled. You'll take the apartment and I never have to think about this town again."

"Look Bernice, if you really don't want the apartment, we could sell the place and split the money. You won't even have to come back to town."

Bernice thought that over for a moment. "What's a dump like this worth?"

"Hundred fifty thousand probably. The real estate market has started inching back up. Carla got it for a lot less, at the insider price."

Bernice looked at me like I was nuts. "Yeah, right, don't make me laugh. A hundred fifty thou for one lousy room and a four-by-seven kitchen in a big ugly old building in a neighborhood full of weirdos with spiked blue hair, artists, actors, and writers in a decaying, dangerous city. Who do you think you're kidding? I wasn't born yesterday, you know."

Actually, she was wrong; the blue-haired weirdos pretty much stayed over in the East Village.

Bernice had come prepared with papers signing over her half of Carla's estate to me. "Sign this and we'll be done with it."

"You're sure this is what you want?"

"I'm sure."

I signed.

"Well," said Bernice, "that's a great burden off my shoulders. Now, I'm sure you won't mind if I look around for some things."

"No, of course I don't mind."

7

The legal mumbo jumbo about Carla's apartment kept me tied up for the next couple of days. When it was all done and the apartment officially mine, I went over to take a look around the place. The same doorman was on duty as the morning Carla had been killed. To test his attentiveness, I ignored the ALL VISITORS MUST BE ANNOUNCED sign and tried to slip by.

"Just a minute, please," he said when I was two feet away from the elevator. "Who do you want to see?"

"I'm the new owner of Carla Haley's apartment."

When he heard Carla's name the color drained out of his face. He swallowed hard. "Oh."

I took advantage of the fact we were alone in the lobby to ask him some questions. "Did anyone ask to see Carla the morning she was murdered?"

He shifted his weight in his chair this way and that, jiggled his leg up and down, scratched his nose, pursed his lips, and finally mumbled, "No."

"Were you at your post all morning?"

"Look lady, the cops already asked me. If you mean to give me a chewing out, the super took care of that. Besides, my lawyer—"

"Your lawyer?"

"Well my sister's husband's brother, he's a law student. He says to me, 'Ralph, you better clam up if anybody starts asking you questions.' "

"Well, Ralph, I'm not going to chew you out. I'm not going to sue you. Are the cops trying to say you neglected your duties and let drug heavies into the building?"

He nodded.

"The cops are nuts. What I think might have happened is that you let a woman slip by, a well-dressed woman. You probably thought she was a tenant. No one can blame you for that."

"It was my first week on the job," he said. "Over two hundred apartments. That's a lot of people."

"Sure is," I said. "I was hoping maybe you could help me out. Do you remember seeing a woman that morning, dressed head to toe in shocking pink, with big round sunglasses?"

"I don't remember anything."

After that he clammed up.

What struck me most about being alone in Carla's apartment with no cops, no Bernice, and no Carla was how normal everything looked. No bloodstains on the floor, no bullet holes in the plaster walls, no signs of a struggle. The blood was on Ashley's dress; the bullets in Carla's head.

Though I never told her so, I'd always thought Carla's apartment was a little spooky. Now it was even spookier. The walls and ceiling were painted bright white, every flat surface piled high with fluffy white tulle. Bolts of white satin leaned against the walls; lace remnants hung from lamps. She'd made her curtains from yards and yards of sheer white cotton that cascaded past the windowsills into a swirling mass of white on the floor.

In this sea of whiteness stood dark heavy flea market furniture: a five-drawer carved walnut bureau, a bulky worktable, a collection of big solid chairs, and a brown leather sofa bed. This would take some getting used to.

The yellow crime scene tape was down, but I checked with Detective Turner anyway to make sure it was okay to move in.

"You can do whatever you want," he said. "We're through with the apartment."

"Thanks. Any leads in the case?"

"We're following up on a couple of things. Nothing I can tell you about yet."

"The Lady in Pink?"

"No, Detective McKinley and I are homicide detectives; we don't do robberies."

I started to say something but he cut me off.

"Before I forget, Ms. Midnight, congratulations on the apartment. So far, it looks like you're the only one who had anything to gain from Carla Haley's death."

My heart skipped a few beats. "What do you mean by that? Do you think I killed Carla?"

"Let's just say that Detective McKinley and I are pursuing many avenues in our investigation."

Unfortunately, the traffic only moved one way on Turner's avenues.

As soon as I hung up with Turner, I dialed Johnny's number and blurted out "Detective Turner thinks I killed Carla," before I realized I was talking to Johnny's machine.

In all the time Johnny had spent at the precinct, he'd come up with a big fat nothing. I finally got sick of waiting for results and thought to hell with him, I'd investigate on my own.

Driven by a sense of urgency to find the Lady in Pink, I headed down to Soho to see Margo in person. She probably knew a lot more about the Millards than she'd revealed when I first asked. After all, her ear for gossip was every bit as good as her eye for fashion. I hoped she'd picked up on something about Ashley Millard that would lead me to the Lady in Pink.

Einstein's Revenge took up the entire ground floor of a renovated warehouse on Wooster Street. Margo had decorated the store in high-tech style using lots of brushed aluminum partitions and glass brick. It was filled with the kind of clothing Margo herself wore, mostly sleek, mostly black with an occasional shot of bright color. It looked great in the silver gray industrial environment. Margo was her own best advertisement. Model tall and almost as thin, she wore her blue-black hair in a severe short hairstyle. Her eyebrows curved elegantly over a narrow face with dramatic high cheekbones and bright red lips.

"Wait till you see," she said, leading me back to her office. "Fall has arrived."

In her office fall garments spilled out of a jumble of cartons, hung on hooks along the walls, stretched out across chairs, and piled up everywhere.

She held up a streamlined long black dress. "Great, isn't it?"

"Beautiful," I said. "Bias cut?"

"Sure is. Very clingy. I could sell dozens. That is, I could if the manufacturer had sent the sizes I ordered, but these days that would be expecting too much. Is it just me, or have you noticed that no one does anything right anymore? Sometimes I think they must have put something in the drinking water. The whole thing gives me one powerful migraine. I may just pack it all in and take off for distant climes."

Once Margo got started it was hard to shut her up, which was exactly why I wanted to talk to her in the first place.

"Enough of my problems," she said. "Let's see the fabulous fall collection you've brought me today. I'm in desperate need of hats. Dramatic hats for the windows, not-so-dramatic hats for sales, and I need them all like yesterday."

"I'm a little behind on my fall line. What with—"

"Oh, Brenda, you poor thing. I forgot. I'm so sorry. Here I'm going on ranting and raving. Carla Haley was a friend of yours, wasn't she? I couldn't believe it when I heard about her. Drugs, of all things. It just shows you never really know anyone. I had no idea. I've even recommended Carla to my customers who were looking for custom bridal wear. If I'd known, I never would have—"

"Carla had nothing to do with drugs."

"The papers said—"

"The papers are wrong. The police are wrong."

"Then why was Carla murdered?"

"That's what I'm trying to find out. I think it had something to do with Ashley Millard's wedding. I think someone had a grudge against Ashley and wanted to ruin her wedding. The very same morning Carla was killed, a woman dressed in pink robbed me at gunpoint. She took all the hats for the Millard job. That's it. Nothing else, no money, no nothing. I think she also went to Carla's to steal the bridal gown and dresses. When Carla resisted, the woman shot her."

"A noble reason to die," said Margo. "I doubt I'd resist if someone came in here waving a gun around, though I have considered getting a gun myself. Lots of shopkeepers around here have guns stashed under their counters."

"I thought you might have heard something about someone who'd want to ruin Ashley's wedding. A jilted lover, perhaps."

Margo closed her eyes and rubbed the acupressure points on her forehead. When she'd hit all the points she smiled and said, "This is really, really delicious. You'll never believe in a million years."

"Never believe what?" I asked, wishing she'd hurry up.

"Well, even though Ashley is the kind of person everyone loves to hate—what with her money, her superior attitude, her arrogant lawyer friends—I can only think of one person who might want to ruin her wedding."

"Who?" I asked.

"Ashley herself."

I walked along Bleecker Street on the way home from Soho. When I passed by Johnny's building I pushed the buzzer mounted on the door next to his name.

A fuzzy voice crackled from the speaker. "Who is it?"

"Brenda."

He buzzed me into the building.

I smelled garlic. As I climbed the four flights to his apartment, the odor got stronger and stronger, reaching a peak in front of Johnny's door.

"So you're the source of the garlic," I said.

"Black bean soup," he said. A giant stainless steel pot simmered on his stove.

"Kind of a hot day to make soup," I said.

"Gotta have my beans," he said.

He set up a folding chair for me by the door of his tiny avocado green kitchen. "Sit right here and watch me squash garlic. Never know, you might pick up a useful household tip."

"I talked to Detective Turner today to make sure it was okay to move into Carla's place."

"What did he have to say?"

"He thinks I killed Carla."

Johnny kept right on squashing garlic. "That's what your phone message said. Don't worry about it, Brenda. Turner thinks no such thing. Like I told you, I've been asking questions over at the precinct. They're pretty sure the doer is this dealer from Chelsea."

"The doer?"

"Yeah. The one who did it."

"Turner told me that I was the only one with something to gain from Carla's death. What an insult."

"Turner knows the realities of New York real estate."

"Come on, Johnny."

"Seriously, Brenda. Turner doesn't think you did it. He was merely trying to intimidate you."

"Why?"

"It's part of the fun of being a cop." Finished with the garlic, he hacked open a red pepper with a long knife, dug out the seeds, and threw them into a Balducci's shopping bag on the kitchen floor.

"He's not a very good cop. While he's been hunting down drug dealers in Chelsea, I've been asking questions in Soho. You won't believe what I found out."

"Oh yeah? Tell me."

"I went down to see Margo at Einstein's Revenge. Remember her?"

"Sure, she's the tall one with the short hair who never stops talking."

"That's Margo. She makes it her business to know everything that happens in Soho. I asked her if Ashley Millard had any enemies, you know, like someone who'd want to mess up her wedding."

"What did Margo say to that?" He threw two tablespoons of ground cumin into the black bean brew.

"Ashley sabotaged her own wedding. She hired the Lady in Pink."

"Oh come on, Brenda. Why would she do that?"

"Mainly because she can't stand her betrothed, Gil Davison. Margo claims Gil doesn't think too much of Ashley either."

"Don't people usually wait until after the wedding to start hating each other?"

"It wasn't exactly a match made in heaven. It was arranged."

"You're kidding. In this day and age?"

"Maybe 'arranged' isn't quite the right word. It's more complicated than that. It all began, according to Margo, when Gil Davison became unhappy with the commission structure at the Millard Gallery and started talking to other gallery owners. Word got back to Simone and Walker Millard and they were afraid their biggest-selling artist was about to jump ship. To keep him in the gallery's stable they pushed Ashley at him."

Johnny looked puzzled. "From what you've told me, Ashley doesn't seem the sort to be pushed into anything. I can't believe she'd marry someone she didn't like just to please her parents."

"You're right. Ashley's not pushable. However, she's quite bribable. Her parents promised her a big chunk of profits from sales of Gil's work."

"Margo told you all this?"

"It's an educated guess."

"What about Gil? If he can't stand Ashley, what's in it for him?"

"He's got a reputation in the art world as being extremely difficult. Remember those other gallery owners he went to see? None of them would have anything to do with him. They all turned him down. When the Millards pushed Ashley at him, he thought he had to accept the bait in order to stay with the one gallery that would have him."

"So Ashley's pretending to be in love with Gil to keep him with the gallery and Gil's pretending to be in love with Ashley to stay with the gallery. That's pretty funny when you think about it," said Johnny.

"Except that Carla's dead."

"Sorry," said Johnny. He thought for a moment, then shook his head. "Wait a minute. I'm confused. I still don't see why Ashley would sabotage the wedding. No wedding, no percentage."

"I figure Ashley freaked. The closer the wedding got, the more she realized she couldn't go through with it. After all the money her parents poured into a storybook wedding, she could hardly cancel. She came up with the Lady in Pink scheme to give her a way out that her parents would accept. Who knows? Maybe they'll still let her have the profits."

Johnny covered the pot of black beans, turned down the flame really low, turned to me, and said, "Brenda, I think you've got a screw loose."

8

I'd won the big prize, beat the number one New York problem. Without lifting a finger I owned my own apartment. All I'd done was to have a best friend who got killed and she had a sister who hated New York. As far as I was concerned it was still Carla's apartment. I didn't want to move in. I felt like an intruder. Plus, the fact that she'd died in the apartment kind of creeped me out. After an agonizing, gut-wrenching talk with myself, I decided to go ahead and make the move. It finally came down to this: I could sell the place for a pretty good chunk of change and feel guilty and creeped out for the rest of my life for letting a stranger desecrate the apartment, or I could move in myself and feel guilty and creeped out for the rest of my life that I lived there. Once I'd made the only possible choice, I wanted to get it over with quickly.

I borrowed a collapsible shopping cart from Carla's neighbor Elizabeth, who was still taking care of that little dog, and my accomplice, Jackhammer. While Elizabeth got the cart out of her hall closet, he zipped around me, a tiny packet of pure energy.

"I'm glad you decided to move in," said Elizabeth. "I was afraid Randolph, the guy in the apartment next to yours, would somehow manage to finagle Carla's apartment. He's been bugging Carla for years to sell it to him, so he can expand his own place. He's the one who always complains about me boarding dogs.''

''You don't have to worry about me,'' I said. ''I love dogs, especially this little guy.'' I reached down and patted Jackhammer on the head.

Johnny dropped by Midnight Millinery and caught me in the middle of loading up the shopping cart.

''I wanted to apologize for yesterday,'' he said.

''Apologize for what?''

''For saying you had a screw loose. I've reconsidered and concluded that your screw is no looser than Turner's and McKinley's respective screws.''

''Thanks. I knew you'd see it my way.''

''I don't exactly see it your way. I'm still not sure you're right about Ashley Millard, the Lady in Pink, and all that, but you're no more wrong than Turner and McKinley thinking they can find drugs under every rock and behind every crime.''

Johnny stuck around and helped me move. He pushed the shopping cart; I made sure nothing bounced out. I didn't have much stuff. My quilt, some clothes, a few books. The whole move took only four trips with the cart.

After we dumped out the last cartful onto the floor, Johnny asked, ''Want me to stay to help you put this stuff away?''

So far, I'd avoided thinking about that. There was no place to put anything, at least not without disturbing Carla's things. I sat on the couch, hung my head, and sulked.

Johnny, a man of action, opened up the foyer closet. ''Where do you want me to put Carla's clothes?''

''I don't know.'' The closets and drawers were stuffed full of Carla's clothes. Her sister Bernice barely took anything home with her. She'd said Carla's taste was ''bizarre urban trash'' and that she'd be a laughing stock if she wore any of Carla's clothes back home in South Carolina. Not that she could have fit into Carla's clothes anyway, but I'd kept my mouth shut. We both felt bad enough already. All she'd taken was a six-yard length of embroidered heavy white silk. "In case Billy Junior knocks up that delinquent girlfriend of his and has to marry her," she'd said, "at least we'll be ahead a few bucks on the dress."

Johnny tapped me on the shoulder. "Come on, Brenda. I know it's hard, but you're going to have to deal with this sooner or later."

"Later's soon enough for me. For the time being, I'll leave my stuff in the middle of the floor."

"Okay, Brenda. Call me if you need anything."

"Thanks, Johnny."

For hours I moped around the apartment, dragging an empty plastic garbage bag behind me. I opened up drawers and closets, thinking maybe I could find a few things of Carla's to store. I picked up the floppy-brimmed straw hat I'd made for her, put it in the bag, and took it out again. In fact, nothing made it into the bag; the task was too morbid. I folded up fabric, rearranged piles, but changed nothing. I found a couple of beads that had rolled into a crevice along the baseboard, beads from the bodice of Ashley's gown. Beads from the gown upon which Carla had died. I put them into a porcelain bowl on top of Carla's bureau.

Eventually I sat down on the couch and drifted off. When the phone jangled it startled me back to consciousness. I let Carla's machine pick up the call.

Through the speaker, a male voice. "Hey, Carla. It's me. I just blew back into town tonight. You free for dinner anytime this week? Surely you're all done with that big wedding by now."

I froze. I didn't know what to do. Pick up and tell the voice that Carla was dead? My first instinct was to ignore the call and let him find out some other way. But if I let him do that, he'd find out the newspaper version, not the truth. Couldn't I at least do this for Carla? By the time I decided to act responsibly and do the grown-up thing, it was too late. I dove for the phone but the caller had clicked off.

After that call, I felt even worse. I gave up trying to make room to put my things away and ended up stuffing them into the plastic garbage bags. Carla's things could stay put for a while longer.

I pulled out the sofa bed, stripped Carla's sheets off, quickly put them into her laundry bag, and made the bed up with my own white cotton sheets. That night, even though it was much too hot, I slept curled up under the quilt my grandmother had made for me when I turned sixteen. She called it a crazy quilt, pieced together from large scraps of richly colored velvets and smooth satin brocades, all sewn with a decorative hand stitch. When I asked my grandmother where she got such fancy fabric in her tiny rural town, she answered, "From the funeral director. It's casket lining."

9

I tossed and turned most of the night. Finally, in the early morning hours, I fell into a nightmare-filled sleep only to be awakened at six A.M. by the sound of the *New York Times* as it skidded along the hallway floor and whomped into the neighbor's door.

Wide awake after that, I got up and foraged in the kitchen for food. Carla usually kept a well-stocked kitchen, but she'd let things slide while she worked on the Millard job. I found a box of stale granola in the cupboard and some milk in the back of the refrigerator, but the milk had turned sour. Pouring it down the drain made me sad. As I watched the white liquid swirl away, I pictured Carla running to the Sloan's on Hudson Street to grab a few items. Had she studied the expiration dates on the milk cartons or simply grabbed the frontmost one? Certainly she had bought the milk in good faith, with the full expectation of finishing it. Instead, the milk had turned rotten and Carla was a clump of ashes buried beneath a willow tree somewhere in the middle of South Carolina, where the boy next door had grown up to own a fried chicken franchise.

I lost my appetite. Okay, Carla, I thought, from now on I'll devote myself full-time to tracking down the Lady in Pink.

*   *   *

Hoping it wasn't too early, I knocked on Elizabeth's door. I wanted to return her shopping cart and also ask her some questions about the morning Carla had been killed. She might remember something.

Elizabeth opened the door dressed in a flowered chenille robe and bright yellow rubber flip-flops on her feet. A large woman with strong features, she carried herself regally even in that get-up. Her long black-and-gray hair hung in a single thick braid down her back. Jackhammer scrambled out in the hall and hopped up and down to greet me. Fully extending himself, he almost reached my knees with his front paws.

I scooped him up and let him lick my cheek. To Elizabeth I said, "I thought you might need your shopping cart."

"Thanks," said Elizabeth. "As long as you're here, why don't you come in for coffee? It's a special high-test blend of ridiculously strong beans. I grind them myself."

"Sounds good to me." I wheeled the cart into her foyer.

"Make yourself at home. I'll be a minute with the coffee." Her flip-flops slapped along the floor as she retreated to the kitchen.

I looked around her apartment. It was laid out exactly like Carla's, only flipped over, a mirror image. As far as the interior design went, it was hard to imagine that two apartments as dissimilar as these could occupy the same galaxy at the same time and be inhabited by the same species. From her kidney bean–shaped blond wood coffee table to her bright primary-colored biomorphic chairs and the boomerang-shaped motifs in the curtains, Elizabeth's apartment came straight out of the swinging sixties. Hanging on every wall were large abstract paintings. It was like I'd been sucked into a time warp, and it was surprisingly comforting.

Elizabeth returned carrying two yellowish green ceramic coffee cups and a banana. "I thought a banana might do you some good. You're looking a little peaked if you ask me."

"Thanks. I haven't had much of an appetite ever since . . . ever since Carla . . ."

"Of course you don't. But you really must eat. Have you lost weight?"

I slipped my thumb under the waistband of my jeans and pulled out the slack. "Judging from this, I'd say three pounds." To make her happy, I peeled the banana and took a bite. "I was just admiring the paintings. Who's the artist?"

"Except for that little red one hanging over there by the bookshelf, I painted them all."

I looked again at the paintings and back at Elizabeth. I felt like a complete fool for not making the association earlier. "I can't believe it," I said. "You're Elizabeth Franklin Perry, *the* Elizabeth Franklin Perry. I had no idea; Carla never mentioned it. I mean, wow, I studied you in art school, twentieth century art history." In the sixties Elizabeth Franklin Perry was one of the most well-known and well-loved painters in America. Then, at the height of her career, she blew it all off, quit making art to protest the war in Vietnam. This was a year or so before such acts were commonplace, and it got her a lot of media attention, most of it bad. Bold for her time, Elizabeth became notorious for yelling "screw the media" and giving the finger to a television camera during a protest march.

"That all seems two lifetimes ago, maybe three," said Elizabeth. She shook her head and leaned back in her chair that looked like an amoeba on spindly metal legs.

"What do you do now?" I asked. "Play chess like Marcel Duchamp?"

Elizabeth laughed. "No chess. I read; I write a bit. For money, I take care of the dogs." She patted Jackhammer. He raised his head, licked her hand, then went back to gnawing on a gooey rawhide knot that must have weighed more than he did.

"It's hard to imagine you stopped making art like that, cold turkey. Wasn't it difficult?"

"Not at all. I discovered that the real art is in my head.

It doesn't matter that it never gets committed to canvas. When I feel the need to commit to something more solid than brain waves, I whip up a batch of cookies. I never use a recipe; each batch is essentially an experiment, combining flavors, textures, colors, and odors Betty Crocker never dreamed of. I'll bring some around next time I make them.''

"That'd be great," I said.

"So tell me," said Elizabeth, "how was your first night in the apartment? Did you sleep well?"

"Awful. Terrible. I don't expect it to get any better until I find out who killed Carla."

"Don't you trust the police to do that? Those two who interviewed me, Turner and McKinley, seemed quite competent."

"Competent. You've got to be kidding. Turner and McKinley completely ignored everything I told them about the Lady in Pink."

"Who's the Lady in Pink?"

"She robbed me that same morning Carla was murdered. I'm positive Ashley Millard hired her to steal her wedding gown and hats from Carla and me. Did you see a woman around here that morning dressed in all pink? With big round sunglasses?"

"No, I don't think so. I'm confused. Why would Ashley Millard pay someone to steal her wedding attire?"

"Ashley had reasons to ruin the wedding, although I doubt she planned for anyone to get killed. Turner and McKinley think I'm nuts. They're convinced Carla was murdered because of her involvement with drugs and prostitution."

Elizabeth looked stunned. "What kind of crazy talk is that? Carla didn't have anything to do with drugs or prostitution."

"I know. That's why I'm going to find the real murderer and clear her name."

"I don't understand. What do you mean clear Carla's

name? Who besides the police thinks Carla had anything to do with drugs?''

"Only about eight million people. Didn't you see it on the news? Or in the papers?''

Elizabeth buried her face in her hands. "I'm so sorry. I didn't know. I don't watch television and I never read the papers, not since my screw-the-media days. My god, how could anyone say such terrible things about Carla?''

"I don't know," I said. "But I intend to find out.''

Elizabeth took a long slow drink of coffee, closed her eyes, and sat very still. Minutes passed, I finished my coffee, and then as I was getting ready to leave, she slammed her hand on her chair and jumped up. "That goddamned Randolph has gone too far this time. I'll bet you anything I know exactly what happened. Goddamned yuppies will be the end of us yet. Come with me, Brenda. We'll get to the bottom of this. It's time for you to meet your next-door neighbor, Randolph.''

With Jackhammer and me trailing behind, Elizabeth stormed out of her apartment and pounded on the door of the apartment across the hall, next door to Carla's. "Randolph,'' she yelled, "you sniveling, conniving uptight sleazeball, get your ass out of bed right this goddamned minute before I knock your door down.''

Jackhammer took full advantage of the situation, racing around the hallway. I just stood there feeling foolish. Finally a round-faced, half-bald man dressed in baby blue pajamas opened his apartment door a crack.

"Bringing me my morning paper?'' he asked sarcastically.

Elizabeth picked up the *Times* outside his door and threw it at him. "Randolph, we need to have a little talk.''

"You better keep that dirty, obnoxious dog away from me. Who do you think you are, getting me out of bed like this? I should have you arrested for harassment. Better yet, I'll sue you.''

Elizabeth pushed the door the rest of the way open.

"We'll see who sues whom, Randolph. Ever hear of slander?"

With those magic words Randolph stood aside and let us into his apartment, another mirror image of Carla's. A treadmill, stationary exercise bike, and large-screen television took up most of the room.

Elizabeth turned to me. "Brenda, I'd like to introduce you to your next-door neighbor, Randolph. He's famous around the building for complaining. If it's not the dogs, its the noisy elevator. If it's not the noisy elevator, it's the squalid condition of the incinerator room, or the insipid color of the walls in the lobby, or the unaesthetic flower arrangements in the hallways. Randolph always has some gripe."

Randolph turned his back to us and draped a white towel around his neck. Then, hiking up his pajama bottoms, he mounted the exercise bike and started pedaling.

Elizabeth raved on. "I bet Randolph can enlighten us about how the police got the idea that Carla was involved in drugs and prostitution."

Randolph pedaled faster. Droplets of sweat formed on his forehead.

"Come on, Randolph, tell us about that little story you made up about Carla two years ago."

I walked around the front of the bike, gripped the handlebars, and tried to make eye contact with Randolph. "Did you tell the cops Carla was a drug-dealing hooker?"

Randolph pedaled even faster, refusing to meet my eyes.

Elizabeth explained. "No, Randolph didn't tell the cops anything. That would be too risky for this lousy excuse for a human being. What Randolph did two years ago was make a formal complaint against Carla to the condominium board, claiming that she dealt drugs out of the apartment and had men visitors at all hours. I thought all that had blown over. I completely forgot about it, but it's part of the official records. No doubt the police found out about it."

Randolph's face was bright red, sweat thoroughly soaked through his pajama tops. He pedaled faster and faster.

I shook the handlebars. "If you don't stop pedaling and start talking, I'll kick out your damned spokes."

He stopped pedaling. "All right, all right." He struggled to catch his breath. "I didn't mean anything by it. I wanted to buy Carla's apartment and knock down a wall so I could move all my exercise equipment over there. Year after year after year she refused to sell. So, I did what anyone in the same situation would do: I tried to get the board to throw her out."

"You made up lies. What an incredible, arrogant jerk you are."

He cocked his head to the side and jutted out his chin. "Hey, for all I know she did sell drugs. There were always people tramping in and out of there. I didn't mean any harm. I deserve an exercise studio. I wanted room for serious weightlifting equipment and maybe one of those little trampolines."

"Didn't mean any harm!" I screamed. "The story was plastered all over the papers, the TV news, not to mention that your lies got the cops going off in the wrong direction. Did you hear or see anything that morning, anything you didn't tell the cops about for fear it would ruin your little lie?"

"No. I was working out with headphones on. Whitney Houston, I believe, turned up loud."

We went on like that for a good half hour, Elizabeth and I venting our anger, Randolph defending himself, Jackhammer growling and joining in the fracas. Finally Elizabeth said, "I'm going to call the Sixth Precinct. It's time for you to tell the police your story."

Randolph smirked. "The police aren't going to pay any attention to a wacky old bat like you."

"That's where you're wrong, Randolph," said Elizabeth. "I know the captain. Whenever he goes on vacation, I take care of his bulldog, Elmo."

My nerves were frazzled from Elizabeth's strong coffee and the blowup with Randolph. I sought refuge back in Carla's apartment. Trying to calm down, I sprawled out on my back on top of the unmade sofa bed and studied the cracks in the plaster ceiling. Little by little the morning's amazing events replayed themselves in my head.

Elizabeth was Elizabeth Franklin Perry. I thought back to the time when I'd first heard of Elizabeth. The art history professor had spoken with great reverence of her antiwar stance and her bravery, and he'd shown slides of her work. Back then I never would have imagined that one day I'd end up living across the hall from her and borrowing her collapsible shopping cart. For that matter, back then I rarely thought beyond my next portfolio review.

I thought about rotten Randolph. How could anyone be that arrogant, that deceitful, that insensitive?

None of this should have amazed me. New York is, after all, a city full of famous and formerly famous people; they all have to live next door or across the hall from someone. And New York is a city full of people driven to extreme acts of desperation in pursuit of a larger apartment. Unfortunately, they, too, have to live next door or across the hall from someone.

Nor should I have been amazed that Elizabeth was pals with the police captain. Networking is serious business in this town. It's all in who you know, who they know, who knows who you know, and who—of all these whos—owes whom a favor.

Because Elizabeth took care of his bulldog, the captain not only agreed to talk to Elizabeth but he listened to what she had to say. Before they even hung up, a squad car was on the way to pick up Randolph for questioning. The police were not pleased to find out their murder investigation had been screwed up by a fast-pedaling real estate freak.

Elizabeth promised to let me know as soon as she heard back from the captain. Confident that Carla's name would soon be vindicated, I felt relieved. Maybe Turner and Mc-Kinley would give up their search for nonexistent drug connections and begin to search for the real murderer, the Lady in Pink.

Once again I turned to the task of deciding what to do with Carla's belongings. Again I dragged a large heavy-duty plastic garbage bag around the apartment. Again I opened closets and drawers. I remembered Carla in the baggy faded jeans now folded and stored neatly. I remembered Carla looking in her mirror, demonstrating how to put on mascara without wrinkling her forehead. I got yet another lump in my throat. Again I put nothing in the bag.

In the midst of looking through her sketchbooks, the phone rang. I picked up and a soft-spoken woman introduced herself as a student from Carla's Wednesday-night sewing class and asked me who I was.

"Brenda Midnight," I said, "Carla's friend."

"I'm sorry to bother you at a time like this about such a trivial matter," she said, "but do you have any idea what became of our student projects? We were making ties out of this beautiful silk Carla gave us. My boyfriend's birthday is next week, the big three-oh, and I'd like to give him the tie I made. Carla had finished grading, but I didn't get a chance to pick it up before, well you know, before."

I took her phone number. "I'll call you if I find anything."

"Thanks. I'm really sorry. Carla was a wonderful teacher. We'll all miss her."

I continued my rounds of the apartment, getting nothing accomplished, only to be interrupted again when the doorman buzzed me on the intercom. He announced that I had visitors, of all people, Ashley and Simone Millard.

"Send them up," I said, caught totally off guard.

Ashley. Here. Anger surged through my body. If not for Ashley sabotaging her own wedding, Carla would still be alive. I couldn't forget that. I wanted to scream, make Ashley understand what she'd done. I wanted to shake her, squeeze her neck until she became limp. I wanted to shoot her in the head. I wanted to see her crumble to Carla's floor and die.

I took a deep breath and tried to compose myself. Ashley's visit could, after all, very possibly simplify my search for the Lady in Pink. I'd already plotted and rejected dozens of convoluted, impossible schemes to get Ashley to talk to me, to get her to say something to connect her with the Lady in Pink. Now here she was, right on my doorstep, wanting to see me. If I played my cards right, acted cool and calm, maybe I could squeeze some information out of her. I might be able to wrap this whole thing up much sooner than I'd ever hoped.

It was weird they should come. What the hell could Ashley and Simone Millard possibly want with me? I opened the door, caught a whiff of too sweet perfume, saw their matching mother-and-daughter scowls, and knew this wasn't exactly going to be a friendly let's-stop-by-and-chat-with-the-milliner visit.

Simone entered the foyer first, Ashley right behind. Both were dressed in beige linen. Ashley, presumably coming from her midtown law firm, wore a conservative suit, gold button earrings, and black patent leather pumps. Simone, presumably coming from Soho, wore an ankle-length sheath with a long slit up the left side, sandals, and a big blob of gold hammered into a sun motif pinned to her chest.

Neither bothered to say hello.

Ashley looked around me, straining to see into the apartment.

At first, I had a knee-jerk reaction to unexpected guests. I was mortified, sorry the place was still such a mess, with my stuff all over the floor and Carla's in disarray. I was quickly brought back to the reality of the situation when Simone pushed by me into the apartment. "We want our deposit back from Miss Haley's estate," she said.

"Deposit?" I shrank back to let her by. I hadn't thought about it before, but of course there must have been a deposit. Carla never would have taken on a job of that size without at least something up front.

Ashley followed her mother into the apartment. "The two thousand dollar deposit," she said.

What kind of people could demand their deposit back so soon after Carla was murdered? If I was right about Ashley's hiring the Lady in Pink, her behavior was truly despicable. I wanted them out of Carla's apartment. "You mean the deposit for the wedding gown, the veil, the hats, the other dresses, right?"

"Of course that's what we mean," said Simone. Hands on her hips, she surveyed the apartment. "We don't look like Miss Haley's *drug* clientele, do we?"

"Nor did we require her services as a hooker," said Ashley.

My hands formed fists, fingernails digging deep into my palms. But I successfully bit my tongue. "Carla wasn't a hooker," I said. "There never was any drug clientele. That was all a mistake. Randolph, the guy next door—"

"Of course it was drugs," said Simone. "It's always drugs. The police say it was drugs; the papers say it was drugs. Everybody knows it was drugs."

"Well—" I said, tempted to bring up the Lady in Pink and Ashley's role in the whole affair.

Ashley interrupted me. "I've got a good mind to sue Miss Haley's estate for all the grief and humiliation her irresponsible behavior caused me."

"Irresponsible?" I said, dumbfounded. "Because Carla

was murdered, you're calling her irresponsible?"

Ashley nodded. "My name was splattered all over the news also."

"Not to mention the other damages," added Simone. "The caterers, the Plaza ballroom, the limousines, the photographers, the videographers, the flowers, the list goes on and on. All canceled at the last minute with no refund. All because Carla Haley failed to finish her job. We lost almost half a million on the deal."

Deal. That's exactly the right word. "You didn't have to cancel the wedding," I said, failing to keep my voice as calm as I would have liked. "You could have gone to one of those Madison Avenue wedding boutiques and picked up another dress, another veil. You had enough time for that."

"You've got to be kidding," said Ashley. "Off-the-rack. No way. This was to be my special day."

I wondered if Simone had any idea that Ashley had sabotaged her 'special day' to get out of marrying Gil Davison. I wondered if Ashley cared that her sabotage had ended up costing Carla her life. I wanted to confront Ashley, but chickened out. I took a deep breath. "How much was the deposit?"

"I already told you," said Ashley.

"Two grand," said Simone.

"I'll see what I can do," I said, swallowing back my anger.

"Just remember," said Ashley, "this in no way settles anything. I can still sue the estate for complete damages."

I could no longer restrain myself. "Get out of here, both of you. Right now."

"We were just leaving," said Ashley, a self-satisfied smirk on her face.

"Yes," said Simone, looking at her Rolex. "I have a meeting with an important collector."

On their way out I heard Simone say, "I doubt it's worth your trouble to sue this estate."

"Mother, it's no trouble at all. One of the paralegals can

handle it. Anyway, don't forget about the drugs. There's got to be money somewhere.''

After they left I was too riled up to stay in the apartment any longer. I was about to go over to the shop when Elizabeth knocked.

''The precinct captain called,'' she said. ''That conniving, sniveling twit Randolph broke down real quick and gave the cops the straight story. They've seen to it that Randolph's real, real sorry. That's the good news. Unfortunately, there's not a whole lot the police can do besides release a statement to the media, saying those things about Carla were all a bunch of damned lies. You and I both know it'll never get printed. The truth doesn't sell papers.''

Before I could spit out the stream of curse words my lips had started to form, the telephone rang. It was Johnny.

''They've got Carla's killer.''

11

A hard hot wind blew in from off the Hudson River, kicking up the sand and greasy grit loosened by the digging up and re-digging up of Hudson Street for the ongoing, seemingly perpetual water main project. I saw Johnny as soon as I turned onto West Tenth Street. He was sitting on a stoop waiting for me across the street from the Sixth Precinct. He ran his fingers through wind-whipped hair and smiled. "I think we should wait here. I checked it out and it's the best spot to see the perp walk."

"The what walk?" I asked. Johnny was in his Tod Trueman, urban detective cop talk mode again.

"The perp walk. You know, perp for perpetrator. It's when, in high-profile cases like Carla's, after booking, the police parade the alleged perpetrator in front of TV cameras and reporters to show off their trophy on the way to the hoosegow."

I gave him a questioning look. "Huh?"

"The slammer, Brenda, the slammer. Anyway at the perp walk, everybody's happy except the perp."

"I know the meaning of 'hoosegow.' I just thought the word was perhaps a little dated. Don't you think we should get closer? I've seen these perp walk things on TV and the bad guys always stoop over, hide their faces behind a hooded sweatshirt, or drape a coat over their heads. We won't be able to see a thing this far away."

Johnny shook his head. "No. We're better off over here. Any closer, and we'll get caught up in the tangle of video equipment and frenzied reporters."

"Reporters," I said. "You should hear what Elizabeth from across the hall has to say about the media. She's got good reason too. You'll never in a million years guess who she is."

"Who?"

"Elizabeth Franklin Perry."

"Who's that?"

Before I could explain to Johnny, the show began. Through the front doors of the precinct flowed a sea of blue-uniformed cops. In their midst a bubble-headed platinum blond perp smiled at the cameras and waved and blew kisses at the reporters, basking in the bright lights.

As Johnny had predicted, the reporters and camera crews rushed forward, jockeying for the best position. This perp was a special case, lots better than the usual run-of-the-mill killer. This perp didn't shrink away from the lights. This perp craved their attention. Even better, there was still plenty of time to get her on the six o'clock news.

"See," said Johnny, "we have a great view, and nobody's shoving us around."

I had a clear view but didn't like what I saw. I looked hard at the perp, tried to imagine her without the platinum hair, with half her face covered by sunglasses, wearing a pink suit. It was no good. "That's not the Lady in Pink," I said. "Turner and McKinley have got the wrong person."

"Are you sure?" asked Johnny. "I thought you didn't get a good look at her face because of the sunglasses."

"I'm positive. The face doesn't matter. The Lady in Pink was about my size. This woman is at least a size twelve."

Emotionally, the day had gone like a roller-coaster ride. When I'd heard the cops had Carla's killer, I was on the top of the last crest. I'd thrown my arms into the air and thrilled at the downhill ride. But now the ride was over, the little train had coasted to a stop, and the Lady in Pink was farther away than ever.

Johnny tried to cheer me up. We walked around the Village, sat on a bench in front of the bakery, and shared a custard napoleon. Then we headed over to Johnny's apartment in time to catch the perp walk on the six o'clock news.

"I don't want to see it," I said. "Once was enough. That woman is not the Lady in Pink."

"Maybe not," said Johnny, turning the key in his lock, "but she could still be the murderer. Did it ever occur to you that you might be wrong about the Lady in Pink?"

Johnny opened his door. Immediately I saw a big bare space in the middle of the floor where his orange-and-yellow shag rug had formerly festered. Had Johnny finally realized I was right about the rug? Was he starting to come around to my sense of style?

Again my bubble burst. "In case you're wondering," he said, "the rug's at the cleaners. I spilled pizza sauce." He flicked on his old black-and-white television just as the story was being aired. We saw the same platinum-haired woman blow the same kisses to the same reporters in front of the same precinct.

"Weird, isn't it," said Johnny, "how much more real it looks on television. Television gives it that stamp of authenticity."

The station's dashing crime reporter came on-screen. "Today in a dramatic, tearful confession, Laurel Tipton, a Greenwich Village actress known for her many Off-Off-Broadway appearances, admitted to the murder of Carla Haley. . . ."

"Way, way Off-Off-Broadway," said Johnny.

"Police have issued a statement saying that their earlier theory that Ms. Haley was involved with drugs and prostitution was apparently unfounded. It now appears that Ms. Haley, a seamstress, was murdered over a wardrobe dispute of some sort. Ms. Tipton, in her confession, claims to have acted in self-defense."

Abruptly a commercial for a local car dealership came on. Johnny flipped through the channels, but the story had already wrapped up.

"Well," said Johnny. "What do you think now?"

"I think it's a crock. Not only is that woman not the Lady in Pink, but the idea of a wardrobe dispute is even stupider than the drug-and-hooker theory. Carla hated theatrical costumes. She said they were nothing but facades. Carla designed real clothes, clothes to be worn, clothes with integrity."

"Maybe that's what the dispute was about," said Johnny. "Maybe Laurel Tipton wanted Carla to make costumes, Carla refused, and it turned nasty."

"Don't be ridiculous. The whole thing stinks to high heaven. Do you think Detective Turner is still at the precinct?"

Johnny shrugged his shoulders and handed me the phone. "Go ahead and see."

Turner was there, and I got put right through to him. He cleared his throat. "I guess we owe you an apology, Ms. Midnight. You were right all along; there was a Lady in Pink. Although, you must understand, Laurel Tipton vehemently denies having robbed you. Says she's never heard of Midnight Millinery."

"Laurel Tipton did not rob me. Laurel Tipton is not the Lady in Pink. Laurel Tipton did not kill Carla."

"Of course she's the Lady in Pink. Not only did she confess to Carla Haley's murder but when we searched her apartment we found the pink suit, the pink shoes, pink handbag, big sunglasses—just like you described."

"No," I said. "When you searched her apartment you found *a* pink suit, not *the* pink suit. There's a lot of pink suits in this city and Laurel Tipton looks just the type to have one of them. She's at least four suit sizes larger than the woman who robbed me."

"Are you positive?" asked Turner. "As a rule, people look larger and more authoritative on television."

"I'm positive, all right. I saw it live. I was across the street from the precinct when Laurel Tipton took the perp walk. I know a size twelve when I see it."

"Hmmm," said Detective Turner. "Then I guess we're

right back to where we started with two separate incidents. Incident one: Carla Haley was murdered. Incident two: You were robbed. No connection. Right back where we started except we have a confessed murderer in custody.''

"You've got the wrong person," I said. "I'd bet anything that Laurel Tipton made it all up so she could get her smiling mug on TV. You say you found a pink suit in her apartment. Did you happen to find the murder weapon?''

"We've got a team out looking for it now. We believe she ditched it somewhere, probably right around the neighborhood.''

"How'd Laurel Tipton react to the information that you held back from the press?''

"What do you mean?''

"My ex-boyfriend Johnny Verlane, who studies police procedure . . .''

"I'm well acquainted with Mr. Verlane. He's visited the precinct many times.''

"Well, Johnny says the cops always hold back some piece of information. You know, to weed out the nutcase confessors like Laurel Tipton.''

"Mr. Verlane would be more accurate if he said that sometimes we hold back information. In this case we did not.''

"Why?''

"We forgot.''

"Great. So this is it? Case closed?''

"Unless something else turns up.''

"Are you actively looking for something else?'

"It's not our highest priority, but we are looking. Meanwhile we've got seven other murders. No one has confessed to them.''

Johnny was incredulous. "You're kidding. Turner actually told you they forgot to hold something back?''

"That's what he said. Guess it's a day for confessions. They'll never find the Lady in Pink. From now on I'm stepping up my effort to find her myself.''

"How do you plan to do that?" asked Johnny.

"I'm positive Ashley holds the key to this whole thing, so I'm going after her."

"Ashley will never talk to you, especially after what happened today with her and her mother."

"You can say that again. That's okay, though. I don't want to talk to her. What I have in mind is sort of a sneak attack. I've got an idea how to uncover her connection to the Lady in Pink."

12

The best way for me to get to Ashley was to put on my temp hat and slip into Bateman & Crews, the law firm where she worked. After all, way before I became a milliner, way back when I still believed that one day I'd make it as an artist, I'd supported myself as a freelance temporary word processor. It was a silly profession, but the pay was decent, jobs were plentiful, and if a particular assignment was unbearable, I never had to go back: There was always another waiting just around the corner. I'd processed words every which way—full-time, part-time, day shift, lobster shift, double shifts. I processed words at every possible kind of organization from big fancy law firms to seedy hole-in-the-wall copy shops and everything in between. They all needed words processed.

In fact, it was on one of these jobs, typing up an inventory list for a mom-and-pop feather importer, that I discovered hatmaking in the first place. To this day I can remember the odor. Mothballs from Needleson Bros. stank up the entire eighth floor of a dark rickety building in the West Thirties devoted to the wholesale trimming trade. I didn't see how Mom and Pop, that is Zorema and Howard Needleson, or for that matter the ribbon importer next door, could stand to work around the fumes.

"Oh, you'll get used to it," Zorema had said when I complained of dizziness and nausea.

Meanwhile Howard took inventory. Wielding a baseball bat, he'd stomped around the storeroom and whacked the lumpy taped-up cardboard cartons until feathers flew out of the cracks. Then he'd yelled out the name of the feathers. "Carton of red ostrich, one of nine-inch green pheasant, and another turquoise hackle pad." My part in all this was to type up whatever Howard yelled out. Then Zorema would give me the price breakdown for each item and I'd type that to the right of each listing.

After two hours in the mothball stench I'd told Zorema I had to leave.

She'd looked at me sympathetically. "Why don't you take a break, dear. It's a nice day. Walk around the block and get some fresh air. We can finish up when you come back."

"Better yet," Howard had said, snapping his fingers, "she can drop off these hackle pads at Frank's on Thirty-eighth Street and kill two birds with one stone."

He and Zorema had both doubled over laughing at his pun.

Back then, before wholesale costume jewelry stores and emporiums of rayon knockoffs took over the block, Thirty-eighth Street between Fifth and Sixth Avenues was the millinery block, the place to find stores for buckram frames, felt hoods, straw braid, wooden blocks, silk flowers, all manner of hatmaking supplies. Frank's Millinery Supply was the largest and most comprehensive on the block. After delivering the hackle pads I hung out for a while to avoid going back to the mothball fumes. A display of antique veiling caught my eye and all of a sudden I wanted to make hats. I bought one of the buckram frames, half a yard of black velvet, some very fine intricately patterned black veiling, and two long red plumes and started my millinery career.

That's one of the best things about New York. If one thing doesn't work out, there's always something else to do. Your whole life can change, well, at the drop of a hat.

Ever since that day at Needleson Bros., I've been a milliner. Now, seven years later, I needed to dredge up my word processing skills to get myself into Bateman & Crews. Once there I hoped to find something to connect Ashley with the Lady in Pink.

My half-baked plan to get into Bateman & Crews would work a whole lot better if I could get an agency to back me up, give me legitimate credentials, make me feel official and confident. Going through an agency also meant I'd get paid. Unfortunately, my old agency was out of business, a casualty of the stock market crash.

I opened the yellow pages and called the first temp agency listed. "Do you place experienced word processors?"

"Certainly," said the receptionist in a syrupy sweet voice, "we can *always* use word processors. What software packages do you know?"

I'd never heard the term software package before. When I told her the system I'd last used, she snorted and refused to let me through to a representative. "Honey, you'd better get yourself some training. I'm afraid that stuff went out with disco and quiche."

I flipped through the entire temp agency section in the yellow pages. Not one of the ads mentioned my old system. At random I called another agency. The receptionist laughed and hung up. Obviously the truth was not going to get me an agency.

Back to the yellow pages. Robin's Early Bird Temporary Service had a half-page ad that featured a line drawing of an unlikely looking pigeon holding a droopy worm in its beak. I liked the pigeon and decided to call. First, I did my homework. I got the *New York Times,* combed through the help-wanted section, and made a list of every word processing and desktop publishing program mentioned. This time I was prepared. When the receptionist at Robin's asked me about my software packages, I quickly rattled off the names of every program I could pronounce. It worked. She put me through to Robin herself.

"Fabulous," said Robin when I ran through the list of programs again. "How well do you know them?"

"Expert level," I answered. "All of them."

She could hardly contain her gushing enthusiasm. "Fabulous, fabulous, and more fabulous," she said. "You're too good to be true."

That, at least, was on the mark. "Thank you," I said.

"I can place you in no time. How soon can you start?"

"Immediately," I said.

"Just one thing, though," said Robin. "You absolutely must come in for testing. Here at Robin's we pride ourselves on our extensive testing procedures. We never send an underqualified temp out. Our clients depend on our temps to get their jobs done efficiently, correctly, and with a smile. We like to think of ourselves here at Robin's as generals sending fresh troops into the battlefield each day."

What a crock, I thought. "Testing's no problem," I said confidently. I made an appointment to take their battery of tests early the next morning. Of course, I had no intention of going. I'd never pass the tests.

Once I had Robin's Early Birds backing me, it was time to move to phase two of my plan: creating an opening at Bateman & Crews. The problem was where. The word processing center was out. There my lack of skills would be noticed immediately. I wouldn't last a minute. Same was true of the litigation department. Too many deadlines. I needed a more relaxed area of law, where maybe I'd last a couple of days before anyone would discover I didn't know what I was doing. I needed something easy, something like trusts and estates.

I dialed Bateman & Crews and asked the receptionist the name of the partner in charge of the Trusts and Estates Department.

"That'd be Mr. Duggins," she said.

"How do you spell that?" I asked.

"D-U-G-G-I-N-S. Robert Duggins."

"And his secretary's name?"

"Alice Caslon. Shall I put you through to Miss Caslon?"

"No thanks." First I had to execute phase three of the plan.

Armed with this valuable information, I called Robin's Early Birds again, only this time I disguised my voice and pretended to be Alice Caslon, executive secretary to Robert Duggins, Esquire, the senior partner in charge of the Trusts and Estates Department at Bateman & Crews.

"Mr. Duggins will need someone first thing tomorrow—someone with excellent skills and a professional manner," I said to Robin in my best law secretary voice. I ran down the list of all the currently popular software packages that Brenda Midnight had claimed to know.

Naturally Robin responded with enthusiasm. An account with a prestigious firm like Bateman & Crews was a big juicy worm for her Early Birds. An account like B&C could mean the difference between plodding along every day fitting eighty-word-a-minute typists to desks and the kind of wild, runaway success Robin had probably never dared dream of. "I have someone in mind who is perfect for such a position," she said, fighting to keep her voice calm and professional.

I hated to burst her bubble. "Oh, I almost forgot to mention," I said, still in my role as Miss Caslon, "Mr. Duggins is a wee bit old-fashioned. He insists that all his girls know shorthand."

"No problem," said Robin, but her gasp was audible. "No problem at all."

Robin had lied about it being no problem. I, posing as Miss Caslon, had asked Robin to do the impossible. Shorthand *was* a problem, a definite problem. Shorthand had gone out even before quiche and disco. I'd have been willing to bet that no more than two people in all of New York City knew shorthand anymore, and neither of them used computers.

Ten minutes later Robin called me—not the me posing as Miss Caslon but the real me, Brenda Midnight, the one who knew all the software in the world. There was panic in her voice. "Do you know shorthand?" she asked.

"Of course," I lied. "One hundred twenty words a minute."

Robin let out a long sigh of relief. "You're a dear, a blessing." She told me the arrangements. Robin admitted it was far too late in the day for me to take the required software tests. However, in the interest of sending a temp who knew shorthand to a very important new client, a senior partner at Bateman & Crews, Robin waived her testing requirement. "It's really just a formality," she said. To further facilitate the assignment, she sent a messenger over with a stack of Robin's Early Bird time cards and a promotional ballpoint pen on a neck string.

I was especially proud of the shorthand ploy. It not only ensured that Robin couldn't fill the position with anyone else, it boosted my pay by $3.75 an hour.

13

I was in at Bateman & Crews, or at least I would be first thing tomorrow if I didn't chicken out. Determined to stay there long enough to find something that would connect Ashley Millard to the Lady in Pink, I took the next logical step. Picking up the phone, I called my friend Chuck Riley.

Chuck knew everything there was to know about computers—hardware, software, and a couple of wares that didn't have names yet.

"God, Brenda, I've been meaning to call you. I heard about Carla and all and . . . I didn't know what to say."

"It's all right," I said. "There's nothing you can say. However, you can help me catch Carla's murderer."

"Cool," he said. "What do you need?"

I told him about Ashley, the Lady in Pink, and my Bateman & Crews assignment. "If I'm going to pull this off, I need a crash course on word processing. It's been over seven years."

Chuck let out a low whistle. "Seven years, huh? That's a lot of territory to cover by tomorrow morning. Maybe you'd better bring a pizza with you. It's going to be a long night and we may get hungry." Chuck thrived on chocolate-covered donuts, barbecue potato chips, and pepperoni pizza, a diet that kept him stick thin, wired, and reasonably healthy except for an occasional bellyache.

He lived in a dicey part of Alphabet City in a boarded-up storefront on East Fifth Street near Avenue B. Before going into his building, I whirled my head around to check behind me for muggers. The coast was clear so I went in. As usual, Urban Dog Talk, the band who rented the entire third floor, was rehearsing. The piercing scream of their trademark distorted guitar greeted me with a wallop. I liked Urban Dog Talk. In fact, it was at one of their gigs years ago that I'd met Chuck in his role as their sound engineer. Even so, I didn't think I'd like to hear them rehearse twenty-four hours a day. I pushed Chuck's buzzer and wondered if he would hear it over the racket. He did and buzzed me in.

"Oh boy, I smell pepperoni," said Chuck through his door. It took him a couple of minutes of fiddling with the police lock before he got the door open. He grabbed my arm and guided me over the thick cables that snaked along the linoleum floor. His apartment looked like the inside of a television set. A tangled mess of wires, small electronic components stored in baby food jars, oscilloscopes, broken down stereos, and computer equipment filled every square inch. He had old computers stacked on top of brand-new computers and Frankenstein computers pieced together from spare parts. He had computers that ran twenty-four hours a day extracting data from god knows where, and computers that would never ever run again. And he had computers that kept an eye on all the other computers.

Chuck looked a lot like his apartment. His curly carrot red hair stood on end, and his green-toned complexion looked like that of someone who ate junk food and stared at computers all day in a boarded-up storefront. He explained the two ratty T-shirts he wore at the same time. "The holes in one sort of annihilate the holes in the other, like in wave theory."

I didn't ask about the wave theory. He also wore two earrings: one, a simple gold stud; the other, a dangly piece of electronic something or other. Chuck could look pretty much however he wanted to. He very rarely worked, and when he did it was as a highly paid, highly respected consultant.

"Don't worry, Brenda; we'll get you up-to-date." I sat down in a very comfortable chair that conformed to every bump in my body and Chuck rolled me over to a gigantic computer monitor that must have been at least a foot and a half across. Then, between stuffing bites of pizza into his mouth, he tech-talked to me. Mega-this and mega-that. He clicked with his mouse and colorful shapes filled the monitor. Then he clicked again and everything completely changed around.

I was intimidated. Too much had changed in the seven years I'd been making hats. I was left so far behind, I couldn't even see the dust. I tried out the mouse but didn't get the hang of it.

"Double click it," said Chuck.

"I did click it," I said. "Nothing happened."

"Then you didn't double click. If you'd double clicked, something would have happened."

I slid the mouse across its mouse pad. "I'll never be able to learn all this new stuff by tomorrow." I banged my head on the keyboard.

Chuck carefully removed all the pepperoni from a slice of pizza and handed it to me. "Here you go, Brenda, the vegetarian version, specially for you."

"No thanks," I said, looking at the circles of grease the pepperoni left behind.

"Well, have one of these, then." He grabbed a box of donuts from a small shelf over the monitor and offered me one. "You'll feel much better."

It occurred to me that all my friends were constantly trying to get me to eat something or other to make me feel better. I bit into the donut. It did make me feel better.

"Now that you're fortified," said Chuck, "try clicking again. It's not that difficult."

Finally, a successful double click.

Chuck smiled. "Great, Brenda. You're halfway home. You're lucky Ashley is a lawyer; they have simple doofus work, no layout or graphics. It would be much harder to fake it if you had to sneak into someplace like an advertising agency. At Bateman & Crews you're not going to have to do anything fancier than type a letter or a brief and print it out. That's about it. Easy stuff.''

He gave me a quick tour of the most popular word processing programs and told me how to get on-screen help. ''Hit the F-3 key in this one, the option F-8 in another, and the command question mark in yet another. Or, now that you know how to use a mouse, you can just go up to the menu and pull down. See how easy it is?''

Right. Easy for him to say.

''You'll do fine, Brenda. Just remember that lawyers use long paper. That's why they call it legal size. So, set your page size for fourteen inches. Oh, and one more thing. Don't reformat their hard drive. That kind of stuff really pisses people off.''

With that taken care of, it was time to scare up a proper costume for Bateman & Crews. According to family legend, one day my great-great-grandfather tied a red bandanna around his neck and went for a walk in the woods to collect kindling. A hunter saw the flash of red through the trees, mistook my great-great-grandfather for a turkey, and shot him dead. From that day on, generation after generation, my family has stressed the importance of what we wear. As my mother always said, ''If you don't want to be mistaken for a turkey, don't dress like a turkey.'' On the other hand, sometimes you need to look like all the other turkeys, which was why I carefully picked my clothing for Bateman & Crews. In order to fool anyone there, I'd have to find a way to dress the part. Problem was, I was fresh out of appropriate office wear.

On the way home from Chuck's, I plucked a pair of taupe panty hose from a revolving display at the corner deli, figuring they'd stay runless about as long as I'd stay at Bateman & Crews. I was going to need a hell of a lot more than panty hose to pull off the right look. I foraged through my clothes, still in garbage bags on the floor, and came up with a too short black silk skirt. A search through Carla's closets yielded a passable green blazer only a size too big. I let down the hem on the skirt as far as it would go and tried it on with the blazer. Instant dowdy. To keep my Urban Dog Talk T-shirt from showing, I tied a length of ivory silk from Carla's scrap pile around my neck, fluffed it up, and tucked it under the blazer. As long as I kept the blazer on, no one would ever know the difference.

While rooting through the deepest darkest part of Carla's foyer closet I stumbled onto a box of ties made from wildly patterned and exotically colored silk. Each tie had a paper with a name and a grade pinned to the lining. I found the tie for the girl who'd called. Carla had given her an A on the project. I called her and said she could pick the tie up from the doorman anytime. I made a mental note to return the others when I had a chance.

Before I went to bed I called Johnny and told him how I'd maneuvered to get into Bateman & Crews.

"What for?" he asked.

"It's probably a big waste of time," I said, "but I can't think of any other way to find out anything about Ashley that would connect her to the Lady in Pink."

"Be careful poking around that place," said Johnny. "What if Ashley recognizes you?"

"I've already thought of that. I'm tying my hair back and wearing a suit. She'll never recognize me."

"Promise me, Brenda, if you find out something about the Lady in Pink, call Turner and McKinley before doing something stupid yourself."

"Of course," I said.

That night I dreamed of a chorus line of pudgy turkeys, all wearing red bandannas tied around their wattles. Over a screeching guitar, they sang a song in three-part harmony: "Gobble, gobble megabyte. Your skirt's too short to get it right."

14

I tossed and turned all night long, disturbed by the singing and dancing turkeys in my dreams. When Chuck called around six in the morning I was happy to officially get up.

He sounded excited. "With the idea that information is power, I've been online all night, Brenda. I surfed the Net, cruised the information superhighway, and you won't believe the cool stuff I found out about Bateman & Crews and your Mr. Duggins."

"I don't get it. Why would there be information about them online?"

"If you know where to go and how to ask, all the information in the world exists in cyberspace. Someday I'll show you. Meanwhile, here's the poop. This first part you probably already know. Any way you look at it, Bateman & Crews ranks as one of the top ten law firms in New York City. They've got a list of corporate clients that'll knock your socks off—everything from international banks to record industry moguls and television networks. What you probably don't know is that Bateman & Crews had been founded in the early 1900s by two corrupt horse traders, Elijah Bateman and Wendell Crews, who married into the same wealthy family and became brothers-in-law. The rumor is that they started the firm to defend themselves against theft charges."

"You're saying they were horse thieves?"

"More or less. As the firm got bigger and bigger, they left their shady background farther and farther behind. They probably figured out that they could earn more money defending crooks than being crooks, and with a lot less risk. Ever since Wendell Crews croaked thirty years ago, there hasn't been a Bateman or a Crews in the firm. However, the current partners proudly carry out the mission of the founding fathers: 'Bill everything.' "

"Sounds like a typical law firm to me. What did you find out about Mr. Duggins?"

"Ah, yes, the not-so-typical Mr. Duggins. You probably remember the story but don't remember his name. Robert Duggins has been with Bateman & Crews long enough that he probably remembers shaking hands with both Messrs. Bateman and Crews. Early in his career he was a star litigator, but in the mid–nineteen seventies he kind of went wacky on drugs and alcohol. One beautiful spring day he took a walk through Grand Central Terminal during the morning rush hour, ripped out of his mind and stark naked."

"I remember now. The Streaking Lawyer, naked with briefcase."

"Right. None other than Mr. Duggins. It wouldn't have been such a big deal—back then streaking was pretty commonplace—but one of the partners of a rival firm recognized Mr. Duggins, ran to a pay phone, and ratted to the media. Since it was a slow day for news, the story hit big."

"I don't remember what happened after the story died down. Did they disbar him?"

"No. He got himself into a bunch of twelve-step programs and willingly handed over the litigation department to a younger, more stable partner. Once he'd dried out sufficiently, Bateman & Crews found him a place as head of the Trusts and Estates Department, a dead-end kind of job. He's been there ever since."

The bus ride uptown lasted long enough that I almost chickened out a dozen different times. What if Ashley recognized me? What if I got caught? Was I committing fraud? Maybe I should have used a fake name. What was I getting myself into? Did I want to keep company with horse thieves and streakers? Maybe it wasn't worth the trouble. It was far-fetched to think that going through with this would put me any closer to nabbing Carla's murderer.

I got off the bus in the mid-Forties and hoofed it cross-town. It had been a long time since I'd walked through midtown at rush hour. Congested streets, congested side-walks, blaring horns—a nice place to visit but I sure wouldn't want to work there.

Bateman & Crews occupied the top five floors of a thirty-story building on Madison Avenue. I stood outside and watched the traffic for a few minutes to get up my nerve. Then I threw caution to the wind, committed myself to whatever would happen, and whooshed through the heavy revolving door, surfacing in the cool lobby at exactly ten minutes before nine.

The sound of my heels echoed conspicuously in my ears as I crossed the hard black marble floor. The thirty-foot-high ceiling intimidated me. People in suits walking pur-posefully unnerved me. Clutching the time card and work order from Robin's Early Bird Temp Service in my hand, I approached the guard station. The guard, a small man with thick glasses and very little hair left, was turned away from me, busy watching the rows of lights light up on the ele-vator control panel behind his desk.

"Excuse me," I said to get his attention.

He turned around. "Yes. How can I help you?"

I showed him the work order from Robin's. While he looked at it, I looked at my watch. "My agency told me to report to Robert Duggins at Bateman & Crews at nine o'clock sharp."

He waved the back of his hand in the air at me. "Dug-gins, he's not in yet, but his secretary's up there. You can go on up if you want. Top floor."

"Thanks." I scooted onto an open elevator and pushed the button for the thirtieth floor.

I watched floor numbers flash by. The higher the number, the harder it would be to chicken out. When the elevator stopped on thirty, the doors slid open, and I stepped off. I noticed a vague lemony smell that probably came from whatever product they used to keep the somber dark wood paneling well oiled.

To the right of the elevator bank were two heavy glass doors. I approached, and a woman with perfectly groomed glossy shoulder-length light brown hair buzzed me through into the plush beige reception area. The well-padded carpeting was low-key beige; the receptionist's conservative suit was the exact same shade. The only color came from two rich-toned life-size oil paintings. Each depicted a portly red-faced man with a dramatically curved mustache and round wire-frame glasses. The portraits hung on either side of a grandfather clock.

"Bateman and Crews?" I asked, pointing to the paintings of the two horse thieves.

The receptionist smiled tolerantly like she was asked this question often. "Actually that's Mr. Crews on the left and Mr. Bateman on the right."

"Oh, I see," I said. "Nice paintings. A proud tradition I'm sure."

She nodded in agreement with me. "What can I do for you?"

I showed her the Early Bird work order. "I'm supposed to report to Miss Caslon for Mr. Duggins."

She pointed down a long paneled hallway. "Trusts and Estates is all the way at the end. Mr. Duggins has the corner office."

"Thank you." I wondered if I looked as shaky as I felt walking down the hall. I considered that this was my last chance to bail out, but I didn't take it. Steeling myself for whatever might happen, I walked down the hall and found Miss Caslon's area.

As secretary to an important senior partner, Alice Caslon merited her own alcove office. It even had a set of windows that overlooked Madison Avenue, though, except for a two-

inch crack that let in a sliver of light, the heavy beige drap-
eries were closed.

I stood before her large walnut desk and cleared my
throat a couple of times until she looked up from her *Times*.

"Excuse me," I said. "The agency told me I should
report to a Miss Caslon."

She pushed her reading glasses to the end of her narrow
nose and gave me a thorough looking over. "I'm Alice
Caslon." She was prim, small-boned, around fifty-five, and
had perfect posture, salt-and-pepper chin-length hair, and a
precise manner of speech.

"I'm the temp," I said. "You know, from the agency.
Robin's Early Birds."

"Temp?" She shook her head. "There must be a mistake. Neither Mr. Duggins nor I requested temporary help."

"Are you positive? They've never made a mistake before
and it was Robin herself who called me late yesterday. She
said I should be here first thing today." I showed her the
time card and work order from Robin's. Both her name and
Mr. Duggins's name were clearly printed on the Report To
line.

She pushed her glasses back to the bridge of her nose,
squinted carefully at the work order, and frowned. "Perhaps Mr. Duggins called for someone himself after I'd gone
for the day. Yes, that must be it. He probably has another
one of his special projects in mind."

I jumped right on that one. "Yes, a special project.
That's exactly what the Robin told me. A special project
for Mr. Duggins."

"All right, then," she said. "You'd better take a seat
over there until Mr. Duggins gets in." She pointed to a
small desk in the corner of her office. It had a brand-new
computer on it. I noticed that Ms. Caslon's desk was conspicuously computer-free.

In the uncomfortable silence that followed, I tried to
make myself at home at the desk. I raised the chair, lowered
the chair, tilted the chair, folded my hands, unfolded my
hands, and rearranged the ballpoint pens. Miss Caslon re-

turned to the business pages of the *Times* and occasionally glanced over to see what I was up to. Finally she spoke. "You may as well turn that thing on." She nodded her head toward the computer. "Let's get it warmed up before Mr. Duggins arrives."

"Good idea," I said. My smile beamed confidence I did not feel. According to Chuck the worst part would be figuring out how to turn the computer on. He told me there were a thousand different ways to turn on a computer and a hundred different components to turn on. Sometimes the order mattered; sometimes it didn't matter. The computer could be a Mac. If so, it would turn on from the keyboard unless it was a newer Mac, in which case I should look for a button under the opening for the floppy disk drive. Of course, if I got stuck with a PC, the on button could be anywhere because nine times out of ten it'd be a clone and who knew who the hell had manufactured it or where they put the on buttons.

I studied the box. My finger hovered in front of a likely looking button. Please, god, I thought, this one's for Carla. I held my breath and glanced over at Miss Caslon. She wasn't looking. I pushed the button and a beautiful guitar chord sounded. Moments later the screen filled with little pictures. I was up and running, though I wasn't sure what. I clicked on some of the pictures with the mouse. Things jumped around impressively enough, though I doubted any of this would be useful on that special project for Mr. Duggins.

Around ten o'clock Mr. Duggins came in whistling a Broadway show tune I couldn't quite place and swinging a weathered leather briefcase. For an old guy, he had a lot of bounce in his step. He was small, almost petite, and had a full head of fluffy white hair that curled down the back of his neck. His two-thousand-dollar gray wool suit fit his body perfectly, his all-cotton starched shirt blazed bright white, his maroon tie pulled the look together. Overall, he looked confident and affluent. Braided leather suspenders added a touch of individuality. Quirky suspenders or not, I couldn't imagine Mr. Duggins prancing naked through Grand Central.

Miss Caslon snapped to attention. "Good morning, Mr. Duggins."

"Morning, Alice."

She folded up her *Times* and put it in her lower desk drawer. "Did you have a nice drive in?"

"Why yes, I did. Thank you, Alice." When he smiled his pale blue eyes twinkled. He got a pad of yellow legal paper out of his briefcase and handed it to Miss Caslon. "If you would please see to these few things. . . ." His voice trailed off when he saw me.

This was it, my big chance. Do or die. Pass or fail. If I couldn't convince Mr. Duggins he'd sent for me, I'd be booted out on the street, or worse, and would have to come up with another way to get the goods on Ashley. I took the bull by the horns. "Good morning, Mr. Duggins," I said, trying to sound calm and collected, hoping my voice didn't betray my terror.

"The agency sent her to work on your special project," said Miss Caslon, gesturing toward me. "I'm sorry, miss, but I didn't catch your name."

Actually, she'd never bothered to ask my name. "Brenda Midnight," I said.

Mr. Duggins looked confused. "Special project?" He looked over at Miss Caslon. She smiled back at him, nodding encouragingly. Then he smiled and said, "Oh yes, *that* special project. Well, then, good morning, Brenda. Happy to have you on board." He pumped my hand.

"It's nice to meet you, Mr. Duggins. I've heard so much about you."

"Hmm," he said, giving me a quizzical look. He turned to Miss Caslon. "Alice, please hold my calls this morning."

"Of course, Mr. Duggins."

"Now, if you'll both excuse me." He smiled and disappeared behind a heavy dark wood door.

15

A voice inside my head echoed, "It's not too late to disappear." I ignored it. The die was cast. Like it or not, I was in.

In at Bateman & Crews. Now what? How long would I have before Mr. Duggins or Miss Caslon realized that neither of them had sent for me and there was no special project? If I got lucky, I'd find out what I needed to know and clear out before they found out I wasn't supposed to be there.

Miss Caslon took the *Times* out of her bottom drawer and spread it out on her desk. I went back to clicking the computer mouse and watched shapes jump around on the computer screen. Somehow I must have goofed and the computer let out with a high-pitched screech that sounded like a small animal getting its foot stepped on. Miss Caslon looked over at me, her brow wrinkled with worry.

"It's all right," I said, smiling serenely. After that I cooled it with the mouse, scared I'd make it screech again. I'd have to remember to ask Chuck about that.

At a loss for what to do, I rearranged the ballpoint pens again and tried to compute the ancient question: If all the ball-point pens in this office were laid out end to end, how far would they stretch? To Miss Caslon's desk and back? To the elevators? Out the door and back to West Fourth Street?

Miss Caslon interrupted my thoughts. "Would you like

to read part of the *Times* while you're waiting? I'm through with the front section.''

"No, thank you. But I was thinking, as long as Mr. Duggins doesn't need me right away, maybe I should walk around a bit and get a feel for Bateman & Crews. You know, to lay some groundwork for the special project. That is, if you don't mind.''

"By all means, go,'' said Miss Caslon. "That sounds like a wonderful idea. Here, take this office directory with you. It'll help you get acquainted with the organization. Don't worry about us up here. If Mr. Duggins needs you, I'll page you.''

"Thanks. I'll see you later.''

Out by the elevators I paused to flip through the pages of the directory. Ashley Millard's office was on twenty-eight. I'd steer clear of that floor. Personnel was down on twenty-seven along with most of the other nonattorney support staff. That sounded like a good place to start.

The support staff didn't rate wood paneling, grandfather clocks, oil portraits of the founders, or even a floor receptionist. I walked around a mazelike hallway looking for the Personnel Department. Finally, past the Word Processing Department, past the Copy Department, past Shipping and Receiving, I found it. The secretary told me the director of personnel was too busy to see me. She clucked her tongue. "No. Not without an appointment. Not today.'' She ran her thumbnail down a list of days in an appointment calendar. "I can fit you in next Wednesday around three. Shall I put you down for then?''

"I'm afraid Mr. Duggins can't wait that long.''

"Mr. Duggins?''

"Yes. I'm working with Mr. Duggins on a special project. He asked me to get some information from the director.''

Dropping Mr. Duggins's name worked magic. The secretary smiled and closed her appointment calendar. "In that case you can go right in.'' She escorted me into the office, introducing me to the director of personnel as "Miss Midnight, from the Duggins special project."

I liked the sound of that.

The director of personnel, Ms. Rogers, was puffy fat and pink-skinned. She stood and shook my hand vigorously. "The Duggins special project, you say? I don't believe I've heard of that. Should I have?" When she smiled, deep dimples formed in her cheeks.

"Not necessarily," I said. "We're still in the planning stages on the project. Mr. Duggins told me I might want to start down here with personnel because, as he put it, 'people are the heart and soul of this organization.'"

Ms. Rogers liked that. "Mr. Duggins is certainly right about that. Here at Bateman & Crews, we ensure that the 'heart and soul' is truly exceptional. We make sure we hire only the cream of the crop by interviewing only the top ten percent of the top ten law schools in the country."

I nodded politely at her glowing descriptions of the stellar individuals that contributed to the heart and soul of Bateman & Crews, but I was really interested in the huge bank of black metal file cabinets that lined the wall behind her. Somewhere tucked in there was Ashley Millard's personnel file. Somewhere in there might be the key that would lead me to the Lady in Pink.

With a rap about how the founding fathers had come up from nothing, her spiel reached its crescendo. "So, you see," she said, flashing a wide smile, "B&C has been quality all the way."

I wondered if she knew that the founding Messrs. Bateman and Crews had been horse thieves. While she continued saying wonderful things about her employer, my eyes glazed over and my mind wandered to more important things, such as: Did she ever leave her office unattended? Could I somehow sneak a peek into those private files? Maybe if I told her Mr. Duggins wanted me to go through the files, culling for special people to feature in the special project, she'd fall for it? I should have been paying more attention to what she was saying, because all of a sudden

I realized she'd stopped talking. It was my turn to say something. "Uh . . . I've been looking at the file cabinets behind you," I said, "thinking how all those wonderful employees you've been telling me about are all reduced to squiggles on a few sheets of paper. When you speak, you give them such life, such dimension."

"Why, thank you," said Ms. Rogers. "I am a people person, you know. That's no doubt why Mr. Duggins sent you to me."

"No doubt," I said, bobbing my head up and down.

She smiled. "Funny you should mention those file cabinets, though." She lowered her voice. "Do you want to know a little Bateman & Crews secret?"

"Sure," I said.

"The file cabinets behind me are empty. Nothing in them but a spare pair of panty hose and a jar of low-cal coffee creamer. As of last month, B&C personnel files are one hundred percent computerized. Everything. All reduced to electronic blips. According to our consultant, in one year we'll save enough paper to equal two acres of old-growth forest."

Oh yeah, sure. Did she really fall for that hogwash? So much for the Personnel Department. A dead end. I checked my watch and stood up to leave. "I should be getting back to Mr. Duggins now. Thank you so much for your time."

"Of course. If there is anything more I can do to help with the special project, just give me a holler."

"Thank you. You've already done more than enough." Then, since I had nothing to lose, I figured I might as well shoot the works. "Actually," I said, "there is one more thing and I bet you know the answer. It's kind of off the subject, but I'm curious. When I looked through the office directory Miss Caslon gave me, I noticed an Ashley Millard listed. Is that the same Ashley Millard whose parents run the Millard Gallery down in Soho?"

Ms. Rogers beamed. "It most certainly is. She's quite a lovely girl, one of our recent hires. Do you know her?"

"From a long time ago. Didn't I read somewhere that she got married?"

The director of personnel sighed. "What a tragedy that turned out to be."

"Tragedy? What do you mean?"

"On the eve of the wedding, Ms. Millard's dressmaker was murdered. You know, another one of those drug-related things. The point is, she bled all over poor Ashley's wedding gown. Ashley was traumatized and postponed the wedding indefinitely."

"What a shame." I started out the door. I wanted to get out of there before I said something I'd regret.

She kept right on talking. "And that exquisite fabric from Mrs. Thackery's textile collection, all ruined. Such a loss."

I stopped in my tracks. "Fabric? Mrs. Thackery?"

"Oh, there I go shooting off my mouth again."

"Who's Mrs. Thackery?"

"A client. I probably shouldn't be saying this, but the fabric for Ms. Millard's dress came from one of the estates handled by Batemen & Crews—Mrs. Thackery's estate."

"Oh, really," I said. I didn't remember Carla mentioning that Ashley had supplied her own fabric.

On the way back to Miss Caslon's alcove I stopped off in the thirtieth-floor ladies' room. It reeked of privilege. The first room was a lounge with a plush velour rose-colored sofa in the center, floor-to-ceiling mirrors covering the walls, and fresh-cut flowers and individual packets of hand cream on a small end table. Beyond this room was the pink-tiled bathroom. While I was in there I heard two giggling women come into the lounge area.

The first woman, who called herself Sherry, had a shrill voice and a Brooklyn accent, quite un-Bateman & Crews-like. "So Mr. Cameron he says to me, 'Sherry, if you play your cards right, I'll send you along with Ellen next time she goes to Europe.' Then he goes on to tell me that Ellen sometimes forgets to play by the rules. Now, you *know* what a witch she is, so I can just imagine.''

The second woman sounded a little less shrill, a little less Brooklyn. ''But Sherry,'' she said, ''what about the part about you playing your cards right. You wouldn't—''

''Heavens, no! Cameron's such a creep. Smarmy. He asked me to call him Wayne. Can you imagine!''

''So what are you going to do? An all-expense-paid to Europe sounds pretty tempting.''

''Girl, never underestimate Sherry Ramone. I didn't go to secretarial school for nothing. I'll lead Waynie-poo on long enough to get the goods on him. Then I'll threaten a sexual harassment suit unless he sends me to Europe.''

''That's brilliant, Sherry, truly brilliant.''

''Thanks. I thought so too. I better get back now before Wayne misses me.''

I stayed in the bathroom until I was positive they were gone. A little sexual harassment mixed with blackmail spiced up the joint. Things at Bateman & Crews weren't quite as rosy as the picture painted by Ms. Rogers in personnel.

I took the long way back to Miss Caslon's alcove, circling the entire thirtieth floor. Most of the secretaries wore ugly neutral-colored suits with skirt hems way below their knees. I wondered if one of them was Sherry Ramone.

''Did you have an interesting little tour?'' asked Miss Caslon when I got back.

''Yes. I had an enlightening conversation with the director of personnel. She's a real people person.''

''She certainly is.''

I spent the rest of the day trying to get the hang of the word processing program on the computer. All the time, Miss Caslon thought I was working on the special project. She smiled when she saw me hard at work. Occasionally I paused, bit my lower lip, and stared at the ceiling as if trying to come up with something. Then I'd go back to the keyboard, typing faster and more furiously than ever.

Around three o'clock Miss Caslon told me that she'd like to leave early. "You don't mind handling things for Mr. Duggins, do you? Sometimes he needs a little extra special care."

"No problem," I said.

Miss Caslon gathered her things and left.

If Mr. Duggins needed anything handled, he sure didn't let me know about it. At five o'clock I knocked on his door and opened it a crack. "Will you be needing me anymore today?"

"No, I don't think so. You can go. Did Miss Caslon mention anything about tomorrow?"

"No."

"Hmmm. Well, you'd better come back, then. She may still need you."

I didn't know if it was worth going back to Bateman & Crews. In one long day I hadn't learned a blasted thing about Ashley except that the fabric from her wedding dress came from some textile collection instead of Carla. Big deal. Carla's clients often supplied their own fabric. On the bright side, I made $226.25. Without the shorthand it would have been only $200.

16

The red light on Carla's phone machine blinked in a pattern of two on, two off that meant two calls had come in while I had been wasting time at Bateman & Crews. Robin from the Early Birds had called; so had Chuck. For different reasons, both wanted to know how my day had gone.

I never got around to taking a lunch break at Bateman & Crews. Now starved, I grabbed a box of graham crackers to keep my stomach from growling while I returned the calls. I called Robin first to get her out of the way. "It went really well," I told her. "In fact, Mr. Duggins wants me to come back tomorrow."

"That's wonderful, Brenda. I'm thrilled. I must admit that I lost sleep over sending you out sight unseen to a partner, without the usual Early Bird battery of tests. I'm glad to hear it worked out. You'd be amazed at the lies some people tell to exaggerate their skills."

I probably wouldn't be surprised. "If it'll make you feel any better, Robin, I'll come in and take the tests."

"No, no, no. That's not necessary. As long as they want you back at Bateman & Crews, that's all that matters. Which brings me to another question. Do you think you'll get a chance to snoop around for me?"

A piece of my graham cracker jammed halfway down my throat. "Snoop? What do you mean?"

"With your help, Brenda, Bateman & Crews could turn

into a very lucrative account for us here at the Early Birds. Snoop around. See what you can find out. What other agencies do they use? Which partners request the most temps? That kind of stuff. Get me some useful information and there'll be a little extra in your paycheck for your trouble. When Robin's does well, our temps do well. That's why we think of ourselves as one big happy family.''

"Oh," I said, greatly relieved. "That kind of snooping. I'll see what I can do.''

"We'll make it well worth your while.''

Next I dialed Chuck.

"How'd you do with the computer?" he asked. In the background I heard the rumble of an Urban Dog Talk bass line.

"Thanks to your help, the computer part was a snap. I did exactly what you told me to, and in no time at all I had the machine up and running. I don't think the secretary, Miss Caslon, is the least bit computer savvy. She seemed impressed when I turned it on.''

"What kind of work did they give you? Anything you couldn't handle?''

"They didn't actually give me any work at all. I've got them snowed. Both Mr. Duggins and Miss Caslon think I'm working on an important special project. Miss Caslon thinks I'm working for Mr. Duggins, and Mr. Duggins thinks I'm working for Miss Caslon. Meanwhile, they want me back tomorrow. I'm not so sure I want to go back and waste another day. I may have managed to turn on the computer, which was great for my ego, but I didn't get any closer to finding out who killed Carla.''

"You didn't get anything at all?''

"Oh, sure I did. I found out that the personnel director is a people person, and that one of the secretaries hates her sleazy boss and is setting him up for a sexual harassment suit.''

"Cool.''

"No, Chuck. Not cool. For a while it looked like I might have had something. I got along so swimmingly with the personnel director, whose job it is to get along with people, that for a moment I thought maybe she'd leave me alone in her office and I'd get a chance to peek at her files. But then, when I was trying to figure out how to get her out of her office, she told me that all the files are electronic. The file cabinets I coveted were empty. The whole thing was a washout.''

"Whoa, baby," said Chuck. "Back up there for a nanosecond. She said their files are electronic? Everything?"

"Yep. That's what she said."

"Hot damn, shit on a swizzle stick. Don't you know what that means?" asked Chuck.

"Sure," I said. "It means fewer trees get chopped down. According to some bullshit story a consultant fed them, they've already rescued two acres of old-growth forest from the wood chipper."

"No, Brenda. It means we can peruse the B&C files at our leisure, safely, from the comfort of home, all through the wonders of electronic breaking and entering. It's neater, cleaner, and easier than trying to access paper files. It's the modern way. Get me the telephone number of their mainframe and modems. That's all I need to hack my way in."

"I've already got the numbers you'd need. Miss Caslon gave me a copy of the firm directory. But Chuck, I'm not so sure this is such a good idea."

"It's a *great* idea. I've been looking for an excuse to hack into someplace for a long time."

I munched on another graham cracker and thought it over. "I don't know. I can't afford to close Midnight Millinery again tomorrow. Customers see the place closed and they think the worst. Plus I've got to get going on my fall line."

"Come on, Brenda. Don't punk out on me. Be realistic. You're not going to be able to design hats for any season until you find out who killed Carla. You don't have to worry about Midnight Millinery. I'll watch the store for you. I can set up one of my computers and start writing the password-generating algorithms."

"You really think you can break into the Bateman & Crews personnel files?"

"I can hack my way into anything."

I must have been nuts to even consider leaving Chuck in charge of Midnight Millinery. I'd never left the shop with anyone other than Carla. She knew fashion, knew how to make the customers feel good. Chuck, on the other hand, wasn't known for his social skills or fashion expertise. To be blunt, Chuck was not suave. He was crude, rude, and perpetually glued to his computer. Aside from Urban Dog Talk, Chuck met most of his friends online. They typed back and forth at each other in cyberspace, rarely meeting face-to-face.

On the other hand, Chuck was right about one thing: I'd never be able to concentrate on my fall line with Carla's killer still running around loose. So, after much hemming and hawing, I gave in and agreed to let Chuck baby-sit Midnight Millinery. "This is the slow season," I told him, "so you won't need to open up before noon or so. If someone buys a hat, wrap it in tissue and pack it up in a hatbox. If anyone wants a special order, take their phone number and I'll get back to them."

"Sissy stuff," said Chuck, "but I can do it."

The graham crackers weren't enough to stave off my hunger. I called Johnny to see if he'd eaten yet. "I've had dinner," he said, "but I've got to meet Lemmy in a little while for drinks at Angie's. Why don't you meet us there and grab a grilled cheese? I'm sure Lemmy won't mind. He likes you."

Angie's. In the glittering New York I liked to imagine, an actor did not meet his agent at a joint like Angie's for drinks. In my imaginary New York, an actor would meet his agent in the lounge of an elegant midtown hotel. They would sit in large plush leather chairs and ring little brass bells for service. In real life, though, it was difficult to imagine Johnny's agent, Lemon Crenshaw, anywhere but Angie's.

Lemon Crenshaw was a short, plump, fast-talking, bald guy who dressed in shiny ill-fitting suits and liked his whiskey and his women straight. He had better luck with the whiskey than the women. Both of his ex-wives had left him for another woman. To say Lemmy was a bitter man was an understatement. Johnny said it made him a better agent.

I found Lemmy and Johnny sitting at the far end of Angie's timeworn gouged and dimpled bar. Lemmy climbed off his bar stool and gave me a bearish hug. He smelled of whiskey and citrus aftershave. "Long time no see, Brenda."

"It has been, hasn't it."

He pulled out the stool between him and Johnny and helped me up. "Johnny tells me you're in hot pursuit of the broad who offed that friend of yours."

"In a manner of speaking, though I haven't been making much progress. The cops are no help; they're all hung up on the Laurel Tipton confession."

"I think I can help you out," said Lemmy. "If you let me handle the Laurel Tipton angle, I'll have that third-rate bimbo *un*confessing in no time."

"How?"

"By doing what I do best. I'll become her agent and get her a real acting job, one that she can't do from prison."

"You're brilliant, Lemmy." I gave him a peck in the middle of his shiny forehead.

"Thank you," he said.

The bartender dropped off a dark beer for Johnny and whiskey for Lemmy. I ordered a red wine and grilled cheese.

"Guess what else Lemmy did," said Johnny.

"I don't know, what?"

"He got me a six-episode deal." Johnny raised his fist in the air. "Tod Trueman, urban detective, rides again."

"That's great," I said. "Congratulations."

Lemmy beamed. "This time it's going to fly."

"Plus," said Johnny, "now I've got a good excuse to hang out at the precinct and poke around for you. I'm going to try to get Turner and McKinley to show me the ropes. I'd like to give Tod more depth, make him something of a Turner-type cop. Fallible.''

"You couldn't find a better model," I said.

On the way home I ran into Elizabeth and Jackhammer in front of the building. Jackhammer, nose to the ground, sniffed his way from a NO PARKING sign to a fire hydrant and back again, finally lifting his leg on the fire hydrant.

"Didn't you go to Bateman & Crews today?" asked Elizabeth.

I gave her the short version. "All in all, probably a waste of time. I'm going back tomorrow, though, to give it another try."

"Good luck. I talked to the precinct captain again today. He called to make a reservation for his bulldog, Elmo. I took advantage of the situation and pumped him for information. He claims his detectives are still following up on Laurel Tipton."

"I've got good reason to believe that won't go on much longer," I said. "Laurel Tipton is about to be exposed for the third-rate actress she is."

"How?"

"Lemon Crenshaw's on the case."

"Who?"

"It's a long story. Let's just say that where Lemmy goes, shit happens."

"Speaking of which," said Elizabeth, "good boy, Jackhammer."

Before going to bed, I dragged Carla's notes on the Millard wedding out of the top of her closet. I'd looked through the notes once before, hoping to find something that would lead me to the Lady in Pink. At the time, I didn't pay much attention to the fabric specs. Now, however, I was curious about Ms. Rogers's statement that some of the fabric came from an estate.

Carla kept swatches of the fabrics she used with the pa-

perwork for each project. She stapled each swatch to a
piece of paper with notes about where she got it, price,
color availability, proper care, and any problems she'd had
with it. Of the fifteen swatches catalogued for the Millard
wedding, all but one had come from Carla's usual sources
on Fortieth Street. The odd one out was the fabric I liked,
the lace for the bodice of the dress and the crown of the
veil. Ashley had supplied that lace herself.

I couldn't find a mention of Mrs. Thackery or her estate
anywhere, but off in the margin Carla had written the name
Wayne Cameron. The name rang a bell. I was pretty sure
he was the attorney the two secretaries in the john were
talking about. Wayne Cameron was the sleazeball who was
going to get slapped with a sexual harassment suit if he
wasn't careful.

17

The next morning I got to Bateman & Crews bright and early, but not before Miss Caslon. Like the day before, she had her face buried in the *Times*. She looked up when I arrived. "Good morning. Scorcher, isn't it?"

"Hot and sticky," I agreed, hurrying over to my desk before she had a chance to notice that I had on the same let-down skirt and baggy blazer as yesterday. I made myself as comfortable as possible and, with the confidence of a pro, flicked on the computer.

Miss Caslon turned a page in the *Times* and smoothed it out with her hand. "Mr. Duggins called to say you'd be back today. Unfortunately, he came down with a bad case of the sniffles and won't be in. I'm afraid you'll have to carry on with the special project without his help."

"No problem," I said. "There's no need to bother Mr. Duggins with the petty details and preliminary programming. I'll do fine without him."

"Good. That's what I was hoping. Meanwhile, if there's anything I can do . . ."

"You know, maybe you can help me out. Remember how yesterday I visited with the director of personnel?"

"Of course."

"Well, during our conversation she mentioned something about a Mrs. Thackery. Does she work here?"

"Work here? Hardly. Gladys Thackery never worked

anywhere. We handled her estate a few months back.''

''A big estate?''

''Enormous. Gladys Thackery's estate spanned the globe,'' said Miss Caslon. ''It was a complicated estate. Quite frankly, Gladys Thackery exhausted the resources of Trusts and Estates. We had to hire freelancers to help. Personnel helped in the coordination of that effort.''

''It must have been intriguing.''

''Oh, it was.'' Miss Caslon folded her *Times*, leaned back in her chair, and smiled at the memory. ''Gladys Thackery was what is known as a 'character.' Ninety-nine when she died, filthy rich, and more than a bit eccentric. She blew out a blood vessel screaming at a daytime TV show. She inherited all her money from a long series of husbands, each wealthier than the last, and each dying under mysterious circumstances.''

''Did she kill them?''

''No one knows,'' said Miss Caslon. ''Nothing was ever proved, no charges ever brought against her, but when each husband croaked, tongues wagged all over the world. The estate was further complicated because Gladys Thackery had a vengeful temper and left no human heirs. Many of the institutions and charities mentioned in her will had ceased to exist long before Gladys Thackery herself had departed. As executor of the estate, Bateman & Crews had to sort out the mess. Wayne Cameron's staff needed outside help to handle the on-site inventory and shipping for the estate.''

''Wayne Cameron?'' There was that name again.

''Mr. Cameron is in charge of the day-to-day work of estate dispensation. He's an attorney, but not a partner. He reports directly to Mr. Duggins.''

''Wasn't part of the estate a textile collection?''

''Oh yes. The Gladys Thackery Collection of Medieval Wall Hangings. Famous the world over. It's a good example of why this was such a difficult estate. Mrs. Thackery originally left the collection to the small Ohio college where she met and married her first husband, a professor of art history. By the time of her death, though, the college had merged with another college, and then both of them were swallowed up by a larger institution. Wayne Cameron's staff went all over the world cataloguing the textiles. Until the proper heir could be determined, the entire collection was stored in an empty office here.''

''Did you get to see the collection?'' I asked.

''Everybody in the firm saw it at one time or another.''

''Was there any bridal lace in the collection?''

''Heaven's no. Mrs. Thackery abhorred frilly things.''

Something didn't quite check out. The personnel drector had mentioned Mrs. Thackery's collection in connection with the fabric in Ashley's wedding dress. Carla's records showed that Ashley had provided the fabric herself, and had Wayne Cameron's name scribbled in the margin. There was something weird about this fabric. I needed to talk to Wayne Cameron. He probably knew more than Miss Caslon.

Miss Caslon looked at her watch. ''Oh my, look at the time. I'm afraid I've gone on far too long. You'd better get back to the special project. I'm sure Mr. Duggins will want to see results when he gets back.''

''Don't worry about it,'' I said. ''This is exactly the kind of information I need for the special project. Not that I'll specifically use any of it, you understand, but you've given me a good idea of the kind of painstaking work typical of Bateman & Crews. You've given me a feel for the place.''

When Miss Caslon wasn't looking I sneaked the Batemen & Crews directory into my purse. Chuck said the directory and a little time was all he needed to break into the B&C files. I figured the more computer-type information he had, the easier it would be. So, under the guise of research for Mr. Duggins's special project, I called Ray Marshall, who ran the computer help desk at Bateman & Crews. He agreed to meet with me.

The minute I saw Ray Marshall my heart did flip-flops. Tall sinewy body, dark liquid eyes, strong narrow nose, and

sensuous mouth. I'd expected to find someone like Chuck
in dress and demeanor running the computer department,
but Ray's suit was custom made and he was charming as
all get-out. He had a wide smile, a resonant voice, and a
solid handshake. Though I usually don't like to admit to
such things, it's entirely possible that as I sat down in a
chair opposite his desk and crossed my right leg over my
left, I may have hiked my skirt up a bit beyond Bateman
& Crews protocol and flexed my ankle just so. When I
looked into Ray's eyes I couldn't imagine any yellow-and-
orange shag rugs in *his* apartment.

Too enthralled to speak, I sat there like a jerk and tried
to remember why I'd come to see him in the first place.

He broke the silence. "You say you're working on a
special project."

"Yes," I said, "for Mr. Duggins. It's still in the early
stages. Right now I'm gathering background material. I've
heard that Bateman & Crews has a very sophisticated computer filing system."

"Bateman & Crews was the first major law firm in New
York to automate to this extent. The personnel records are
totally automated. Plus we're fully networked. We've got
PCs, Macs, laptops, workstations, and mainframes, some
here and some off-site, all working together seamlessly."

"Fascinating," I said. Mesmerized by his voice, I felt
like we were having a romantic dinner by candlelight discussing anything but a computer network.

"Is there anything specific you'd like to know?" he
asked.

Nothing I could think of besides marital status. A quick
check of his naked ring finger perked me up. "I'm interested in the people behind such a state-of-the-art system,"
I said, not lying for once. "People like you, people who
make the computers click. You must face all sorts of fascinating problems."

He looked straight at me with those riveting dark eyes.
"You better believe it. I get distress calls all hours of the
day and night. Distress calls from people who can't remem-

ber how to turn their systems on, and at least as many from people who can't remember how to turn their systems off. Then there are those who've forgotten their passwords. We have two-part passwords. The first part is a six-digit code generated by an algorithm written specially for us. We change these every couple of months to be on the safe side. The second part is a four-to six-digit code made up by the individual employee. It takes two keys to open the system, like a safe-deposit box.''

''Most people forget the first part?''

''Right, those are easy to fix. I can look up those records. You'd be surprised to find out how many people forget the codes they made up. I can't help at all in those cases.''

''What do you do then?''

''Sometimes we have to start all over from scratch.''

The phone on his desk jangled, breaking the mood. He picked up, listened for a moment, frowned, and mumbled something into the receiver. ''I'm afraid I've got to cut this short,'' he said, pushing his chair back and standing up. ''One of the new associates screwed something up. It's amazing. Bateman & Crews hires only the best of the best, starting pay is over eighty thou, and still they don't know a damned thing about computers. I don't know what they teach in law schools these days, but it sure ain't computers.''

Too bad, I thought. It would have been nice to spend more time with Ray Marshall. ''Thank you for your trouble, Ray. I appreciate it.''

''My pleasure. I hope we'll be seeing more of each other.''

Now, what did he mean by that? I felt positively giddy. For the first time since Carla had been killed, I remembered that I was still alive.

When I got back, a note on Miss Caslon's desk said she was out to lunch and would return in an hour. I took advantage of the time alone to call Chuck at Midnight Millinery.

"Yo, this is Midnight Millinery where we block around the clock."

My god, I'd created a monster. "Chuck," I said, "you can't answer the phone that way."

"Give me some credit, Brenda. I knew it was you."

"How'd you know it was me before I said anything? Are you psychic or something?"

"Afraid not. I installed a caller ID box on your line."

"Oh. I see. How are things going?"

"Swell. Don't worry about a thing. Did you get the Bateman & Crews directory for me?"

"Not only that. I got some other information you might find useful." I told him about my talk with Ray Marshall, leaving out the part about how he made my pulse quicken and my knees weak.

"Thanks, Brenda," said Chuck. "That's a big help. Do me one last favor. See if you can find out Mr. Duggins's birthday."

"Why?"

"He probably uses a permutation of it as his personal access code."

While we were talking I heard the bells on the shop door jingle, then voices in the background.

"Who's there? A hat customer?"

"No," said Chuck, "not exactly. That's a résumé customer. Your neighbor Elizabeth is taking care of it."

"Elizabeth? What's she doing there?"

"I'd rather explain in person."

"Has anyone come in for a hat today?"

"Like you said, Brenda, it's the slow season."

I peeked down the hall to make sure Miss Caslon wasn't on her way back. The coast was clear, so I flipped through the calendar on her desk until I got to a page with a day circled in red. She'd neatly printed inside the circle "Mr. Duggins's Birthday."

I called Chuck back. I figured the sooner he had the

information the better. This time Elizabeth answered. "Midnight Millinery."

At least she answered properly. "Where's Chuck?" I asked.

"He went home to get his laser printer."

"Laser printer? What for?"

"He'll explain when you get here."

"He'd damned well better. Meanwhile, when he gets back tell him I found out Mr. Duggins's birthday. It's May twenty-second."

"I'll make a note of it," said Elizabeth.

No sooner had I hung up than Miss Caslon came back from lunch, gathered up her things, and announced that she was leaving for the day. "There's no reason for me to stay, is there? You seem to work quite well independently, Miss Midnight. A good self-starter. I believe I'll put in a good word for you with your agency."

"Thank you. I'd appreciate that."

I didn't see much reason for me to stick around either. It probably wouldn't be worth the trouble to talk to Wayne Cameron about the Thackery textile collection. As far as I was concerned, it was far more important to get back and see what Chuck and Elizabeth were up to at Midnight Millinery. Résumés? Laser printers? Something had gone awfully wrong.

As I headed out, the phone on my desk rang. I debated whether or not to answer and finally picked it up on the fifth ring. A good decision on my part, because it was Ray Marshall. "I feel as if we didn't get to finish our conversation," he said in a voice that melted me. "What I thought was that maybe we could get together for dinner or something."

It took me by complete surprise. My heart pounded. When I could finally speak I said, "Dinner? That would be nice."

"Tonight?" asked Ray.

No hesitation on my part. "Sure."

"Around eight?" he asked.

I gave him my address.

I stopped in my tracks, did an about-face, and retreated around the corner. A bunch of attorneys stood by the elevator bank, talking. Among them, one Ashley Millard. I was pretty sure she wouldn't recognize me in my law firm getup but could see no reason to push my luck. I wouldn't want to have to explain what I was doing at Bateman & Crews. As I peeked around the corner two elevators came and went but the attorneys didn't get on. All of a sudden it didn't seem like such a good time to leave.

As long as I was stuck at Bateman & Crews awhile longer, I figured I may as well stop by Wayne Cameron's office.

"You got an appointment?" asked his secretary.

I recognized the voice as that of Sherry Ramone, the woman I'd heard gossiping yesterday in the john. I pegged her at about twenty-five, a few years younger than most of the women I'd seen around the firm. With an incredible inch-long red-and-black-striped fingernail, she picked at a fleck of mascara adhered to her cheek.

I introduced myself and explained that I was working on a special project for Mr. Duggins. "Do you think I could have a moment of Wayne Cameron's time?"

"I'll check," she said. "He's not doing much of anything." She pressed a button on her telephone. "Brenda Midnight would like to see you."

Through a tinny speaker I heard Wayne Cameron's voice. "Brenda who? Does she have an appointment?"

Sherry smirked. "Mr. Duggins sent her."

Again, the magic words.

Wayne Cameron, though well over forty, was puffed up with about forty pounds of baby fat. His thin light brown hair was styled in a left-to-right comb-over that exaggerated his baldness.

He stood up and shook my hand. His palm felt cool and spongy. "What's this about a special project?"

I didn't like the way he looked at me. It wasn't exactly a leer, but it wasn't exactly not a leer either.

"I'm working with Mr. Duggins on a special project. During my preliminary research I learned that you handled the Gladys Thackery estate. *The* Gladys Thackery with the famous textile collection. I'm in awe. You see, I'm kind of a textile enthusiast myself. I know that Mrs. Thackery's collection was famous for its medieval wall hangings, but I've heard through the grapevine that there was also beaded lace in the collection."

Before answering, he drummed his sausage-like fingers on the desk. Shaking his head, he said, "No, you've been listening in on the wrong grapevine. Mrs. Thackery collected medieval wall hangings, not beaded lace. Now, if you'll excuse me, I have work to do."

That's pretty much what Miss Caslon had told me.

On my way out Sherry Ramone held her forefinger to her lips, walked into the hall, and beckoned me to follow.

"Look, it's none of your business why, but I'm trying to get something on Cameron, so I listened in just now. Cameron's full of shit. There was a piece of lace in Mrs. Thackery's collection. Real pretty beads all over it. Cameron's a sleazebag. He sold it to one of the attorneys and pocketed the money. That's why he won't admit it was there."

"Do you know who Mr. Cameron sold the lace to?"

"Sure," said Sherry. "Ashley Millard, a rich bitch attorney, to use for her custom-made wedding dress. Please don't tell Mr. Duggins. If he ever found out, he'd fire Cameron."

"If you're so anxious to get something on your boss, why don't you go to Mr. Duggins yourself?"

"'Cause I have something better in mind. If I play my cards right, I'll get an all-expense-paid trip to Europe out of it."

18

The thought of Chuck Riley in charge of Midnight Millinery so terrified me that I splurged on a cab from Bateman & Crews to the shop. When I got there and saw what he'd done, my first instinct was to scream. He'd set up his computer in the back of the shop on the long smooth-surfaced table I used for production cutting and pattern drafting. A bulky laser printer sat on top of my good strong blocking table. Chuck and Elizabeth sat with their heads close together staring at the computer screen. Occasionally Elizabeth typed a few words.

In my haste to strangle Chuck, I tripped over a thick ugly wire that stretched between the two machines about four inches off the floor.

"Careful, Brenda," he said, catching my forearm to keep me from falling on my face.

"What the hell are you doing to my store?"

"Sorry about the cable, Brenda, but it's only temporary. I'll bring a longer one and tape it to the floor so you won't have to worry about tripping."

I looked at Elizabeth. "What's your part in all this?" I asked, immediately sorry because I saw that my words hurt her feelings.

"When I walked by this morning with Jackhammer, I saw Chuck through the window. I didn't know if he was a burglar or a friend of yours, so I watched him for a while.

When I saw he wasn't stealing anything, I stopped in and introduced myself.''

For the first time I noticed Jackhammer curled up on the vanity stool. In the few hours I'd been away, my so-called friends had taken over Midnight Millinery. I felt out of place in my own store.

Oblivious to my distress, Chuck babbled on. "When we got our first résumé customer," he said, "I showed Elizabeth—"

"Back up a minute," I said. "What do you mean by résumé customer?"

Chuck gave me a look like I was stupid. "Well, this morning when I was setting up the computer this guy comes in and asks what the computer's for. Now I'm in this weird position. I can't tell him the truth, so I tell him that during the slow season Midnight Millinery does desktop publishing. The guy's real happy, has a résumé he needs done right away, and asks if I can get it to him this afternoon. I tell him I can and then start typing it up. Then Elizabeth comes in and that's even better because I can't get the résumé to look good but she's this artist; did you know she was an artist?"

"Yes, I knew she was an artist."

Chuck continued. "So Elizabeth may not know the computer but she knew how to make the résumé look good. We made like this great team. The guy picked up his résumé and was so happy with the results that he sent two of his friends in who also needed résumés. Then this lady comes in and she wants a brochure and this other lady comes in for a lost cat poster. We did the lost cat poster for free. You know, to build up goodwill in the neighborhood. After we finished the work I showed Elizabeth how to go online, and she's been having a blast."

"It's fascinating," said Elizabeth. "Right now I'm having a stimulating conversation, talking—well, not really talking—typing actually . . .''

Chuck helped her out. "Virtually talking," he said.

"Yes," said Elizabeth "virtually talking to Dude Bob Forty-three in Montana about—"

"Who?"

"Dude Bob Forty-three," said Elizabeth. "That's the name he goes by online, his cyber handle so to speak. See?" She tapped the screen with her finger. Words scrolled by, among them "Dude Bob 43." She tapped the screen again. "That's me. I signed on as 'Luscious Liz.' With that name I've been quite the belle of the ball. Of all the guys typing at me, I like Dude Bob Forty-three the best. Right now he's trying to entice me into a private discussion area. Chuck won't let me go, though; says Dude wants to talk dirty."

"Dude Bob Forty-three's a pig," said Chuck. "I've seen him around before. Nothing but a cyber pervert." He pushed his chair away from the computer, leaving Elizabeth to handle Dude by herself. "Did you get the Bateman & Crews directory for me?"

I handed him the directory.

"This is great, Brenda. With this, Mr. Duggins's birthday, and that information you pried out of that computer guy, I'll get into the files pronto. You should get a job as a corporate spy. I'll bet it pays better than millinery." He scooted his chair back to the computer and took the mouse away from Elizabeth and started the sign-off procedure. "Sorry, Liz, we've got to get to work. It's time to hack into Bateman & Crews."

"Okay. Let me say good-bye to Dude Bob Forty-three." Elizabeth's fingers tapped a few more words on the keyboard; then she turned over the computer to Chuck. "Do you think I'll ever see him online again?"

"Don't worry," said Chuck, "Dude Bob Forty-three's always around somewhere in cyberspace. He'll be back."

I didn't see any point in staying at Midnight Millinery. I wouldn't get any work done with the two of them there, and I didn't feel up to throwing them out. "Do you need me to hang around anymore?" I asked.

"Nah," said Chuck. "Go home and rest. If you want,

you can meet us at Angie's later for dinner.''

"Thanks, but not tonight. I have dinner plans.''

Chuck grinned. "Super. I knew you'd get back together with Johnny sooner or later.''

"It's not Johnny,'' I said. "I'm going out with Ray Marshall, the guy who runs the computer help desk at Bateman & Crews.''

"What about that nice young man I've seen you with?'' asked Elizabeth.

"Tall, dark, and dashing?'' asked Chuck.

Elizabeth nodded.

"That's Johnny,'' said Chuck. "Brenda and Johnny broke up because of some stupid rug that Brenda can't stand.''

"There's more to it than the rug,'' I said.

"Oh, right,'' said Chuck. "Brenda doesn't like the color of his walls either.''

"The rug is a symptom. It shows that Johnny and I are fundamentally incompatible,'' I said.

Chuck wouldn't give in. "That's a crock, Brenda, and you know it.'' He turned to Elizabeth. "Johnny's a cool guy. Brenda's a fool. She's going to end up an old maid.''

"Not possible,'' I said. "I've already been married twice.''

"Two times! You've got to be kidding,'' said Chuck.

"That's nothing,'' said Elizabeth. "I've been married four times.''

Chuck jumped up. "I can't believe it. What's the matter with you ladies, anyway?''

"Nothing,'' said Elizabeth. "It's just we marry men, and men are bums. Right, Brenda?''

"Well . . .''

My exes hadn't been bums exactly. They were more like jerks. Much as I'd like to blame them for the breakups, deep down I knew at least forty-nine percent of the blame was mine. Of course, I'd never admit that in mixed company. I didn't have to. Chuck and Elizabeth were embroiled in a discussion about men bums and women bums and forgot all about me. I patted Jackhammer on the head and sneaked out.

I'd walked halfway to the corner when Chuck came running after me. "Hang on a minute, Brenda. I almost forgot." He handed me a small brown envelope with a hundred dollars inside.

"What's this for? Did you sell a hat?"

"No Brenda. You said it yourself. It's the slow season for hats. This is your third of what we took in for the résumés and the brochure."

"My third?"

"Elizabeth and I figured that's about fair—a third to you since it's your store, a third to Elizabeth for design, and a third to me for equipment and production know-how. If you want more . . ."

I put the envelope in my pocket. "A third is fine." I couldn't remember the last time the shop had taken in three hundred dollars in one day.

"We'll do even better tomorrow, now that the word is out."

"Tomorrow?"

"Aren't you going back to Bateman & Crews tomorrow?"

"I hadn't planned on it."

"Oh." Chuck looked down at the sidewalk. "You see, we kind of figured, you know, the brochure lady, she's coming back to proof her job . . ."

In the end I agreed to let them come in and finish up the jobs they'd started. "But after tomorrow, Midnight Millinery is just that—a millinery store."

"Thanks, Brenda. I knew you'd see it my way. I'll call you as soon as I hack into the files."

I foraged through the plastic garbage bags on the floor until I found both of my black going-out-to-dinner-with-a-new-guy dresses. A dress in each hand, I stood in front of Carla's full-length mirror. First I held the long one up, then the short, then alternated long, short, long, short and finally settled on the long one.

I could wait until after Ray came to accessorize. If he came in a suit, I'd put on a necklace and heels; if he came casual I'd wear cowboy boots.

At eight on the dot the doorman buzzed me. ''Mr. Marshall is here to see you.''

''What's he wearing? A suit?''

''No, jeans.''

I pulled on my cowboy boots.

Once guys get over thirty-five or so they fall into two distinct groups—those who can still wear jeans and those who can't. Ray Marshall definitely fell into the first group. He looked great in jeans.

''Nice building,'' he said. ''Is it a rental?'' I didn't know where Ray was from originally. His accent reminded me a little of the Midwest, but he'd been around New York at least long enough to become obsessed with real estate.

''No, it's a condo. This is my friend's. . . . I mean it was. What I really mean is, excuse the mess. I recently moved in and am not quite settled in yet.''

''Well, it's a nice place.''

''Thanks.''

I recommended Joey's, a charming neighborhood Italian place in the opposite direction of Midnight Millinery. I couldn't risk Ray's seeing the shop and associating me with it, not while Chuck was in there trying to hack into the Bateman & Crews computer.

We walked down a flight of crumbling cement steps to the entrance of Joey's a few feet below street level. When we opened the door, Joey himself rushed over. ''Well, well, well, come in, come in,'' he said, buzzing my cheek. ''It's been awhile. What's the matter? You didn't find pumpkin ravioli any better than Joey's, did you?''

''Never,'' I said. ''You're the best, Joey. I've been sticking kind of close to home for a while.''

While we bantered about ravioli, Joey gave Ray a good looking over. When he'd finished he raised his bushy eyebrows in a quizzical look. I shrugged my shoulders. Like everyone else in the Village, Joey expected to see me with Johnny. And, like everyone else in the Village, Joey was insufferably nosy. He led us to a corner table in the back of the room, making a point of avoiding the table Johnny and I had regularly shared. He recited a long list of specials, then turned us over to a green-jacketed waiter. We chose a bottle of red wine and asked for a few minutes to look at the menu.

"What do you recommend?" Ray asked.

A whirlwind romance, short engagement, and happily ever after, I thought. "It's all good," I said, "but as a vegetarian I'm partial to the nonmeat dishes."

The waiter came back with the wine and a basket of hot garlic bread. I ordered my usual pumpkin ravioli; Ray got the linguini with pesto.

We clinked glasses and sipped the excellent wine. Ray leaned over the table, looked me in the eye, and said, "So tell me, Brenda, what do you *really* do?"

I almost spit my wine across the room. "What do you mean?"

"Well, you're a temp, right?"

I nodded.

"I thought all temps were actors, singers, dancers, or artists."

"Oh, that," I said. "I do a little of this, a little of that. I went to art school, studied painting. I make some hats. I definitely don't sing and dance."

After that, things went well. The meal was delicious, the company stimulating. It turns out that Ray, whose passion was the tenor saxophone, wasn't a permanent Bateman & Crews employee either. "I play in a jazz band. You'll have to come to our next gig."

"I'd love to."

Ray walked me home and gave me a cheek peck in the

hallway. I wondered if my neighbor Randolph was watching through his peephole.

I wasn't inside more than two minutes before Johnny called and broke my dreamy mood. ''I called before but you weren't home.''

''I went out to dinner. Did you hear from Lemmy yet about Laurel Tipton?''

''He's working on it. So, what did you have for dinner? Anything good?''

''I went to Joey's, had the usual.'' I didn't think it was a good idea to tell Johnny about Ray, so I changed the subject. ''That's really exciting about the reprise of *Tod Trueman, Urban Detective*. Have you started shooting yet?''

''No, but today I met with the writers. We went over the first script. How'd it go at Bateman & Crews?''

''Lousy. Another waste of time. I'm not going back. Chuck thinks he can get the information I need with his computer.''

''I know. When you didn't answer here, I tried calling you at the shop. The phone was busy for such a long time, I got worried and stopped by Midnight Millinery on my way to dinner. Chuck showed me what he was doing.''

I hoped Chuck had kept his mouth shut and not blabbed to Johnny about Ray.

At two o'clock in the morning the doorman buzzed me and put Chuck on the intercom.

''I'm in,'' said Chuck.

19

I dragged myself out of bed, threw on a T-shirt and an old pair of cutoffs. Half asleep, I rode the elevator down to the lobby to meet Chuck. He looked like hell, frizzed carrot-colored hair stuck out five inches from his head, rings of darkness circled his red watery eyes, and his pale whisker-stubbled skin was tinged gray-green in the lobby light. He had a huge grin on his face like he'd won the lottery.

"I told you I could hack my way into anything," he said, wired with excitement. "I'll bet you didn't think I could do it, did you?"

I considered that for a moment before answering. "To be honest with you, no, I didn't think you could do it." Now that he had, it occurred to me that maybe it wasn't such a good idea after all. "Chuck, just how legal is this?"

His mouth formed a crooked smile. "It's not the least bit legal, not the tiniest bit imaginable, not even a femtobit legal. That's what makes it so cool."

"Oh." In my head, I heard a jail door clang shut.

"Why?" asked Chuck. "You're not getting cold feet, are you? Remember, even though it's fun, we're not hacking in for fun or profit. We've accessed the Bateman & Crews files for one reason and one reason only—to find out who killed Carla. Morally speaking, right is on our side."

"I suppose so." Tell that one to the judge and jury.

*   *   *

New York's not the twenty-four-hour city it used to be. At two in the morning the Village streets were pretty much deserted. The few people who slinked by were dressed unseasonably in heavy sweatshirts with the hoods up.

We stopped at the all-night deli on the corner and got two black coffees and a box of powdered sugar donuts. A fidgety counter man in a sweat-stained Mets cap never took his eyes off us for a second except to look suggestively at a baseball bat that leaned up against the ice cream freezer.

"What was his problem?" I asked after we'd paid and left. "You'd think we were going to rob the place or something."

Chuck rolled his eyes like I didn't know anything. "Don't take it so personally, Brenda. It's two o'clock in the morning. The guy's all alone in there. He thinks everyone is out to bop him over the head."

On the way to Midnight Millinery, Chuck ate two of the donuts. Powdered sugar stuck to his upper lip and left a streak down the front of his T-shirt.

I'm not sure what I had expected to see, but when I looked at Chuck's computer monitor, I felt let down. Where were all the colorful icons? A jumble of words scrolled by in not-so-dazzling black and white. "Doesn't look like much to me," I said. "Are you sure you're in the Bateman & Crews computer?"

Chuck sat down at the computer and grabbed the mouse. "Oh yeah, we're in all right. Tell me where you want to go."

We dug through Bateman & Crews's electronic personnel files all night long. Finally at sunup we decided to pack it in. Chuck loaded a stack of paper into his laser printer. "I'll print out the information we downloaded and you can take it home with you."

Downloaded. I liked that word. It sounded better than

ripped off, pilfered, or stole. It sounded much less like a felony.

While the printer spit out page after page of Bateman & Crews secrets, I climbed in the store window and rearranged the hat display, strategically moving two large-brimmed hats so that, to someone standing outside the shop, Chuck's computer junk would be less obvious.

Chuck joined me in the window. "You know, Brenda, if you'd let me tape a sign in the window about résumés and brochures and letters and stuff, we'd get a lot of walk-in business."

If looks could kill, Chuck would be six feet under.

He pleaded. "Not even a little bitty sign stuck in the corner?"

I put my hands on my hips and spoke very slowly, making sure to pronounce each word precisely. "Chuck, Midnight Millinery is a millinery store. Midnight Millinery sells hats. Got it?"

"Yeah, but . . ."

"Chuck." I gave him another one of those looks.

"All right already," he said. "It was just an idea. Forget I even asked. I guess I'm being a royal pain in the ass, huh?"

"You're the king, Chuck."

When the last page came out of the printer Chuck and I flipped through the printouts. "I don't know, Brenda. This stuff doesn't look very interesting to me," said Chuck. "Do you really think it'll help you find out who killed Carla?"

"I sure hope so. It's all I've got."

As we were leaving the shop Chuck slapped his forehead with his hand. "Dammit," he said, "I forgot to tell you that Johnny stopped by the shop last night looking for you."

"I know. He called later and told me. You and Elizabeth didn't tell him anything, did you?"

"Tell him anything about what?"

"About my dinner date with Ray Marshall."

"Well . . ."

"Well what?"

"I might have mentioned real casual like that you had dinner *plans,* but I'm pretty sure I didn't actually mention the word "date" or drop any names. What difference would it make anyway? You said you and Johnny were just good friends."

"Right, that's all we are. Good friends. I'd just rather he not know about Ray right away."

"So, your date must have gone well if already you're wanting to keep it a secret."

"It went okay, I guess."

"Just okay?"

"All right. Dinner was divine."

"Divine? Did you really say 'divine'?"

"Yes. I really said divine."

"Well, after your 'divine' dinner, then what?"

"Nothing."

"That's it? You mean deep down in the most secret part of your brain, you're not working on the design of your own bridal veil?"

"Come on, Chuck. I only met Ray yesterday. Anyway, something you should know if you're going to hang around a millinery shop—a veil is not appropriate for a third marriage."

"Tell me something, Brenda. Have you seen *Ray's* rugs yet?"

I took an icy cold shower to wake up long enough to make a pot of coffee, which kept me awake for the rest of the morning. I pushed aside some of the junk on Carla's worktable to make room to spread out the printouts. Then, with the pot of coffee within easy reach, I read and kept reading until I'd gone through everything, bit by boring bit. I'd never tell Chuck because it would break his larcenous heart, but nothing in the downloaded files came close to justifying his effort and the risk involved. We'd broken a whole bunch of laws to find out that Ashley lived in Soho, Mr. Duggins far out on Long Island, Miss Caslon on the Upper

East Side, Wayne Cameron on the Upper West Side, and Sherry Ramone in Brooklyn and that they were all well paid. I could have guessed as much.

I spent the most time perusing Ashley's files and learned she'd gone to NYU for both undergraduate and law, that her middle name was Anne, and that Bateman & Crews was her first real job. Aside from that, nothing. Nothing to prove that she hired the Lady in Pink to steal her bridalwear in order to sabotage her own wedding. Nothing to prove that the Lady in Pink screwed up and killed Carla. Nothing to tell me who the Lady in Pink was. Nothing to get Detectives Turner and McKinley interested in the case again.

I checked out Wayne Cameron's files, hoping to unearth something his secretary, Sherry Ramone, could use as leverage in her quest to get him to send her to Europe. Another strikeout.

I saved the best, Ray Marshall, for last. His file didn't actually say he was unmarried—personnel departments aren't allowed to ask that question anymore—but the person he'd listed to notify in case of an emergency was his brother. Also, it looked like Ray did okay for himself when not playing saxophone. I recognized his previous employers as major Wall Street investment banks and a couple of other big law firms.

Thinking of Ray, I put my head down on Carla's worktable and drifted off to sleep. Around eleven Robin of Robin's Early Birds called and wakened me. She sounded mad as all get out.

"What are you doing at home at eleven o'clock in the morning?" she screamed. "Did you oversleep? You were expected at Bateman & Crews two hours ago. The secretary to the partner you've been working for called to see why you didn't come in today. Now look here, Brenda, Bateman & Crews is an important new client for the Early Birds. You either take this assignment seriously, or I'll find someone who will."

Like she could find someone else who could claim to know every currently popular computer program *plus* shorthand. I took a deep breath and counted to ten before answering. "Don't you worry about a thing, Robin. I'll call Miss Caslon right now and straighten everything out. It's a misunderstanding. Miss Caslon's a little daffy, if you know what I mean. I told her I'd be out in the field today gathering facts. She probably forgot."

"Facts? What kind of facts?"

"Facts for Mr. Duggins's special project."

"Oh yes, the special project. Well then, see that you call Miss Caslon right away, and be sure Bateman & Crews gets billed for every minute you work in the field."

"Of course."

"One more thing, Brenda, before I sign off, did you ask around yet which other partners could use the services of Robin's Early Birds?"

"There might be one," I said, "Wayne Cameron. I don't think he's a partner, but he's pretty high up. He supervises the nitty-gritty day-to-day estate work for Mr. Duggins. I know he has at least one freelancer."

"Find out if he needs more. Find out what agency he uses now."

Fortunately Robin was interrupted by another call she "absolutely had to take" before I could tell her to go fly a kite. However, I did call Miss Caslon, who sounded relieved to hear from me.

"Thank goodness it's you, Miss Midnight. Mr. Duggins has been asking about your special project. When you didn't show up, I didn't know what to tell him."

"Tell Mr. Duggins that things are moving along right on schedule. I'm working outside of the office today gathering facts for the special project."

"That's a relief. Mr. Duggins will certainly be happy to hear that. When shall we expect you back in the office?"

"I'm not sure yet, but I'll keep you informed."

"Be sure to send me your time cards for all the hours you put in. I'll sign them and send them over to your agency."

"Thanks. I appreciate that."

"Don't mention it."

20

A rumble from deep within my stomach sent me to the kitchen to scare up something for lunch. Slim pickings. Someday I'd have to get around to food shopping. Meanwhile, I ate two graham crackers smeared with peanut butter, then called Johnny to see if he'd had lunch yet. No answer. I couldn't remember his schedule. Maybe they were shooting one of the new *Tod Truemans* today.

On my way to Midnight Millinery I stopped at the deli and picked up a green bean salad. When I got to the shop, Chuck, Elizabeth, and Jackhammer were already there, sitting in front of the computer. A large pizza box was balanced on the keyboard.

"Want some pizza?" asked Chuck. He still looked like hell, though he'd changed into a fresher T-shirt.

"No thanks."

Chuck held a slimy piece of pepperoni between his thumb and forefinger, waving it around to tease Jackhammer who anxiously tracked the moving pepperoni with his eyes. Back and forth, back and forth. When the time was right, Jackhammer jumped for it.

"Ouch," said Chuck. "You got some finger there along with the pepperoni."

"You deserved that," I said. "Good for you, Jackhammer."

Chuck took the last piece of pizza out of the box, rolled

it up to keep the sauce in place, and stuffed it in his mouth. Once Jackhammer realized there was no more pepperoni he licked his lips, sauntered over to the vanity, spun around a few times, and settled on a pile of fabric scraps he'd dug out from god knows where. Some of that fabric I hadn't seen in years.

Elizabeth closed up the pizza box and took it to the trash. I marveled at her adaptability. One minute she's this formerly famous ex-artist who walks dogs around the Village, the next minute she's hanging out with Chuck, who's probably twenty-five years her junior, eating pizza, and cruising cyberspace.

I doodled in my sketchbook trying to come up with ideas for my fall line. I'd never been this far behind schedule before. The big department stores had been showing fall for over a month already.

I watched Chuck and Elizabeth work together. They sat close, like two peas in a very weird pod. His carrot red frizzball touched her long gray braid. Elizabeth's fingers flew over the keyboard. She stopped to grab the mouse.

"That's the way," said Chuck, encouraging Elizabeth. "Now, if you want to change the type to bold or italic, all you have to do is . . ." He tapped at the monitor with his finger.

"Like this?" asked Elizabeth.

"Perfect," said Chuck. "Will you get a load of this, Brenda. Elizabeth's a natural. She's taken to the computer like a fish takes to water, like a fourteen-year-old boy takes to the electric guitar, like . . ."

I stopped him. "Chuck, I get the point."

"Oh," he said. "Okay. Anyway, tomorrow I'm going to start Elizabeth on this fantastic new graphics program. With her art background—"

"Tomorrow?"

"Well, yeah. It's too much to get into today."

"You two promised to clear out after today."

"We thought, if you didn't mind, maybe we could extend the deal. Please. I promise we won't be any trouble."

I tried to explain. "Computers don't exactly fit in with my vision of Midnight Millinery."

Chuck pulled a calculator out of the canvas bag he carried everywhere. "What's Midnight Millinery's income per square foot of store?"

"I don't know. I never thought of it that way. I don't even know how many square feet I have."

"That's easy enough to figure out."

Chuck measured and calculated and offered me a deal that was hard to refuse. "Let Elizabeth and me stay here for one month. If we don't triple your income, you can throw us out."

"I'll think about it."

I considered Chuck's proposition while I got out my head block and roll of pattern drafting paper. I thought about it while I went through the motions of designing, and while I stared into space, and while watching Chuck and Elizabeth seemingly having a ball at the computer.

"It's a deal," I said. "One month."

"That's wonderful, Brenda," said Elizabeth.

"You won't regret it," said Chuck.

Jackhammer woke up, stretched, ran over to the trash, and pawed at the pizza box.

I picked him up. "Sorry, little guy, pizza's all gone. Here, have a green bean." I opened up the plastic container with my lunch. Jackhammer swallowed the green bean whole and begged for more. I let him have another, then put him down on the floor. With a few forlorn looks over his shoulder, he headed back to his bed, where he nuzzled his way under the pile of fabric again, this time kicking up a scrap that looked an awful lot like Ashley's lace.

I picked it up. It was Ashley's lace. "Will you look at this," I said. "I didn't think there was any of this left."

"What is it?" asked Chuck.

"Ashley's lace. The stuff that supposedly came from Mrs. Thackery's textile collection, although Wayne Cam-

eron, the attorney in charge, denies it.'' I brought it over
so he could see.

He rubbed his finger over the lace. ''Nice, I guess, if you
like that kind of thing.''

''I usually don't, but this was kind of special.''

''It's very pretty,'' said Elizabeth. ''Especially the beads.
Is this what Carla used for the bodice of the wedding gown?

''Yes, and I had a small piece for the veil's headpiece.
This is what was left over.''

We all went back to work. At least I pretended to work. I
cut out paper and held it up to the head block, cut some
more, taped the pieces together, tilted it this way and that,
turned the whole mess upside down. Nothing clicked. Fall
was a pipe dream.

I looked up when I heard the bells on the door jangle.
An intense man carrying a briefcase strode into the shop.
In a really loud voice he said, ''I'm here to proofread my
résumé.''

Oh boy, I thought. I was in for another month of this.
All because I'd let Chuck and Elizabeth talk me into it. A
big mistake. For the moment I just had to get out of there.
I decided to go to the garment center to look at wool. Perhaps I'd be inspired. Weirder things have happened. I
shoved the scrap of Ashley's lace in my pocket. If fall
failed, I could always go back to my idea of getting some
more lace like it and making dressy little cocktail hats.
What difference did it make that Midnight Millinery had
never done a holiday line? It had never done résumés either.

The number ten bus lurched and rattled its way up Eighth
Avenue. My fellow passengers—degenerate, slumping,
nose-picking men with glazed-over eyes and women who
mumbled curse words under their breath—didn't seem to
notice that the bus driver was doing his damnedest to smash
up the bus. I was relieved to get off safely at Thirty-ninth.
On my way out, the bus driver, a fat man with a shaved
head and a gold cross dangling from his right ear, told me

to have a nice day. I smiled, and then stepped right into the path of a fast-moving garment rack crammed with fall clothes.

The guy pushing the rack along the sidewalk at break-neck speed yelled at me, "Watch your back." Then, mut-tering under his breath something about stupid tourists, he bumped the rack over the curb into the street and propelled it across Eighth Avenue. To prove I wasn't a stupid tourist, I called him garment breath. To prove he wasn't a gentle-man, he gave me the finger.

I thought about Chuck and his calculator. Maybe he could figure out how many crimes per square foot were commit-ted in the garment center on any one day. There were the simple you-pay-cash kind of white-collar crimes, which led to buyers with ten thousand dollars stuffed in their designer carryalls, which led to inevitable muggings. Also, there was industrial espionage and the occasional entire shipment that managed somehow to fall off a truck. These fashion-specific crimes took place against the ever present back-ground noise of drug deals, prostitution, and porn hustling.

Virtually every ground-level store sold fabric. Wholesale, retail, it didn't matter to me. Since I didn't have to crank out hundreds of dozens of the same hat, I could buy either. Looking for the elusive inspiration for fall, I stopped in a dozen stores along Thirty-ninth and then a dozen more along Fortieth Street. Nothing hit me. I got a few sample swatches to take back to the shop and stare at. Did I really want to make plaid caps? Or fuzzy orange mohair berets? Maybe I should forget flat patterns and just go over to Thirty-eighth Street and get some felt for blocking. Maybe I should admit defeat, skip fall, and go ahead with a quick holiday line.

With that thought in mind and Ashley's lace in my pocket, I ended up in one of the storefronts devoted exclu-sively to bridal fabrics. Carla hated this kind of store. She said they were far too retail for her taste. Her sources were strictly wholesale and always an elevator ride off the street.

I could hear Carla's voice as I opened the heavy glass door. "Brenda, this place sucks. It's for home sewers and amateurs who want to make puffed-up purple polyester taffeta bridesmaid's gowns and matching purple men's cummerbunds." So vivid was the image I'd conjured up that I felt a little guilty even going in, like it was disrespectful of Carla's memory.

"Can I help you?" The proprietress, a large cinderblock-shaped woman with a tape measure draped around her neck, stood behind a glass counter that displayed wedding doodads—stretch lace gloves, elastic garters, and clip-on shoe decorations.

"I'd like to match this," I said, and put the scrap of Ashley's lace on the countertop.

"Hmmm." She bent over and took a close look. "Is this your first marriage?"

I laughed, remembering my discussion with Chuck and Elizabeth. "Actually it's not for a wedding. I'm a milliner. I thought this lace might make up nicely into dressy little holiday cocktail hats, maybe with a sculptured bow on the side, a pouf of veiling. Of course, I'd have to have it dyed unless it comes in bright colors."

She unlatched a large display case behind her and selected several laces. "Do you like any of these? I could have them dyed for you whatever color you want."

I opened out each lace and compared it with Ashley's. The new laces had glitzy sequins and lots of beads. I preferred the more subtle beadwork on Ashley's. "They sure don't make them like they used to, do they?"

The woman looked puzzled. "What do you mean 'used to'?"

"Used to—like a long, long time ago. This lace"—I pushed Ashley's lace across the counter to her—"is antique."

She picked it up and rubbed it between her thumb and forefinger. "Antique, you say?"

"Yes. It came from the Thackery collection, which is

famous mostly for its medieval wall hangings. Have you heard of it?''

She shook her head. ''No, I haven't. But if this lace is antique, then I'm Marilyn Monroe having a bad hair day. Here, I'll show you.''

Before I could stop her she grabbed a pair of shears off the counter, snipped off a piece of the lace and lit a match to it. In amazement I watched it melt. When the puff of black smoke cleared, all that was left of the lace was a dark little bead.

''See?'' said the woman, ''not antique, depending of course on what you consider antique. This lace is almost a hundred percent polyester, which wasn't even invented until sometime in the fifties. If you asked me, judging by the pattern, this lace is almost brand-new.''

''Polyester? It can't be. I worked with the stuff and didn't even know.''

The woman looked at me sympathetically. ''Don't feel too badly, dear. They're making them so good these days it's almost impossible to tell unless you're a chemist.''

I felt like a fool. Now that I knew, it was obvious that Ashley's lace was a petroleum product, derived from dead dinosaurs. It looked punched out and flat and sleazily glossy. Still, though, I preferred its more subtle beadwork with fewer beads, prettier beads, and no sequins.

I tried to save face. ''Don't you think this beading is nice? That's what I liked about the fabric in the first place.''

The woman looked at me. ''Of course you like the beading, dear. Didn't you know these are real pearls?''

21

I stumbled out of the bridal store in a daze. That woman had to be either crazy or lying. Real pearls? That would change everything. First off, polyester or not, Ashley's lace would be worth a fortune. All along I'd assumed the lace cost about $250 to $350 a yard. If it's polyester, that would knock the price down about ninety percent. Add real pearls to cheap lace and the price shoots right back up again. God knows how high. Real pearls were worth plenty.

If the pearls were real, then the Lady in Pink must have killed Carla to get her hands on the pearls, which would mean that Ashley hadn't engineered the robbery at Midnight Millinery after all. It would mean that the Lady in Pink had nothing to do with Ashley and that Ashley had nothing to do with Carla's murder. It would also mean that I'd been wrong about the motive from the get-go. I was no better than Detectives Turner and McKinley.

Before totally derailing I had to find out positively if the pearls were real. I needed to get back to Midnight Millinery, regroup, and decide the best way to do that.

Focused and driven by a new sense of urgency, I ran out into Fortieth Street and jumped into a spiffy new cab that reeked of pine deodorant. "Step on it," I said to the ponytailed cabby.

"Step on it?" he asked, surprising me with his command

of English. He twisted his head around and smiled. "You mean like on TV?"

I leaned forward and spoke through the six-inch open section of the bulletproof plastic divider. "That's right, like on TV. Fast as you can without breaking any laws of physics."

He flipped on the meter. "I've been driving this cab ever since I got the ax in that insider trading scandal down on Wall Street a couple of years ago. Until now, nobody ever told me to 'step on it.' They tell me their problems with their boyfriends, they confess to all sorts of indiscretions, they bitch about the weather, the traffic, the mayor. But 'step on it'? Never. You got it, lady. Better hang on to your hat."

Before I had a chance to tell him how funny it was that he should tell me, a milliner, to hang on to my hat, we screeched around the corner on two wheels and tore down Seventh Avenue. Four harrowing, honking, cursing, cutting-in-and-out-of-traffic minutes, and five dollars plus tip later, I stood in front of Midnight Millinery and tried to stop my knees from shaking.

Through the shop window I saw that Chuck and Elizabeth were still around and someone else was in there with them. The last thing I needed at a time like this was one of their résumé customers taking up space. As I got closer I saw that the someone else was Detective Turner. An unsmiling Detective Turner.

I stopped dead in my tracks. My worst fears had come true. We were busted. I must have been out of my mind to allow Chuck to hack into the Bateman & Crews computer. What could I have been thinking? Now Chuck and I would go to prison, all for a few stinking lousy addresses I could have found in the phone book. I could see the tabloids: VILLAGE HACKER DUO BEHIND BARS. I wondered where exactly up the river really was.

I considered running for it. Missing and presumed dead had a nice ring to it. I could grab another cab, hightail it up to the Port Authority, jump on a bus, and disappear.

Only first I had to figure out where to disappear to. Back to the Midwest? Never. California was out because of the earthquakes, mudslides, raging fires, and its laid-back, psychoanalyzed population. Florida was too hot, too humid, and too tacky. I tried to remember how far north Montana was and how cold it got, but it was too late. Chuck spotted me through the window and waved.

Like a lamb going to slaughter, with a lump in my throat and tears welling up in my eyes, I took a deep breath, held my head up, and walked into Midnight Millinery. I hoped that Turner would at least have the decency not to embarrass me by leading me away in handcuffs.

"How'd it go in the garment center?" Chuck asked, all smiles, not acting at all like a man in police custody.

"Okay, I guess." I looked around, waiting for the ax to fall.

"We're almost finished here," said Elizabeth. "As soon as Detective Turner's résumé comes out of the printer we'll be out of your way."

I looked at Detective Turner. "Résumé? You're here to get your résumé?"

"I dropped by to let you know that Detective McKinley and I are back on the Carla Haley case. It looks like we owe you an apology. That Laurel Tipton is quite a piece of work. Turns out her whole confession was nothing but a publicity stunt she and her boyfriend cooked up to get her mug on the six o'clock news. Funny thing is, the strategy worked. Early this morning some theatrical agent talks his way into the jail, claims to be her lawyer, gets to talk to her, and tells her he's got her this acting job. Only she's got to get out of the pokey because the job can't wait. No sooner than you can say 'break a leg' Laurel Tipton takes back her confession. We had to let her go."

Thank you, Lemmy Crenshaw.

I relaxed. It looked like Detective Turner wasn't there to bust us after all. "A publicity stunt, huh," I said. "You never know what they'll think of next." I was willing to bet that whatever they did think of next, Detectives Turner and McKinley would be the absolute last ones to figure it out.

"So," said Detective Turner, "that's what I came to tell you. When I saw your partners in here typing up résumés, I figured what the hell, I might as well get one. I'll be retiring in a few months and might need a part-time job to beef up my pension."

"Retiring, really? Well, congratulations, Detective Turner."

After Detective Turner left with his brand-new résumé I told Chuck how scared I'd been that we'd been busted for electronic snooping.

"Don't sweat it, Brenda," said Chuck. "Detective Turner is a New York City cop. I'm almost positive what we did was a federal offense."

"Do either of you know anything about gems?"

Chuck and Elizabeth both shook their heads no. "Why?" asked Elizabeth.

"When I tried to match the scrap of lace Jackhammer found, this woman who runs a bridal fabric store told me that the lace is junk but the beads are real pearls."

"No kidding," said Chuck.

"She seemed to know what she was talking about."

"Let me see them again," said Elizabeth.

We all looked at the beads.

"So, what do you think?" I asked.

Elizabeth plucked a straight pin out of my pin cushion and dragged it across one of the beads. "The only thing I can say for sure is that these are not painted. Pearls, though? I don't know."

I looked at Chuck. He shrugged his shoulders. "Don't ask me. Jewelry's not my department."

"How am I going to find out if these are real?"

"Take them to Forty-seventh Street," said Elizabeth. "Any of the jewelers there could tell you."

"Too risky," I said. "Until I know what the deal is, I don't want it blabbed all over town."

"Good thinking," said Chuck.

"Wait a minute," I said. "I just remembered. Johnny's got this friend he met while researching his role as the fence in the *Fence Who Knew Too Much*."

"Johnny played a fence?" said Elizabeth. "He doesn't look seedy enough to play somebody who deals in stolen goods."

"Well," I said, "he got bumped off in the first five minutes. Anyway, he stayed friends with the real fence. Max I think his name is."

I picked up the phone and dialed. Johnny answered on the second ring.

I explained the situation. "I thought maybe your friend Max would take a look at these beads and tell me if they're for real."

"Sure," said Johnny. "Max will help out. Max knows gems."

Johnny and I took the subway to the Upper West Side. "Wait till you see Max's apartment," said Johnny. "It's got a great view of New Jersey, the Bronx and Queens."

"Apartment? Aren't we going to Max's, um . . . store?" I didn't pretend to know what it was that fences like Max did, but I'd always figured they did whatever it was from some seedy hole-in-the-wall storefront while chomping on a big smelly cigar.

Johnny looked at me. "Max doesn't work out of a store."

"Oh."

Max lived in a brand-new forty-story mixed usage chrome-and-glass building. The only tenant so far in the street-level retail stores was a Seattle-style coffee shop, one of the dozens invading the city.

Johnny put his hand on my elbow and ushered me through a huge revolving door into the building's lobby. The doorman's elaborate chrome-trimmed station filled an entire wall. Across from him, on a purple patch of carpeting, two fake leather chairs were arranged, facing a lavender-and-green painting that spanned at least twenty feet of wall space. According to a brasslike plaque the painting was done "in the style of Monet." A small waterfall trickled down the back wall and splashed into a shallow pool where plastic lily pads bobbed.

The doorman's uniform matched the deep purple of the carpeting and was trimmed with gold braid. As we passed by, his thick black mustache twitched. He nodded to Johnny. "Good to see you, sir. Max is expecting you."

Max may have been expecting us, but I sure as hell wasn't expecting Max, or I should say, Maxine. Maxine who opened her faux marble door wearing loose-fitting, elegantly draped, peach-colored silk lounging pajamas and feather-trimmed peach satin slip-on mules. Maxine whose wavy bleached blond hair cascaded several inches past her shoulders. Maxine who kissed Johnny hello—on the lips. Maxine. I hated her on sight.

Through the dense fog in my head I barely heard Johnny say, "Maxine, this is my old friend Brenda. Brenda, this is Maxine."

How could this be happening? Johnny? Maxine? I had to get a grip on myself. I went on autopilot. "Nice to meet you," I heard myself say. To me, my voice sounded very far away.

"I'll bet it was a wig," said Elizabeth.

"What?" I said, still in a fog.

"I'm telling you that Maxine's shiny long blond curls were probably fake."

"Not only that," said Chuck, "but she's probably a porker underneath that outfit. In my experience, women who wear loose baggy clothes have something to hide, usually a bad ice-cream-and-cookie habit."

From Max's I'd cabbed it straight to Midnight Millinery, where I found Chuck and Elizabeth hunched over the computer. They were online again, goofing off, typing at Dude

Bob 43. I must have looked bad. As soon as they saw the expression on my face, they signed off.

"Brenda," said Elizabeth, "what's wrong?"

Sputtering venomous words, I told them all about Johnny's friend, Max the fence. Max the female fence.

"In all the years I've known you, held your hand through thick and thin, I've never heard you use that kind of language," said Chuck.

"Colorful," said Elizabeth.

"You'd be colorful too if you'd been there. You should have seen Maxine. She fawned all over Johnny. Simpered. The most disgusting display of, of—I don't know what. I almost puked."

It took me a while to settle down and tell them the whole story. "Maxine slithered around her decorator-decorated apartment making sure Johnny was comfortable, making sure Johnny's champagne glass was filled, making sure Johnny was as happy as a pig rolling in the mud. She sat on the arm of his chair and kicked her foot so that her satin slipper teetered on the end of her big toe, which, I might add was polished bright red. At Johnny's every word, she giggled like he was the funniest man in the universe."

"Let me get this straight," said Elizabeth. "She both slithered and giggled?"

"Yes, she slithered and yes, she giggled. When I finally showed her the beads, she transformed into a businessperson. She gave Johnny a peck on the cheek, shut the heavy floor-to-ceiling drapes, sat me down in a satin-brocade-covered chair across from her desk, and flicked on a bright light. She took the beads from me and laid them out on a piece of black velvet and looked at each one through a jeweler's loupe."

Maxine rolled one of the beads between her thumb and forefinger. "Where'd you get these?"

"From a friend." I figured it was none of her business that the friend was dead.

"Are there more?"

"Yes, but I'm not sure how many."

"Can your friend get hold of the rest?"

"No, I don't think so." I tried to account for the beads. I'd found a couple on Carla's floor. The Lady in Pink had the beads from the veil she took from me. I didn't know what had happened to the beads on the dress. Either the Lady in Pink cut them off after killing Carla or they were in an evidence bag at the Sixth Precinct.

"Well," said Maxine, pushing her chair back from her desk, "these are definitely real pearls. If they're the pearls I think they are, your friend is in deep trouble. Word on the street is to keep an eye out for pearls like these. They're stolen."

"My friend didn't steal the pearls. Why would the cops want . . ."

Maxine shook her head and waved her forefinger in the air in front of her pouty red mouth. "No no no no no. You misunderstand. When I speak of trouble, I don't mean police kind of trouble. This is far more serious than police business. The party who wants them back operates quite outside the law."

"What do you mean?" I asked.

"You better warn your friend that Snake Mezuna wants his mom's pearls back."

"Wow," said Chuck when I'd finished the story.

"What's a Snake Mezuna?" asked Elizabeth.

"Real bad guy," I said. "Ruthless international hitman. Maxine says the pearls came from a necklace somebody stole from his mother while she vacationed in Paris."

22

Chuck and Elizabeth invited me to join them for a grilled cheese and glass of red wine at Angie's, but I turned them down. I wanted to be alone to wallow in self-pity. And that's exactly what I did. As soon as I got home I threw myself facedown on the couch and pulled my quilt over my head to shut out the world. After a half hour or so of pathetic self-indulgent moping, I forced myself to concentrate on the significance of the pearls. Unfortunately, it was hard to think about the pearls without thinking about Maxine—a revolting recurring vision of simpering Maxine plumping up the pillows behind Johnny's head—and that got me too upset to think.

When the phone rang I figured it was Johnny calling to apologize for his disgusting behavior with Maxine, so I let it ring until the machine picked up. Let him leave a message. It didn't much matter to me if I never spoke to him again. I didn't want to hear his stupid voice either, but it boomed out surprisingly loud and clear from the little speaker.

"... you have to understand about Max. Sometimes she's ..."

I fumbled with the switches and dials until I got the sound on the blasted machine turned off. One thing I'll say for Johnny, at least he was sensitive enough to know I was mad. Maybe it had something to do with the way I'd left them sipping their champagne and spreading caviar on crackers. Maybe it was the way I stormed out of Maxine's apartment, slamming the door behind me without saying good-bye or thanking Maxine.

I stuck my head back under the quilt and resumed thinking about the pearls. If Maxine was right about their having been stolen from Snake Mezuna's mother, who sewed them to the lace? That had to be the thief. Why? To hide the stolen goods from the authorities and sneak them out of Paris.

So the pearls left Paris, stitched to the lace. They next surfaced at Bateman & Crews mixed in with the Thackery estate textiles. Then Wayne Cameron sold the lace to Ashley. She gave it to Carla to make into a dress, which the Lady in Pink attempted to steal, killing Carla in the process.

How did the Lady in Pink know about the pearls? The only thing I could figure was that she was the thief who stole them from Snake Mezuna's mother. If so, how'd she lose track of them? How did she find out Carla had them? She could have traced them to Carla through Bateman & Crews, which brought up another question. Why did Wayne Cameron sell the lace, with the pearls, to Ashley? Something mighty strange was going on at the esteemed law firm.

I got Sherry Ramone's home telephone number from the electronically pilfered Bateman & Crews personnel files. It wasn't all that easy because after Chuck told me that downloading the files had been a federal crime, I'd stashed them high up in Carla's foyer closet under a carton of ivory-colored satin. In retrospect, it seemed pretty stupid, like the feds wouldn't think to stand on a step stool and look in the closet. Who did I think I was kidding?

I dialed Sherry's number in Brooklyn.

"Brenda who?" she asked.

"Brenda Midnight. I met you the other day at Bateman & Crews. I'm working on a special project with Mr. Duggins."

"Sure, I remember, the special project. Hold on a minute. Let me turn this thing down." Seconds later the disco music thumping in the background stopped and Sherry was back. "Exercise tape," she explained. "If I'm not careful, I'll get a fat butt from sitting at a desk all day typing up lists of dead people's worldly goods for Wayne."

"That's what I wanted to ask you about," I said.

"Don't bother," she said. "It's all privileged information. God knows what would happen if word got out that some dead guy gave one bratty kid more than the other bratty kid and shortchanged his second wife."

"I don't care about who left what to whom," I said. "I'm interested in something you said about a trip to Europe."

"Oh, sure, I can talk about that. I've got some dirt on Mr. Cameron. He's like sexually harassing me, you know. So far I'm letting him get away with it, but come the next European trip, I'm gonna change my tune. I'll make it so he has to send me to Europe instead of Miss Ellen Stuck-Up Suttlan."

"Who's that?"

"The freelance bitch who goes on all the European trips for Cameron. She travels to estates all over the world, oversees the inventory procedure and distribution, and racks up humongous expense account charges. Only the best for Miss Ellen. Luxury-class hotels, four-star restaurants, all charged to Bateman & Crews. She does a lousy job too. You'd think an inventory would be pretty straightforward. But not hers. She's always coming around after the fact and makes a million changes to the lists after I've typed them up. Put this in, take this out. She drives me nuts. I mean, why can't she get it straight in the first place? It's just a list. What's so hard about that?"

"Has Ellen Suttlan ever gone to Paris for Mr. Cameron?"

"Sure," said Sherry. "All the time. The last one must have been some doozy of a trip. You should have heard the fight she had with Wayne when she got back. I can tell you one thing, when I finally get to go to Europe, I'm sure as hell not gonna come back and yell at the boss like she did.''

''What did she yell about?''

''It was that lace from Mrs. Thackery's estate. Ellen was pissed that Wayne had gone and sold it to Ashley Millard for a pittance. She went absolutely ballistic when he told her Ashley was having it made into a wedding dress. Wayne yelled right back. He told Ellen she'd stepped out of line for the last time. They're still mad at each other.''

''What does Ellen Suttlan look like?''

''She looks bitchy. Other than that, I don't know. About five six maybe, okay bod, short hennaed hair, penciled-on eyebrows.''

My heart beat fast, muscles tensed in anticipation of Sherry's answer to my next question. ''Ever seen Ellen Suttlan in a pink suit?''

''Could be. She's got a million suits, every color of the rainbow.''

I hung up from Sherry and let out a big whoop. I'd figured it all out. Ellen Suttlan, freelance estate handler, had to be the Lady in Pink. She and Wayne Cameron must have had some kind of smuggling operation working out of Bateman & Crews. What a perfect setup. They shipped entire estates all over. If occasionally they tossed in some goods of dubious pedigree, who'd ever know? The way I figured it Ellen got the stuff and Wayne sold it. One thing still didn't make sense. How come Wayne sold the lace to Ashley for, as Sherry said, ''a pittance''? Even if they'd got their signals crossed, he should have recognized the pearls were real. I'd have to give that some more thought.

Meanwhile, it was enough to know I had a motive that Turner and McKinley would go for. Not only that, I had a name for the Lady in Pink—Ellen Suttlan.

I tried to squelch my impulse to call Johnny and probably would have succeeded if it had been twenty years ago and Carla's phone had been a rotary dial. But it wasn't twenty years ago and Carla's phone had a memory dial feature and I only had to push one button to get to Johnny. He answered in half a ring. At first I was flattered, thinking he'd probably been sitting right on top of his phone waiting for me to return his call. But he wasn't waiting for me at all. As soon as he heard my voice he said, "Brenda, I'll have to call you back. I'm on another call now."

"Don't bother," I told Johnny. "I won't be home. I'm going out." I slammed down the receiver, but the feather-weight piece of plastic gave me little satisfaction. I wanted an antique phone, one with a rotary dial, no memory, and a receiver heavy enough to slam.

I decided to let my new theory percolate in my brain a couple of days before bugging Detectives Turner and McKinley. I didn't have a whole lot of credibility with them and wanted to be a thousand percent sure this time. If I wasn't careful, they'd end up thinking Carla was mixed up with jewel thieves and smugglers. I didn't need them to drag her reputation through the mud again.

I felt like I'd burst if I didn't tell someone what I'd found out. So I walked over to Angie's, hoping Chuck and Elizabeth would still be there.

Ten o'clock, prime time for a weeknight, and Angie's was packed with neighborhood types. I squeezed my way through the smoky front room. Chuck and Elizabeth were in the back in a small booth for two next to the jukebox which, of course, played Sinatra.

I grabbed an unused chair from a table across the way and scooted up to the booth. "I figured it out."

"What?" said Chuck. "That you couldn't resist our company and Angie's grilled cheese and decided to join us after all?" From the litter on the table it looked like Chuck was already on his second order of fries.

"I know who murdered Carla. I know who the Lady in Pink is and why she did it."

The waiter stopped at the table. Elizabeth ordered coffee

with anisette; I got a red wine; Chuck asked for more ketchup.

"She's got something to do with the pearls then," said Elizabeth.

"She sure does," I replied. I told them the rest of it and that I was positive that Ellen Suttlan was the Lady in Pink.

"Congratulations," said Elizabeth. "Have you told the police yet?"

"Well, I'm positive, but not that positive. I don't want to make any mistakes this time, so before I go running to Turner and McKinley, I want to get a look at Ellen Suttlan to see if I can ID her as the Lady in Pink."

"How are you going to do that?" asked Chuck.

"I have a plan."

"Here's the deal," I said. We'd gone to Elizabeth's apartment to sample her latest batch of cookie experiments—a not bad combination of peanut butter, coconut, and orange. "According to the Bateman & Crews personnel files, Ellen Suttlan lives way east on Ninety-first Street. Chuck, I need you to pose as a bicycle messenger. Scraping together a costume should be easy, but can you get a bike?"

"No prob. Urban Dog Talk's got one. I'm sure they'll let me borrow it."

"Great. Early tomorrow morning, you're going to deliver a package to Ellen Suttlan. You've got to insist that she come down personally to sign for it."

"What can I do?" asked Elizabeth.

"Two things. Make up a credible-looking package, something that looks like it came from a swank jeweler."

"With Chuck's computer and laser printer, that's a snap. What's the second thing?"

"I need to borrow Jackhammer for the morning. I'll be outside Ellen's building posing as a dog walker. When she comes down to sign for the package, I'll get a look at her face."

"That kills two birds with one stone," said Elizabeth. "I was going to ask you anyway. Jackhammer's owner called this morning to tell me he's stuck out of town for a few more days. He was supposed to be back tomorrow morning. Normally I wouldn't mind except I've got this seventy-pound chow coming tomorrow. Jackhammer hates chows. So, it would be wonderful if you could take the little guy off my hands for a few days until his owner comes home.''

"What's Jackhammer got against chows?'' asked Chuck.

Elizabeth thought for a moment. "Maybe its their bruise-colored tongues.''

"Come here, Jackhammer,'' I said. "You're coming home with me tonight.''

When Jackhammer and I got home there was a message from Sherry Ramone asking me to call her back if I got in before one o'clock. It was, so I did.

"I remembered something I thought you might want to know,'' Sherry said. "Someone else asked me questions about Mrs. Thackery's textile collection.''

"Who?''

"A new guy. He's got something to do with the computers. Ray Marshall.''

I almost dropped the phone.

According to Sherry, soon after Mrs. Thackery's textile collection arrived at Bateman & Crews for storage, Ray came around with a tool case to perform what he called routine maintenance on her computer. "No one had ever done that before,'' said Sherry. "He had the computer open and everything, and I'm looking in there with him thinking how smart he must be to know what all those little parts do, when he looks over at me—he's kind of cute, you know?''

"I've met him,'' I said.

"So he looks at me with those sexy eyes, and asks real casual if I'd seen Mrs. Thackery's textile collection. I remember thinking it was a little weird, you know, that this computer guy would even know about any textile collection. But, hey, who am I to say? So, anyway, I told him that sure, I'd seen the collection.''

''Did he ask specifically about the lace?''

''I don't remember. I really didn't pay much attention. I guess I forgot all about it until your questions reminded me. Mostly what I remember was checking out his ring finger. You know, to see if he was married.''

I smiled remembering how I'd done the very same thing myself. Good strong hands, prominent veins, long fingers, no rings. What the hell was he doing asking questions about Mrs. Thackery's textile collection?

''Thanks, Sherry. I owe you one.''

Just when I thought I finally had a handle on the case, things got all confused again. This Ray Marshall thing threw a wrench into my theory. What was he really doing at Bateman & Crews? The computer consultant bit was probably a cover story. Maybe he was involved in some shady deal with Wayne Cameron and Ellen Suttlan. Even worse, maybe he was involved with Snake Mezuna.

The most troubling thought of all was: What did he know about me? Was going out to dinner part of his act?

For the second time that day I teetered on a ladder in a struggle to get at the Bateman & Crews personnel files. This time I looked more carefully at Ray Marshall's file. His former clients were prestigious, all right. Prestigious, perfect, uncheckable references. Every last one of them had gone belly-up in the last few years. I didn't find anything to link Ray with Ellen Suttlan, Wayne Cameron, Snake Mezuna, or Mrs. Thackery's textile collection.

23

Something icy cold pressed against my cheek. Terrified, I lay very still and pretended to be asleep. However, my brain revved into analytical overdrive and screamed at me to get it more feedback. "Okay, brain," I said, "the diameter is half an inch, maybe a little more."

"Hmmm," said my brain, "that's too large to be the tip of a knife. Could it be the barrel of a small cold gun?"

"No," I said, "it's too wet for a gun."

"Too wet?" asked my brain. "What do you mean too wet?"

Dog nose. Dog nose. Dog nose. I sat straight up in bed. "Jackhammer, am I ever glad to see you."

He jumped off the bed, ran over to the door, slammed against it, ran back, and jumped up on the bed. I got the hint. "Want to go for a walk?"

He did.

In the very early morning hours, the Village resembled a peaceful little community of a hundred years ago. The cobblestoned streets, devoid of honking traffic, glistened with dew. Bright flowers in window boxes stretched their faces toward the sun, leaves rustled in the breeze coming off the Hudson River. The breeze smelled vaguely of dead fish.

While I took this all in, not paying enough attention to Jackhammer, he broke through a Chinese restaurant's curb-

side garbage bag and gulped down a big glob of cold ses-
ame noodles. I pulled him to the other side of the street.
On the way home I stopped at the newsstand to pick up
the paper. The guy who ran the place pushed my change
across the counter with his forefinger, in slow motion, a
dime at a time. "There's a good-sounding recipe for sea-
sonal creamed-corn-and-spinach soup in today's home section," he said. "You oughta check it out."

"Thanks, I will," I said. Right, I'd check it out just as
soon as they put it in a can.

Jackhammer ate half a banana for breakfast. I dunked some
graham crackers in coffee while looking through the paper.
A feature article previewing the big fall art openings put
Gil Davison's show at the Millard Gallery at the top of the
list of must-sees. It wasn't high on my list, but I taped the
article to the refrigerator anyway, in case I decided to go.
Then, I went back to the paper and was reading the obits
when Elizabeth knocked on my door.

"How's this?" she asked, handing me a package with a
classy-looking label. I had to look closely to make out the
highly stylized logo: Dude Bob's Jewelry Emporium. Elizabeth had given the fake store a tony Park Avenue address.
She'd addressed the label to Ellen Suttlan in a different
type.

"Perfect," I said. "It looks legit." I shook the box.
"What's inside? It feels solid."

"Bubble-wrapped doggie treats."

Chuck put together a convincing costume, so good that the
doorman refused to let him up. When Jackhammer and I
got to the lobby, Chuck, astride the borrowed bike, rang
the bell on the handlebars. He wore black biker's shorts
with a bright red stripe down the side, a bandanna around
his head, a beat-up dented helmet over the bandanna,
clunky leather boots, wrist supports, gloves, and, slung over
his shoulder, a bright blue nylon knapsack.

"Yo," he said.

"Yo to you too," I said. "Here's the package."

He looked at the label. "Wow. Elizabeth did a good job. She's picking up the computer stuff fast."

After a bit of negotiating, we convinced a cab driver to wedge the bicycle into his trunk and drive the three of us to East Ninety-first Street. For the first twenty blocks Jackhammer squealed, squirmed, and, in general, threw a fit. The cab driver cursed. By Thirty-fourth Street, Jackhammer settled down and seemed happy to look out the window at the traffic. The cab driver did the same.

On the way uptown I told Chuck what Sherry Ramone told me about Ray. "He might be in this up to his eyebrows."

"That certainly complicates things," said Chuck. "What are you going to do about it?"

"I don't know."

A block before Ellen Suttlan's building I told the cabby to pull over. I paid him, tipping generously, while Chuck tugged the bicycle out of the trunk.

Jackhammer and I went first. Ellen Suttlan's building, tall, gray, and ugly, was set back twenty feet or so from the street to make room for a large cement area furnished with weathered redwood benches. In a couple of spots, trees poked through the cement.

I walked Jackhammer back and forth, making sure I had a clear view into the building's lobby. Once I felt properly situated, I signaled to Chuck. He rode up, locked the bicycle to a street sign, winked at me, and walked into the building. As I watched, the doorman tried to take the package, but Chuck shook his head and refused to turn it over. Finally the doorman shrugged his shoulders, picked up his desk phone. He held it to his ear for a minute, then hung up and shook his head. I watched him try to take the package from Chuck again. But Chuck held on to the package, walked out of the building, unlocked the bike, and rode to the corner and waited for me.

*   *   *

"What went wrong?" I asked.

"The doorman said Ellen Suttlan is out of town."

"Damn," I said.

Jackhammer lifted his leg on a fire hydrant.

We got back by nine o'clock. Chuck went to Midnight Millinery, but I wanted to go home for a while. What a letdown. I'd been all excited that I'd finally discovered who the Lady in Pink was, but I still hadn't confirmed it. I'm afraid disappointment got the best of me.

I was still sulking when Johnny called. This time I picked up the phone.

"I'm making pancakes, fresh blueberry pancakes. From scratch." He sounded as if everything were completely normal between us. As if there were no Maxine. As if he'd called me back last night.

"That's nice," I said.

"Why don't you come over for breakfast?"

"I already ate."

"I can imagine what you had. What was it? A banana, a graham cracker?"

"Actually, Jackhammer ate my last half banana. I'm taking care of him for a few days while Elizabeth takes care of a chow."

"In that case maybe you should buy some dog food. Meanwhile, bring the little guy over here. I'll throw an extra piece of sausage on the griddle. *He* eats meat, doesn't he?"

"I guess so."

"So, you coming or not?"

"Oh, all right."

Droplets of water sizzled and danced on the hot griddle. "That means it's hot enough to put the pancakes on." Johnny poured the yellow batter. It spread out into disks, then puffed up.

"Here," he said, handing me a pitcher of syrup and a

tub of butter, "take these out to the table. The pancakes will be done in a minute."

Jackhammer followed me out of the kitchen and headed straight for Johnny's orange-and-yellow shag rug. It had come back from the dry cleaner as ugly as ever. Too bad the cleaner hadn't lost it. I hoped Jackhammer would pee on it, but he dived right into the rug, flipped over, and rolled around on his back. There's no accounting for taste, I thought.

Johnny may not have been a great interior decorator, but he sure had a way with pancakes. "Tasty," I said.

"Thanks. It's been a great year for blueberries. I got some from the farmer's market at the height of the season and froze them. I planned to crack them out in the middle of February when the snow piles up and the wind whistles through the air vent, but I couldn't wait."

"Well, I'm glad you didn't."

Johnny dangled a piece of sausage in front of Jackhammer. "Here you go, little guy."

Jackhammer swallowed it whole and begged for more.

Johnny poured more syrup on his pancakes. "You haven't said anything about Maxine."

Actually I hadn't said much of anything about anything, and that was quite intentional. I could hardly tell Johnny about Ellen Suttlan and how she might be the Lady in Pink without admitting how much Maxine had helped.

When I didn't respond, Johnny put it another way. "Maxine's quite a gal, isn't she?"

I had to say something. "I guess she is."

"Was she helpful?"

Damn. I hated this. "Well, yeah. She told me the beads were pearls and about that Snake Mezuna guy. Puts a whole different spin on things."

"That's good. I wasn't sure. You took off so fast yesterday. I think Maxine was a little hurt."

She was a little hurt. What about *me*. "I took off because it didn't look like anyone wanted my company." Or for that matter even noticed my company.

Johnny laughed. "I can't believe it. You, Brenda Midnight, are jealous of Maxine."

"I am not. Why would I be jealous of Maxine? What you do is none of my business. I don't care what you do or who you do it with."

We finished our pancakes in silence.

I helped him carry the dishes to the kitchen. "So anyway," I said, swallowing my pride, "thanks for taking me there yesterday." I might have to thank him, but I still couldn't bring myself to say Maxine's name. "It was a big help. Last night I found out some other stuff. Now I'm almost positive I know who the Lady in Pink is."

"That's great. Who is she?"

"Her name is Ellen Suttlan. She works for Wayne Cameron at Bateman & Crews. I think she stole the pearls from Snake Mezuna's mother."

I told Johnny my new theory.

"Did you tell Turner and McKinley yet?"

"No, I want to be positive first. Chuck and I cooked up this scheme and went to Ellen Suttlan's this morning so I could try to identify her, but she was out of town."

"If you want my opinion, I think you should tell Turner and McKinley right away. They can do things you can't do, like search her apartment. They might find the gun that killed Carla. Or maybe she still has some of the hats. That would at least prove that she robbed you."

"It's even more complicated. Before I go blabbing to the cops, there's one other thing I want to check out."

"What's that?"

"There's this guy who runs the computer help desk at Bateman & Crews. I found out he's been asking questions about Mrs. Thackery's textile collection, and I want to see . . ."

"Do you mean Ray Marshall, the guy you had dinner with the other night?"

I looked down so Johnny couldn't see the expression on my face. "Uh . . . yeah."

*   *   *

I slammed Midnight Millinery's door so hard that the glass rattled. "Dammit, Chuck. You lied to me. You told me you didn't tell Johnny that I had dinner with Ray Marshall." I don't like to think of myself as a person who yells, but I think I probably did. Loud. Jackhammer added a few yips of support.

"What I said was that I was pretty sure I hadn't mentioned any names," said Chuck.

"Well, you must have mentioned names because Johnny knew Ray Marshall's name, and he knew I'd had dinner with him."

Chuck looked sheepish. "Okay, I guess I maybe mentioned names. For goodness' sake, Brenda, don't make such a big deal out of it."

"You mentioned names and you lied about it."

"I'm sorry," said Chuck. "I didn't mean to upset you."

"It's okay. I guess I'm extra upset because I still don't know how Ray fits into all this."

"Maybe you should ask him."

"Maybe I will. Where's Elizabeth? I thought she'd be here by now."

"She walked up to Twenty-third Street to look at chairs. She says the ones here aren't ergonomic enough. She's scared she'll get one of those repetitive motion injuries."

While Chuck worked on a brochure for an aerobics studio that had opened up on Hudson Street, I moved some things around the shop. Since I'd agreed to let Chuck and Elizabeth stay for a month, I needed to make room so he could get his laser printer off my blocking table. I had almost finished when Jackhammer ran to the door and barked. Elizabeth was outside, cursing like a truck driver, struggling to extract a bulky chair from the backseat of a cab. Chuck helped her drag it to the shop.

It was the ugliest chair I'd ever seen. "Don't bring that hideous thing in here."

They ignored me and bumped the blue tweed monstrosity up the step, over the transom, and through the door.

"There's beauty in its function," said Elizabeth, defending her purchase. "This chair is completely adjustable to assure comfort and support. All at the touch of a button. Allow me to demonstrate."

She sat in the chair and made it go up and down, tilted the entire seat assembly back and forth, pushed the back of the seat lower than the front, changed the angle of the seat to the back support.

"It's ugly," I said.

"It comes in other colors," said Elizabeth. "Maybe I should have bought the maroon one."

"Then it would be an ugly maroon chair instead of an ugly blue chair."

"Brenda's in a lousy mood," said Chuck.

"I don't blame her one bit," said Elizabeth. She looked at me sympathetically. "I'm sorry things didn't go better for you this morning."

"At least the plan worked fine. You should have seen Chuck as a messenger. He even fooled the doorman."

"What's your next move?"

"I don't know. There's also the problem with Ray. Did Chuck tell you about that?"

"Yes he did."

"Before I do anything else, I want to know why he's been asking questions about Mrs. Thackery's textile collection."

"Well then, dear," said Elizabeth, "why don't you invite him to dinner and ask him?"

"You know, that's not a half-bad idea."

24

I liked Elizabeth's idea so much I went right home and called Ray Marshall at Bateman & Crews. He wasn't in but, according to his voice mail, he would be happy to return my call if I'd leave my name and number, which I did. Then I opened my big mouth and invited him to dinner. I regretted it as soon as I'd hung up. Now I had to plan a meal, not even knowing when, or if, he'd get the message or if he'd want to come to dinner.

Food was a problem. I don't eat meat. The whole time my mother was pregnant with me, she worked as a secretary at the stockyards amid the stench and sounds of death. Somehow it sank into my formative brain and I never could stand the taste of the stuff. My parents tried everything to get me to eat it. They stuck small chunks on the end of a fork and flew it into my mouth, airplane style. Nothing worked. As soon as I had a choice, I spurned it totally. This, combined with the fact that I'm a lousy cook, made it a real challenge to come up with a meal somebody else could actually eat.

However, with fresh ingredients, I could throw together a salad that would knock almost anyone's socks off. Lucky for me, the mecca of fresh, locally grown green stuff, the Union Square farmer's market, was still going strong. With a canvas bag slung over my shoulder and Jackhammer scrambling along at my side, I headed out.

Not so very many years ago Union Square Park had been a scary, filthy, smelly, rat-infested, crime-ridden spot of land where drug buyers got together with drug sellers for a quick deal, and muggers roamed free. Then, to the east a shabby discount department store was leveled, a high-rise apartment and office building erected in its place. To the west of the park along lower Fifth Avenue, huge lofts once devoted to the cutting out and manufacturing of men's suits filled up with publishing houses and modeling agencies. On both sides of the park trendy restaurants sprouted. In the dead center of all this activity, the farmer's market grew and grew to four days a week year-round. Additionally, it had become a scene.

When Jackhammer and I got there, the joint was hopping. Tourists marveled that New Yorkers have access to six different kinds of fresh parsley and a dozen different varieties of potatoes. New Yorkers piled collapsible shopping carts high with bunches of basil, velvety green beans, and plump red New Jersey tomatoes.

I have a strict personal code of visual and gustatory aesthetics that dictates which vegetables can be served together. It has nothing whatsoever to do with nutritional science; the complicated rules are based solely on appearance and texture. It's difficult to explain. Let's just say I would no more combine asparagus and broccoli than wear a wide-brimmed straw hat after sunset.

I tried to explain all this to a vegetable vendor from Pennsylvania who wanted to sell me one of everything he had.

"Good food tastes good with any other good food," he said.

"Not if it doesn't match." I handed over my two dollars for a gorgeous bunch of asparagus.

I stopped at several vendors, eventually filling my canvas bag with the makings of a wonderful salad—all carefully color and texture coordinated. Jackhammer did okay for himself too. He scarfed up a portobello mushroom from the ground and successfully begged a broken piece of jalapeño corn bread out of the bread guy. I'd have to remember to stop by Elizabeth's and get him some proper dog food.

On the way home I stopped at the pasta shop on Greenwich Avenue for a meatless entrée. The owner recommended his wild mushroom ravioli. "It's the most satisfying," he claimed. "If you serve it with our cream sauce . . ." He smacked his lips. I got the sauce too.

At home a message from Ray waited. "Yes, I'd love to come to dinner tonight. See you at eight."

I panicked. To buy the ingredients was one thing, to actually make them into an edible dinner, quite another. First, I tackled the apartment. For days I hadn't had the heart to sort out Carla's things, so there was little hope I'd get it done by eight, but at least I could get the garbage bags filled with my clothes off the floor. I crammed them into Carla's closet. It was such a tight fit, I had to lean against the door to get it to shut. This was not a good long-term solution, but would do for tonight.

When I heard Elizabeth come home I went over to get some dog food for Jackhammer. "Oh my god," she said, "I forgot to give you anything last night for him. Has he eaten at all today?"

"Plenty. Half a banana, sausage, Chinese . . ."

"He hasn't puked yet?"

"No."

"No bellyache either?"

"He feels fine."

"You're lucky. Feed him this from now on." She handed me a plastic container full of boring-looking kibbles.

"Where's the chow?" I asked.

Elizabeth pointed to her kitchen. "She's cowering in there. Strangers scare her. Come on out, Penelope. Brenda wants to meet you."

The bear-size Penelope stuck her nose out of the kitchen but refused to budge.

"See, she's nothing but a big baby."

Elizabeth tried once more to coax Penelope out of the kitchen.

"It's all right," I said. "I'll meet her some other time. By the way, I followed your advice and invited Ray Marshall to dinner tonight."

"Good for you," said Elizabeth. "Let me loan you a tablecloth. You'll need to cover Carla's worktable with something. A tablecloth is very romantic. With candles, nice wine . . . who knows."

"No thanks. Don't forget, dinner has one purpose and one purpose only: to find out why Ray wanted to know about the Thackery textile collection. It's not a romantic dinner; it's a fact-gathering mission." The fact that he made me weak in the knees was irrelevant.

"Take the tablecloth anyway," said Elizabeth. "You can't expect anybody to eat on that dumpy old table."

I took the tablecloth.

I did a last-minute inspection before Ray arrived. The apartment was clean, garbage bags off the floor, salad made, and table set.

For wine, I picked a very decent Côtes du Rhone out of Carla's dishwasher. I remember when Carla first moved in she'd been amazed that the apartment had come equipped with a dishwasher. "I don't know how they managed to wedge this appliance into such a tiny kitchen. Who needs it? I can think of a hundred better things to do with these eight cubic feet than pile up dirty dishes." She'd ended up using the dishwasher to stash her wine. It made the perfect studio apartment wine cellar.

I sure did miss Carla but didn't have time to dwell on it. Ray was due any minute and the dress I'd intended to wear clashed with Elizabeth's tablecloth. After much agonizing, I ended up back in black, this time the short dress.

Seconds before Ray was due, Elizabeth knocked on the door. "Very flattering dress," she said. She handed me a pair of silver candlesticks complete with long white tapers.

"Here, put these on the table. Romantic dinner or not, you've got to keep Ray thinking it is."

Ray arrived at eight o'clock on the dot, looking great in a crisp cotton shirt and black jeans. He handed me a bunch of snapdragons and pecked me on the cheek. "I was glad to hear from you."

One look and I was re-smitten. I must have been out of my mind to think that anyone who smiled at me like that and brought snapdragons could have had anything to do with pearl smuggling or Carla's murder.

"Great snaps," I said. "Thank you."

Jackhammer trotted up to Ray, circled him once, then sniffed at his shoes. He looked a bit lopsided. Maybe he did have a bellyache from all the junk he'd eaten.

Ray squatted down and scratched Jackhammer behind the ears. "Nice doggie. I don't remember you from the last time I was here."

"This is Jackhammer," I said. "I'm watching him for a friend."

"Big name for such a small dog."

Jackhammer sauntered off to his pile of fabric, settled down with his head resting on his paws, and stared at Ray.

"Doesn't look like he trusts me," said Ray.

"He's a little grumpy." I found a vase for the snapdragons and set them in the center of the table. "I hope you like wild mushroom ravioli."

"Sounds delicious."

I put a big pot of water on the stove to boil and carried the salad out to the table.

"That's quite a salad."

"Well, you know what they say," I said, feeling stupid saying it. "Vegetarians make a mean salad."

Ray followed me to the kitchen and watched me watch the water. When it boiled I opened the box of ravioli and held it poised over the boiling water, ready to dump them in.

Buzz.

The sound scared me. I jumped straight up in the air. Jackhammer barked. Ray looked surprised.

"It's just the doorman." I pushed the button on the intercom. "Yes, what is it?"

"Mr. Verlane is here to see you. I told him to go on up," said the doorman.

Great. What the hell did Johnny want?

"What are you doing here?" I spoke through a crack in the door, keeping my voice down so Ray wouldn't hear.

Johnny pushed at the door. "Come on, open the door. What's the matter? Got a hot date?"

"No. Well, yes." I didn't know. I let go of the door and Johnny strode in.

"Sorry if my timing is bad," he said, "but I need to borrow one of those ties Carla's students made. Lemmy set up an appointment for me to get some promo shots taken early tomorrow morning. I think Lemmy's even more excited than I am about the resurrection of Tod Trueman. He says this time Tod is going to be really big." Johnny walked right by me and went into the apartment.

"Hi." He walked over to Ray and held out his hand. "I'm Brenda's friend Johnny. Sorry to bust in on you two like this, but I have a fashion emergency."

Ray shook Johnny's hand.

So mad I could spit, I somehow got through the introductions. "Ray this is Johnny. Johnny this is Ray. Ray runs the computer help desk at Bateman & Crews."

"Oh yes," said Johnny, "Brenda's told me all about you."

I kicked Johnny in the shin to shut him up. "I told Johnny all about your impressive computer installation at Bateman & Crews."

Given the awkward situation, I thought Ray was rather gracious. "Oh, you're interested in computers, are you? If you'd like to come see our installation some day, I'd be glad to show you around."

"Thanks," said Johnny. "I may take you up on that

offer. So, anyway, Brenda, where are those ties? I'll grab one and get out of your way.''

While the two of them—the ex-boyfriend and the boy-friend-to-be, if it turned out he wasn't involved with the B&C smuggling operation or Carla's murder—made small talk, I dragged the stepladder over to the foyer closet, climbed up, and pulled at the box of student ties. It was stuck. When I finally yanked it out, the folder of down-loaded Bateman & Crews files came along with it. Printouts scattered all over the floor. I scooped them up and stuffed them back in the box. Ray was so busy listening to Johnny brag about his Tod Trueman role, I don't think he noticed.

I shoved the whole box of ties at Johnny. ''Here, pick one.''

Johnny pawed through the ties. ''These are nice. What do you think, Ray?'' He dangled a blue, maroon, and rust tie in front of Ray's face.

Ray nodded his head. ''Very nice.''

''I think it will be perfect for Tod Trueman. There's dozens of these ties in here, Brenda. What are you going to do with them?''

''When I get around to it I'll return them to Carla's students.''

''That sounds like a lot of trouble,'' said Johnny. ''Why don't you take them over to Midnight Millinery and sell them?''

I kicked Johnny in the shin again to shut him up but Ray had already heard.

''What's Midnight Millinery?'' asked Ray.

Johnny ignored my kick to his shin and the dirty look I gave him and babbled on. ''Didn't Brenda tell you about her millinery shop? Shame on you, Brenda.''

I was mortified. ''I, er, well . . . I was too embarrassed, because the shop's been doing so lousy. It's the slow season.''

''A millinery store,'' said Ray. ''I knew you did some-thing besides work on special projects for doddering old lawyers. Is it close by? You'll have to take me over there after dinner.''

My words caught in my throat. "Uh, uh . . ."

Johnny didn't have any trouble opening his big mouth again. "As a matter of fact, I stopped by Midnight Millinery on my way here. Chuck's still there, pounding away at the computer.''

I could have killed Johnny.

"Really," said Ray. "You use a computer to make hats?''

Before I could explain, Ray's beeper beeped.

Ray looked at the number on the beeper's display. "It's the Bateman & Crews computer calling in an alarm. Someone is trying to break into it again. Brenda, I'm terribly sorry but I have to go. I've got to catch this hacker."

25

As soon as Ray was out the door and down the hall, I dialed Midnight Millinery. The line was busy. That meant Chuck was on-line.

"Dammit," I said.

"What's the matter?" asked Johnny.

"No time to explain. I've got to get to Midnight Millinery and stop Chuck. If he's doing what I think he's doing, we could be in serious trouble. Wait here if you want. I'll be right back."

"I'll put the salad back in the fridge," said Johnny.

I tore across Eighth Avenue and almost got hit by a number ten bus as it pulled away from the curb. The driver called me a bunch of names, but I kept on running, not looking back once.

I burst through the door of Midnight Millinery. "Chuck, hang that damned modem thing up."

Chuck spun around in Elizabeth's ergonomic chair. He had a goofy smile on his face that made him look like a four-year-old caught with his hand in the cookie jar. "My god, Brenda, take it easy; you're all out of breath."

"Are you online?"

"Yeah, I thought—"

"Get off. Now."

"All right, already." He turned back to the computer and

tapped at the keyboard. "The connection is broken. Now, tell me what's going on."

"Ray Marshall was at the apartment. I invited him to dinner."

"I know. Elizabeth told me you'd taken her advice."

"So, Ray's there and Johnny opens his big mouth and tells him about Midnight Millinery and how you've got your computer here."

"What was Johnny doing there? Chaperoning?"

"He came barging in to borrow a tie. At least that's what he said. While we're all talking, Ray's beeper beeped him. He said it was the Bateman & Crews computer calling to warn him that someone was breaking into its files again."

"Neat," said Chuck. "I like the way your man Ray works. He's got the computer rigged to dial his beeper whenever it detects a disruption or suspects an invasion."

"Yeah, really neat," I said sarcastically. "Just tell me one thing: Was that you trying to hack in again?"

"Yep."

"You promised we were all done with that."

"Well, I thought maybe if I poked around a little more I could find something. . . ."

"No, Chuck. Do not poke around the Bateman & Crews computer. Ever again. Do not commit any more federal offenses. We have all the information we need. The risk is too great."

"I'm sorry, Brenda. It's such a cool thing to do, I couldn't resist the challenge."

"Remember, Chuck. That cool thing could send cool you and cool me to the cooler for a cool ten to twenty."

"Okay, I won't do it anymore. I guess I kind of messed up your date, didn't I?"

"It wasn't a date; it was a fact-finding mission. And, no, you didn't mess it up. Johnny took care of that."

I started to leave but then had an awful thought. "Chuck, if the Bateman & Crews computer is smart enough to recognize when someone unauthorized is trying to break into its files, and smart enough to dial out to Ray to tell him, wouldn't it be smart enough to know the phone number that dialed in, like with your caller ID box?''

"Don't sweat it, Brenda. You're right, the Bateman & Crews computer probably logs in all incoming calls. But don't underestimate Chuck Riley. I routed that call so it hopped around to hundreds of cities and countries before it ever got to Bateman & Crews. It'll never get traced back to us, at least not in our lifetimes.''

"You're sure.''

"Sure I'm sure.''

When I got back to the apartment, I tore into Johnny. "Thanks a whole hell of a lot,'' I said, slamming the door behind me.

Johnny stuck his head out of the kitchen. "What's the matter, Brenda? Why don't you sit down at the table and take it easy. I'll put the ravioli in now. You'll feel lots better after you eat.''

"I doubt that.'' I sat at the table with Jackhammer on my lap and watched Johnny plop the fat mushroom-filled pillows of ravioli into the water, one by one.

"Why did you go running out of here like that?'' asked Johnny. "I can't remember ever seeing you so focused.''

"You know how Chuck is,'' I said. "He couldn't leave well enough alone. He hacked into the Bateman & Crews computer again because he liked the challenge. This time, his poking around caused the B&C computer to beep Ray. If Ray had gotten to Bateman & Crews before Chuck hung up, we would have been caught red-handed or red-modemed. Whatever you call it, it would have been bad news.''

"It's a good thing you got there in time.''

"You can say that again.''

Johnny came out of the kitchen to light the candles and pour the wine. When the timer gonged he went back into the kitchen and poured the ravioli out of the pot into the colander. I watched the swirling steam surround his head and wished he'd choke on it.

"Sorry your date got all screwed up," he said, putting down a plate of ravioli in front of me.

"Not a date, a fact-finding mission. I wanted to find out if Ray had any links to Ellen Suttlan."

He grated a chunk of fresh parmesan over the ravioli. "It looked like a date to me. You outdid yourself for Ray Marshall. Fancy tablecloth, silver candlesticks, great salad, good choice of wine, mushroom ravioli. Not only that, but you look smashing. I really like that dress. Too damn bad Ray had to leave, though I can't imagine what you see in a guy like that. He's a computer nerd, for god's sake."

"Chuck's a computer nerd."

"Yeah, but Chuck's got soul. Ray Marshall, I'm not so sure about."

"Can we please change the subject?"

"Sure."

I nibbled at my ravioli while Johnny told me all about the latest *Tod Trueman, Urban Detective* adventure. "It's got the requisite car chase with Tod driving a spiffy red Corvette."

I shook my head. "Come on, Johnny, that's not credible. Who'd ever believe a New York City cop driving a Corvette?"

"That's easy," said Johnny. "For one thing, Tod's a detective. They do okay. He's got a healthy stock portfolio, no wife or kids to support. Tod could well afford his own Corvette, but in this case, the script calls for Tod to commandeer the car from a breathtakingly beautiful supermodel who speeds by at the very moment Tod spots the bad guy headed up Park Avenue. Tod grabs the 'Vette and the chase begins."

"I assume the beautiful model and Tod get together at the end."

Johnny nodded his head. "You got it. A long, passionate kiss right over the closing credits."

On his way out Johnny remembered to tell me that Margo had called while I was at Midnight Millinery. "She said it was important. Call her at Einstein's Revenge. She'll be there late." He pecked me on the cheek. "Night, Brenda. Oh, and thanks for letting me borrow the tie."

"Anytime," I said. I almost asked him to please call next time he wanted to barge in when I had someone over, but considering how things had turned out, it didn't seem to make a whole heck of a lot of difference.

I felt awful. Whether it was a date or a fact-finding mission, either way I looked at it, the evening had been a complete bust. I'd found no facts and had ended up eating ravioli with Johnny. That wasn't a date.

To take my mind off my ruined evening, I returned Margo's call.

"Brenda, thank goodness you called. I'm desperate. There's a dead spot in my fall window. You've got to bring me a hat. Something big, something dramatic, something tonight."

"Tonight? I haven't even—"

"Yes, tonight. I've got to get this window finished. The big fall openings are all happening this weekend. Besides Christmas, this is my busiest time of the year."

"I'm sorry, Margo, but with Carla and everything I haven't gotten around to making my fall line yet. It's not even designed."

"Doesn't matter. Make one tonight. I'll be here till the wee hours working on the window. You can bring it by whenever you've finished."

"But—"

"The hat doesn't have to be perfect. I don't care if it's lined, or if it has a band sewn inside. It doesn't have to be hand stitched. Just bring me something to slap on this dummy's head."

"Okay, Margo. You win. I'll see what I can do, but I can't make any promises."

"Brenda, I knew you'd come through; you're a life-saver."

*　　*　　*

Chuck had gone home, so for the first time in a while, I had Midnight Millinery all to myself. If I ignored the résumé prices taped up in the window and didn't look in the direction of the computer, it was almost like the old days.

Jackhammer curled up in his spot beneath the vanity and went to sleep. I went through my trunk scrounging for fabric, found a big piece of black velvet, got out my buckram, and started cutting and wiring and sewing and shaping. Everything kind of fell into place, and the next thing I knew it was two o'clock in the morning and I had a hat for Margo. Its curved brim swept down on one side and up on the other to reveal a chartreuse contrasting underside. I took Margo's advice and skipped some of the hand work.

I called Margo to make sure she was still at Einstein's Revenge. She was, so I put the hat in a box, grabbed Jackhammer, and got a cab down to Wooster Street.

Margo was thrilled when she saw the hat. "Brenda, I knew you could do it. It's absolutely perfect. I love it. It's got the mysterious drama of black and the shock of the chartreuse emerging from the underside." She climbed into the window and put the hat on one of the mannequins, angling the brim so the chartreuse would show from the street. Margo slapped the mannequin on the butt. "Madeline, this hat is exactly what you needed to go with your long sexy black dress."

"The mannequin's name is Madeline?" I asked.

"Yes," said Margo, "after my third-grade teacher. Do me a favor, Brenda, and hop up in the window. I want to take a look from outside."

"Sure."

With Margo outside gesturing wildly and me inside making minute adjustments to the display, we finished the window to Margo's satisfaction.

"That's it," she said. "I think it's going to be a good year for Einstein's Revenge. Now, how about joining me over at Leo D's for a drink, a little something to celebrate the beginning of the fall season? I'm buying."

"I don't know," I said. "What about Jackhammer?"

"Don't worry. It's three o'clock in the morning. We're in the center of bohemian New York. As long as you keep him on your lap, no one is going to say anything. Besides, you're with me; I know the owner, Marc—intimately."

During the day Leo D's catered mostly to the herds of tourists and shoppers who strolled the streets of Soho and needed a place to rest their feet and grab a bite—a rather expensive bite, heavy on the basil. In the evening and on through the night, a steady stream of locals kept the place jumping until late, but by three in the morning, things had pretty much wound down. The taped music was low, the kitchen staff had gone home, and the bartender had nothing to do but dry glasses with a white linen towel. Margo's boyfriend, Marc, was seated at the shiny black bar smoking a cigarette. He was about fifteen years too old for his rock-and-roll haircut and fifteen pounds too fat for his jeans.

"Margo, my love, sit down." Marc patted the bar stool next to him with a professionally manicured hand. "You finished earlier than expected, I see." He spoke with an exaggerated fake-sounding European accent, not specific to any particular country.

"Yes," said Margo. "Thanks to Brenda, I'm finally done. She came through with a fabulous hat on a moment's notice. It pulled my whole fall window together. I am now officially ready for the season."

"Then we must celebrate," said Marc. "Bartender, a bottle of our finest champagne for the ladies, s'il vous plaît."

The bartender popped the cork before I could protest.

"To success," said Marc. He turned his attention to me. "So *this* is the Brenda Midnight I've heard so much about." He looked me up and down with heavy-lidded dark eyes. It made me uncomfortable. Then, as I knew he would, he grabbed my hand and held the back of it to his lips. "It's a pleasure to meet you."

I wiped my hand on my skirt. "A pleasure." Jackhammer, from his vantage point on the floor, made a rumbling noise in his throat.

Marc looked down. "And who do we have here?"

"This is Jackhammer," I said. "I'm watching him for a friend."

"*Tres* cute." Marc reached down and tried to pet Jackhammer.

Jackhammer had other ideas. He took off running in the direction of the kitchen. He made it halfway there before I caught up with him and scooped him up. On the way back to the bar I noticed a couple seated at a round table set off in a little alcove. The woman was blandly pretty and at least twenty years younger than the man. Tears poured out of her eyes. Her tears seemed to have little effect on the man. If anything, he looked bored.

"Don't look now," I said when I got back to the bar, "but the man at the table over there, the one with the salt-and-pepper gray hair, looks an awful lot like Walker Millard."

"It *is* Walker Millard," said Margo. "He comes here all the time. The blond is his girlfriend. Or, I should say, his *latest* girlfriend."

"No," corrected Marc, "you should say *one* of his latest girlfriends, with emphasis on the S. Walker's quite a stud. He's in here every night with a different broad."

I don't know which upset me more: the fact that Margo was hanging out with a sleazy pretentious fake European restaurateur who referred to women as broads and buffed his fingernails, or the fact that Walker Millard cheated on his wife. Such goings-on and fooling around always surprised me. I guess I had a bad case of misplaced faith in mankind.

"What about Simone?" I asked, "Doesn't she care?"

"I should say she does," said Marc. "From what I hear Simone has hired a detective. Walker's got to cool it with all his little friends for a while. That's probably why the girl's crying like that. No doubt she's another artist to whom he promised a show at the Millard Gallery. They're all so naive, these artists."

26

Margo told Marc to go outside with me to help me get a cab. I probably would have been safer alone on the streets. Margo had managed to find herself a real sleazeball this time. As Marc put me in the cab he slipped me his business card. "Call me sometime. We'll get together for a little private dinner."

I left the card on the seat of the cab.

I got home at four in the morning. The lobby was so quiet I could hear Ralph the doorman snore. I tried to tiptoe past him, but when I was halfway to the elevator, he woke up and made a gallant effort to look alert.

"Did they move you to this shift?" I asked.

"Nah. I'm subbing for the regular guy."

Jackhammer was so pooped he fell asleep in the elevator. It was all I could do to make the couch into a bed before I conked out too.

Not too many hours later I woke up to the sound of Jackhammer flinging himself against the door, snarling viciously. I dragged myself out of bed and stumbled over to look through the peephole to see what the fuss was all about. Elizabeth stood in the hallway with Penelope the chow. The poor dog quivered in fear. She had no idea Jackhammer weighed about as much as her front paw.

I didn't dare open the door but called through it, "Hey, there. Good morning, Elizabeth."

She waved at me through the peephole. "I hope everything went well last evening."

"A total disaster."

"I'm so sorry. I thought with the tablecloth, the candlesticks . . ."

She was interrupted when Randolph stormed into the hall. He slammed his door behind him so hard our adjoining wall vibrated. "Will you two *please* shut up? And you"—he kicked my door—"coming and going at all hours of the night, two gentlemen callers at the same time. You may think I don't know what goes on in there, but I do."

"My, my, aren't we a busybody," said Elizabeth to Randolph. She turned to my peephole and said, "Two guys?"

"Long story," I said. "I'll fill you in later."

I couldn't get back to sleep, so I made a cup of coffee and peeled myself a banana. Jackhammer didn't want to have anything to do with the plateful of the kibbles I set out for him. He sniffed at them and pushed them with his nose but refused to eat any. He followed me around the apartment until I finally broke down and gave him a piece of banana.

I'd been much too tired to check the answering machine when I got home. When I finally played it back, there was a message from Ray.

"Brenda, I apologize for tonight. Dinner looked wonderful; you looked wonderful. I promise I'll make it up to you."

That was sweet of him, but what he said next made my heart stop cold. "Whoever's been breaking into the B&C computer is pretty sharp. He did some elaborate routing of the call. Still, I'm positive I can trace it back to the culprit. I'm going to be stuck at B&C most of the night and all day tomorrow trying to track down this hacker, but if you want to stop by around one-thirtyish, I'll take a break. How's the Oyster Bar sound?"

The Oyster Bar part sounded okay. The part about tracking down the hacker, definitely not so okay. I called Chuck and played back Ray's message for him. "Are you a hundred percent sure your call can't be traced back to Midnight Millinery?''

"Ninety-nine percent sure."

"That's all?"

"Got to allow for magic, the uncertainty, the quantum variability."

"What's quantum variability?"

"Don't worry about it. I know what I'm doing. I'll tell you what. If it'll make you feel any better, go to Bateman & Crews a couple of hours before your lunch date and distract Ray. I know one or two more tricks to throw a few more leaves over my tracks, electronically speaking."

"What do you mean by distract?"

"I mean do anything you have to do to get Ray Marshall away from his computer. Give me a chance to hack in there again and make sure he never finds us. So get over there, okay? Elizabeth and I will take care of things at Midnight Millinery."

That's exactly what I was afraid of.

I had a big whopper all ready to tell Miss Caslon, but it turned out I didn't need it. She was delighted to hear from me.

"Thank goodness you called, Miss Midnight. I've been frantic, absolutely frantic. Mr. Duggins is in a total dither. He's anxious for an update on the special project. I don't know anything about it myself and didn't know how to reach you. I must have misplaced my copy of your time cards and I couldn't remember which agency had sent you. I don't believe it's one of our usual agencies."

"Robin's Early Birds," I said.

"Oh yes, of course. How silly of me to forget such a catchy name. Just the other day I talked to Robin herself."

"Don't you worry, Miss Caslon. Tell Mr. Duggins I'll be in a little later this morning."

"Thank you so much, Miss Midnight. I can't tell you how relieved I am."

Next I called Ray.

"Brenda, I'm glad it's you. I was afraid you were mad. After the way I took off last night, I thought you'd never speak to me again."

"Don't be silly," I said. "I understand that these things happen."

"I'm glad you do. So, how about lunch?"

"Lunch would be nice. I am going to be at Bateman & Crews today anyway. Mr. Duggins is getting anxious about his special project."

"See you at one-thirty, then."

Actually he'd see me before that. All I had to do was come up with a way to distract him.

While I waited for the number ten bus in front of the drugstore I watched an aggressive panhandler work the traffic by Abingdon Square Park. He had long greasy blond hair, no shirt, and refused to take no for an answer. When drivers shook their heads and rolled up their windows, he kept right on harassing them until the light changed and they pulled away. No wonder so many cars ran through the red light. One of them, a small black sporty type car, whizzed around the corner and screeched up to the curb in front of me. The dark tinted window lowered a crack and frighteningly loud rap music thundered out. The music stopped and I heard a voice.

"Hey, cutie, goin' my way?"

I recognized that broadcast-quality voice. "Johnny, what the hell are you doing scaring me like that?"

It was weird enough to see him, the man who'd never had a driver's license, who had to have a stand-in drive for him on TV and film, behind the wheel of a real car on a real city street mixing with real traffic and real pedestrians. It was even weirder to see his driving companions. Detective McKinley sat in the shotgun seat, Detective Turner in the back.

Before I could comment, McKinley jumped out and pushed the seat forward so I could get in.

"Hop in," said Johnny. "I'll drop you off."

Detective Turner scooted over and made room for me. Johnny had joined the tens of thousands of pedestrian-terrorizing curb-jumping unlicensed New York drivers, only he did it with a new twist: He had two cops in the car. He had on dumb-looking mirrored wraparound sun-glasses and a tight-fitting black T-shirt. He raised the sun-glasses up over his brow and made eye contact with me. "Don't look so worried, Brenda. I got my driver's permit. The guys here are teaching me how to drive in exchange for the name of my tailor."

"Where'd you get the car?" I asked.

"It's Lemmy's. He had to be in Philadelphia for a couple of days and needed someone to help him out with the al-ternate side of the street parking. It seemed like a good time to finally get this driving thing down pat." Casually, with one hand on the steering wheel, he merged the car into the stream of traffic going through the yellow light and headed up Eighth Avenue.

"You look funny driving," I said.

"I'm working on my style. So, where are you heading?"

"Midtown. I'm working at Bateman & Crews again to-day."

Detective McKinley looked around at me. He sported the same kind of wraparound sunglasses as Johnny, but he didn't raise them up before speaking. "Isn't that the law firm where Ashley Millard works?"

How did he know that? Did that mean he and Turner were finally investigating the Ashley Millard–Lady in Pink connection to Carla's murder? "Yes," I said, "I believe she is one of the associates."

"Why are you working there?" asked Turner. "You said you were a hatmaker."

"Well, yes, but . . ." I was stuck. I could hardly tell Turner and McKinley that I had been fraudulently working at Bateman & Crews, breaking dozens of city, state, and federal laws, trying to uncover evidence in Carla's murder, all because they hadn't done their job.

Johnny came to my rescue. "Brenda is a woman of many

talents. She's been working on a special project for one of the Bateman & Crews partners.''

"I see," said McKinley, "a special project."

A touch sarcastically Turner said, "Brenda does everything. She makes hats, handles special projects for hotshot lawyers, types résumés, not to mention—"

I butted in. "Wrong. I don't do résumés. Chuck and Elizabeth did your résumé.''

"Well, it came out of a shop with your name in the window," said Turner. "Whoever did it, they did a fine job. I handed out your business card to the entire precinct.''

Business card? Since when did I have a business card? Chuck and Elizabeth had some more explaining to do.

As Johnny braked for the red light at Fourteenth Street, a cop car sped by with lights spinning, siren whooping.

Turner gripped the back of Johnny's seat. "Okay, Johnny," he said, "now's the time for Tod Trueman to show his stuff. Follow that squad car.''

"You're the boss," said Johnny. "Better hang on to your many hats, Brenda." Stiff armed and leaning way back, he punched the accelerator and tore through the red light behind the cop car. Behind us, a cab did the same thing. At Eighteenth Street we all ripped around the corner. Halfway down the block the cop car stopped, two cops jumped out, and, with their hands on their guns, ran into a six-story redbrick apartment building.

The cab kept on going.

"Should I stop?" asked Johnny.

"Nah," said McKinley. "It's probably nothing."

"Out of our precinct," said Turner. "Anyway, we've got enough problems here. Johnny, Tod's driving style is all wrong.''

"How?" asked Johnny.

Turner shook his head. "Basically, you look like a jerk. First off, you've gotta learn to relax your shoulders.''

"And bend your elbows," said McKinley.

By the time we turned up Sixth Avenue, Johnny had

learned how to hunker down over the steering wheel, cop-like.

"That's much better," said McKinley. He turned to Turner. "Don't you think so?"

"Oh, yes, much, much better."

I hoped they were off duty.

Tod and the homicide detective drama coaches dropped me off at Bateman & Crews a little before ten o'clock.

"Give Ray Marshall my best," said Johnny. "Tell him he missed a wonderful dinner."

"Who's Ray Marshall?" asked Turner.

"A friend," I said.

"Ray's the computer whiz at Bateman & Crews," said Johnny. "For some inexplicable reason, Brenda's got the hots for him."

"There's no accounting for taste," said Turner.

At least Ray doesn't go around pretending to be someone he's not, I thought.

27

First thing, I checked in with Miss Caslon.

She rested her hand on her chest and sighed. "Ah, Miss Midnight, am I ever glad to see you. Mr. Duggins said to tell you he was pleased as punch to have you back with us at Bateman & Crews. He wanted to talk to you the minute you got here, but unfortunately, he's been called into an emergency partner meeting."

"That's a shame," I said. "I'd hoped to talk to him too." Actually, this was great news for me, since I had no idea what I was going to tell Mr. Duggins about the status of the nonexistent special project.

"I imagine the meeting will end sometime this afternoon," said Miss Caslon. "Mr. Duggins will be able to see you then." She lowered her voice and motioned for me to come closer. "Between you and me, Miss Midnight, I believe Mr. Duggins intends to expand the scope of your special project. He's thinking video, multimedia, CD-ROM, maybe even one of those Web pages. I tell you, that man has vision."

"That he does," I said. "As long as Mr. Duggins is stuck in a meeting, I have some questions I'd like to ask Ray Marshall. You don't mind if I go down to his office, do you?"

"Mind? Heavens no. Mr. Marshall is such a nice young man. Smart as a whip and a hard worker too. Why, just the other night he went way beyond the call of duty to help me computerize the Trusts and Estates records.''

''That must have been a big job.''

''Oh yes. Mr. Marshall stayed here until all hours of the night, even after I left, to finish. It's not part of his job description either. He did it out of the goodness of his heart because he saw how I was struggling with the computer. I doubt I'll ever catch on to those infernal machines.''

''Don't say that, Miss Caslon. You'll learn, especially with Ray to help you.''

''I hope so. You know, Miss Midnight, now that I think about it, when Mr. Marshall was here that night he asked questions about you and the special project. You know what I think?''

''No, what?''

''I think Ray Marshall is sweet on you.''

What I thought was that Ray Marshall was damned nosy.

On the way down to Ray's office I stopped by to see Sherry Ramone. When she saw me she put down the *Shops of Paris* travel brochure she'd been reading. ''Hi, Brenda. How's it going?''

''Not bad. I was wondering, though, about that Ellen Suttlan person you told me about. Has she been out of town again?''

''Sure has. She got back late last night from another all-expenses-paid trip—this time to San Francisco. Not as good as Paris, but an okay little junket. If you want to see her, she'll be here this afternoon going over her latest inaccurate inventory with Wayne.''

''Will you call me when she gets here?''

''Will do.''

''Don't tell her I want to see her.''

''Wouldn't dream of it.''

I could have kicked myself for ever letting Chuck hack into the Bateman & Crews computer. Now I had to distract Ray to give Chuck time to break in again. How was I supposed to do that? Cry, seduce him, call in a bomb scare? I came up with all sorts of sleazy lies and tacky deceptions before it occurred to me that maybe the truth would work. Not the whole truth, of course. It would be incredibly stupid to tell Ray that Chuck and I were responsible for the hack-ins. I figured a half-truth might do the trick. I made up my mind. I would tell Ray Marshall the real reason I was at Bateman & Crews.

The door to Ray's office was open. I stood around outside for a few minutes watching him work while I tried to get the nerve to do what I had to do. He typed in short rapid-fire machine gun bursts using his index fingers. Between bursts he looked at his monitor, frowned, and shook his head. Finally, I couldn't stand it any longer. I took a deep breath. "Hello, Ray."

Startled, he looked up, fingers poised over the keyboard. "Brenda, great to see you." He looked at his watch. "It's a little early for lunch, though."

I kicked the door closed with my foot. "Ray, we have to talk."

The truth is a funny thing. Ever since Carla had been murdered I'd been telling fibs—little fibs, big fibs, big fat jumbo fibs, and super colossal fibs. I'd deviated so far from the truth, swerved so far off the path, it was hard to tell which end was up.

"You're right, Brenda," said Ray, "we have to talk." He motioned for me to sit down. "I don't know where to start. News travels fast at Bateman & Crews. I know you've been asking a lot of questions, so I guess it's time for me to come clean."

Wait a minute. What was happening? That was supposed to be my line. Why were my words coming out of Ray's mouth? I was stunned speechless.

Ray continued. "I know you know who I really am and why I'm here."

"I do?" I didn't. What was he saying? That he wasn't really Ray Marshall, freelance computer consultant?

"It's all right, Brenda. You don't have to play dumb. First, I want you to know that my intentions toward you were always sincere. I like you a lot. That's why I've decided to tell you."

Weird things knocked around inside my head. Lights flashed, alarms sounded, and a tornado whipped through, mixing up everything.

"I don't know if you know it or not, Brenda, but the shit is about to hit the fan at Bateman & Crews."

"Because of the hacker?" I asked. In my head I heard the sound of that prison door slamming shut again.

"No, that's silly stuff. Bateman & Crews has a lot more to worry about than some amateur hacker poking around in their personnel records. I shouldn't be telling you this either, Brenda, but for your own good you should know something. If I really wanted to, I could uncover the hacker in two seconds flat. But that's not why I'm at Bateman & Crews. I'm not here to make sure their computers run smoothly and securely. That's a cover."

"I thought . . . last night when the computer beeped you and you had to leave . . ."

"The emergency was real. But the computer didn't beep me; that was an associate telling me . . . well, I'm not at liberty to say anything more. Trust me, Brenda, after today Bateman & Crews will never be the same. The partners have been in an emergency meeting all morning."

"I know. That's why I haven't been able to see Mr. Duggins about the special project."

"Come on, Brenda. Special project? Don't take me for a fool. I know there's no special project. I don't know why you're here, but I've done enough checking that I know you're not in it with the rest of them. Your Mr. Duggins is hip deep in it, though, without any paddle whatsoever. If I were you, I'd get out of here while the getting's good. Put some distance between yourself, Mr. Duggins, and the Bateman & Crews Trusts and Estates Department. Go make some hats. I'll call you when all this is all over."

I guessed that meant lunch was off. Completely confused

and disillusioned, I left Ray's office in a daze. I would have taken his advice and got the hell out of Bateman & Crews except for one thing: Ellen Suttlan would be in later to see Wayne Cameron. I had to see finally, once and for all, if she was or was not the Lady in Pink.

For privacy, I went down to the lobby and called Chuck on a pay phone. I was afraid I'd get a busy signal, but he picked up.

"Good," I said. "I was afraid you'd still be online."

"I finished what I had to do and logged off a few minutes ago," said Chuck. "Did you distract Ray?"

"A long story. It's more like Ray distracted me. It doesn't matter, anyway. We had the strangest conversation. I'm almost positive he knows the hacker's calls have been coming from Midnight Millinery."

"Impossible."

"No, not impossible. Chuck, get this. Ray doesn't care."

"Huh?"

"The freelance computer consultant bit is just a cover."

"A cover for what?"

"He wouldn't tell me."

When I got back to Miss Caslon's office she was reading a paperback romance, seemingly oblivious to what was about to hit the fan at Bateman & Crews.

"How was your talk with Mr. Marshall?" she asked. She closed the book but kept a finger inside to mark her place.

"Interesting," I said. To say the least.

"If you asked me, Miss Midnight, Mr. Marshall is a real catch."

"I suppose so," I said. "Has Mr. Duggins come out of the meeting yet?"

"He darted out for a second and made a phone call. I don't know what's going on in there, but he didn't look very happy. Profits must be down again. You'd be surprised how many of our clients, big-name clients, simply don't pay their bills."

"Who'd he call?" Not that it was any of my business.

Miss Caslon didn't seem bothered by my question. "He called *his* lawyer," she answered.

"Well," I said, "I certainly hope everything's all right."

"I'm sure there's nothing to worry about," said Miss Caslon, "but it looks as if this meeting will go on all day. I'm afraid Mr. Duggins won't be able to meet with you after all. If you want to go home, we'll pay you for the entire day. It's the least we can do."

"Thanks, but as long as I'm here, I may as well wrap up a couple of loose ends."

"Whatever you like," said Miss Caslon.

I didn't bother turning on the computer or attempting to look busy. It hardly seemed worth perpetuating my special project ruse, so I sat and thought and waited for Sherry Ramone to call and tell me that Ellen Suttlan had come in. When she finally did, I told Miss Caslon where I'd be.

"Go ahead, Miss Midnight. I'll page you if by some miracle Mr. Duggins gets out of the meeting."

The excitement of possibly finding the Lady in Pink made me forget all about Ray Marshall.

"Get a load of this," said Sherry. She turned up the intercom on her desk so I could hear. "They've been fighting like this ever since Ellen got here."

From the little box came an angry male voice and an angry female voice, both calling each other names. Lots of four-letter words came through, but little content.

"What's the fight about?" I asked.

"I think it's a continuation of their last fight. The one they had when she got back from Paris."

I wanted to get into Wayne Cameron's office to see if I could identify Ellen Suttlan as the Lady in Pink. I didn't know what I'd do if she was, but I wanted in there all the same. It occurred to me that maybe I should call Johnny or Turner and McKinley, but before I could do anything, the door to Wayne Cameron's office flew open and the Lady in Pink marched out.

Her mouth was set in an angry scowl, her face red, her eyes narrowed into tiny little slits. Although she wore a bright suit the color of paint used down in the subway, MTA blue, no doubt about it, Ellen Suttlan was the Lady in Pink. She pointed a red-tipped finger at me. "What's *she* doing here?"

Wayne Cameron came out of his office. "She's nothing, just a temp who's been working on a special project for Mr. Duggins."

The Lady in Pink snarled. "Special project my ass. Wayne Cameron, you're even more of a fool than I thought. That's no temp. Special project? Don't make me laugh. That's Brenda Midnight, the goddamned milliner who's got the rest of Snake Mezuna's mother's pearls."

Up until Ellen Suttlan mentioned Snake Mezuna, Sherry had been fighting to stifle a laugh. When she heard that name, her expression changed.

Ellen Suttlan reached into her fake Chanel pocketbook and pulled out a gun that looked exactly like the gun she'd used to rob me, the very same gun she'd used to kill Carla.

"Both of you, inside," she said. She pointed the gun first at me, then at Sherry.

"For chrissakes, Ellen," said Cameron, "you can't do that here. This is Bateman & Crews, a respectable law firm."

"Put a cork in it, Cameron."

28

Damn. I'd been so focused on identifying Ellen Suttlan as the Lady in Pink, it had never occurred to me that she might recognize me, especially the way I looked, in a frumpy suit with my hair all plastered back. I guess she had a good memory for faces.

Using her gun as a prod, Ellen ushered Sherry and me into Wayne Cameron's office. Wayne hung back in the doorway, twisting his head this way and that, nervously looking up and down the hall. It was hard to tell if he was checking to be sure no one else was around or getting ready to bolt.

"Don't be getting any funny ideas, Cameron. Like it or not, you're in this to the end," said Ellen. "Get your fat ass in here."

Cameron looked at Ellen, then at the gun, then back at Ellen again. Meekly he walked into his office.

"Shut the door behind you," said Ellen.

"Ellen, I don't think this is a good idea," he said.

She pointed the gun at him. "Now. While you're at it, lock it."

Wayne Cameron was not a partner in the firm. Even so, he'd done all right for himself at Bateman & Crews. His office had everything a partner's office should: dark wood paneling, a floor-to-ceiling bookcase filled with leather-bound law books, oriental rug, and windows looking out on Madison Avenue. It looked like a cognac ad on the back of a men's magazine.

Wayne walked over to his dark heavy desk and started to sit, but before his ample bottom touched down on the chair's plush black leather upholstery, Ellen stopped him. "Oh, no you don't, Cameron. I can't trust you. Get over there with them." She jutted her chin toward Sherry and me.

"But Ellen, we're partners," said Wayne.

Scowling, Ellen stepped toward him. "Don't 'but Ellen' me, you whiny bastard," she said, waving the gun around for emphasis.

Wayne opened his mouth like he was about to say something but apparently thought the better of it. Reluctantly, he joined Sherry and me where we stood with our backs against the bookcase.

Ellen ran her free hand through her hennaed hair. "You know, Wayne, I'm beginning to think you're more trouble than you're worth. It was your sorry ass that caused all this trouble in the first place.

"But Ellen," said Wayne, "you didn't tell me there'd be pearls in the shipment. Pearls weren't part of the plan. I didn't have buyers lined up for pearls."

Ellen let out an exasperated sigh. "As you *should* know by now, Wayne, in this business the plan frequently changes. You're supposed to adapt, not freak out. You're certainly not supposed to sell the goods to the first little yuppie twit that happens by."

"I've told you a thousand times, Ellen. When Ashley Millard walked in on me and saw the lace she started asking questions, questions that quite frankly got me scared. I thought she was onto us. I thought she was shaking me down. I had to give her a deal so she'd keep her mouth shut."

"Some deal," said Ellen. "Ashley made out like a bandit. For my trouble, I've got Snake Mezuna chasing after me."

"Blame me if you want," said Wayne, "but it was you

who stole the pearls from Snake Mezuna's mother. For chrissakes, Ellen, you put our whole operation here at risk. It's all over anyway. We're in for it as soon as those partners get out of their emergency meeting.''

Fascinating as this conversation was, I tuned them out and tried to assess the situation. What did Ellen have planned for Sherry and me? Kill us? Unlikely. It's not like we were in an abandoned waterfront warehouse in the middle of the night; we were in the offices of a major law firm in midtown Manhattan at three o'clock in the afternoon. If I counted Wayne, there were three of us against only one of her. These thoughts were only comforting if I assumed that Ellen was rational, but she wasn't rational. She was a desperate criminal, who had killed at least once before, when she was caught off guard, without a plan.

Ellen's voice got louder, forcing me to pay attention. ''. . . and I wouldn't be a bit surprised if it was you,'' she shrieked at Wayne, ''who told Snake Mezuna where to find me. You'd sacrifice your own mother for the five hundred thousand reward.''

Sherry nudged me with her elbow. She mouthed the words ''five hundred thou'' and let out a barely audible whistle. Five hundred thousand dollars would pay for a lot of trips to Europe. The pearls weren't worth nearly that much. With Snake I guessed, it was the thought that counted. There was a lesson to be learned here: Never steal anything from a notorious hitman's mother.

Ellen's voice reached a hysterical pitch. ''Can you imagine what it felt like getting off that airplane last night and seeing Snake Mezuna there waiting for me? I almost walked right into his arms. If it hadn't been for that bomb scare and hundreds of extra cops crawling all over the airport, and the fact that I could get a cab faster than a guy who looks like Snake, I'd be a dead duck. I can't go home; I'm risking a lot just coming here.''

''You're a dead duck anyway,'' said Wayne. ''If Snake Mezuna wants you dead, you're dead. That's his job for chrissakes.''

Who knows how long they would have gone on like that. Probably forever, if not for Sherry Ramone, who thought to leave her intercom on. Probably forever, if not for Miss Caslon, who walked by Sherry's desk on her way to the rest room and heard everything.

Sherry elbowed me in the ribs again. Her eyes directed my attention to the door. The doorknob jiggled, then turned. Seconds later, the door burst open and Miss Caslon stepped into the office holding a set of master keys.

She stomped into the room, stopping in front of Wayne. Hands on her hips, she glared at him. "Wayne Cameron, you should be ashamed of yourself. After all Mr. Duggins has done for you, this is how you thank him. I guess I know now what the emergency partner meeting is all about. You and Miss Suttlan have been using Trusts and Estates to cover up smuggling, haven't you?"

Wayne Cameron switched from whiny to smarmy. "Alice, please, it's not at all what you think. I had nothing to do with it. I can explain. Really."

By then Ellen had pointed the gun at Miss Caslon. When Miss Caslon noticed, the color drained from her face. "Oh my," she said. She sucked in her breath and brought a fluttering hand up to her chest.

No one ever accused me of bravery. I don't take subways late at night, Rollerblade down the middle of Broadway, take cash to the garment center, scale tall buildings, or jump out of airplanes. In fact, I don't even fly in airplanes. Clearly, if I'd taken even a second to think about what I did next, I never would have done it. The whole time I was doing it, I kept thinking to myself, no one will ever believe that I did it, not in a million years.

What I did was seize the moment. I put my head down and dived straight for Ellen Suttlan's ankles. Because she wore out-of-date spike heels and a tight skirt that didn't have a kick pleat, it was easy to knock her over. She landed facedown on the ornately patterned rug. It says a lot for the tensile strength of thread that she didn't split her skirt.

Ellen was down, but not out. With her legs thrashing and

arms flailing, she fought to get up. Sherry ran over to help. Even Wayne Cameron, who must have figured out which side his bread was buttered on, plunged into the brawl. He grabbed on to Ellen's right wrist until she let go of the gun.

"The gun," I said. "Somebody get the gun."

Cautiously Miss Caslon approached. While Sherry, Wayne, and I wrestled with Ellen, Miss Caslon reached for the gun. "Got it," she said. She held it flat in the palm of her outstretched hand like she was afraid it might explode. "What do you want me to do with it?"

I was too busy struggling to keep Ellen pinned to the floor to care what Miss Caslon did with the gun. "Put it in a safe place where Ellen can't get hold of it again. Then call building security, the cops, and, if you want, Mr. Duggins."

Finally, remembering a trick Johnny had learned for his Tod Trueman role, I successfully yanked Ellen's right arm behind her back. She could still twist and turn, she could still call me terrible names and threaten to sue me, but she couldn't get up, which made her mad as hell and fight all the harder. Wayne held her feet, Sherry sat on her butt, and I put my knee between her shoulder blades. Still she managed to lift her head up and spit. She was a good spitter, hitting Wayne's wastebasket from at least three feet away.

Fortunately, building security was on the ball. Two beefy weightlifter types who looked like they could be a father-and-son team, arrived seconds after Miss Caslon's call. They wore matching navy blue jumpsuits. A yellow-and-gray emblem sewed above their left breast pockets identified their employer as Men of Steel Enforcement Systems, a local firm with a staff of freelancers known to cause as much trouble as they prevented. "What seems to be the problem here?" asked the older, beefier of the two.

"Keep them here until the police come," said Miss Caslon. She pointed first at Ellen, then at Wayne.

"But, but . . ." said Wayne, blubbering. "It was all her idea. I didn't do anything. I helped capture her."

Miss Caslon turned her back on Wayne Cameron and walked out.

"No problem," said the younger Man of Steel.

Mr. Duggins arrived in time to supervise the Men of Steel as they handcuffed Ellen and Wayne, sat them in chairs, and hulked over them.

"Good work," he said. Then he turned to me. "Nice to see you again, Miss Midnight."

"Nice to see you too."

He looked at Miss Caslon. "Alice, are you all right?"

"A bit rattled is all. I got so mad when I heard Mr. Cameron and Miss Suttlan discussing how they'd used our department to smuggle, I'm afraid I acted without thinking."

"Thank goodness someone did," I said, smiling at Miss Caslon.

Everyone arrived at once: cops in all kinds of different uniforms, partners of Bateman & Crews with concerned looks on their faces, secretaries, and Johnny. . . .

Johnny? What was he doing at Bateman & Crews?

He rushed over and hugged me. "We were right across the street," he said. "Turner and McKinley were showing me how to do a stakeout. We parked in a no-parking zone and pretended to read the newspaper and checked out the people walking by. We saw a couple of small-time drug deals, a possible pickpocket, and a pooper-scooper violator. Then, as we were getting ready to leave, all of a sudden a whole bunch of cop cars pulled up to Bateman & Crews. I was afraid you would be right in the middle of whatever was going down. It looks like I was right. What happened here? Are you okay?"

"It was great, Johnny. I got the Lady in Pink. I tackled her and held her until the Men of Steel came." I pointed to Ellen Suttlan. "That's her over there."

Johnny looked at Ellen Suttlan. "Yeah, right, you tackled her. I'll believe that when the F train runs on schedule."

"I did. You can ask anybody. Where are Turner and McKinley?"

"They stopped off in the john. That's the worst part of a stakeout—having to go."

"I can't wait to see them lead the Lady in Pink away. They'll have to admit I was right all along about Carla's murder."

Johnny shook his head. "I don't think so, Brenda. Turner and McKinley won't be taking the Lady in Pink anywhere. Not this time. They don't have jurisdiction."

"What do you mean? She robbed me and killed Carla."

"Doesn't matter," said Johnny. "See those guys over there?" He nodded his head in the direction of two grim men who were questioning Sherry, Miss Caslon, Mr. Duggins, and one of the other partners. "They're feds."

"Feds?"

"Yeah. Customs I think. This is their bust."

"Miss Caslon called the cops, not customs."

"From what I gather, the customs agents were already on the premises, setting up the bust," said Johnny. "My guess is that they've been investigating the smuggling going on through Bateman & Crews for a long time. It was all coming to a head today. You walked right into the middle of their operation."

So that's what Ray had been talking about. What did that make Ray? An informant? A customs agent? A smuggler? A friend of Snake Mezuna's? In fact, where was Ray? I didn't see him anywhere.

However, I did see Turner and McKinley. They'd joined a group of regular cops laughing it up with a lot of head nodding, back slapping, and gruff noises.

As Johnny and I watched, the Men of Steel handed Ellen and Wayne over to two customs agents. When they started to lead them away, Ellen put up a fight. She screamed and cursed and spat. Wayne Cameron, head down, cooperated completely.

I ran over to Turner and McKinley. "You've got to stop them," I said. "That's the Lady in Pink, Carla's killer.

Can't you arrest her? Murder has got to be a bigger offense than smuggling.''

Turner sighed. ''There's nothing we can do. Even if you're right, we have no evidence against her except your say-so.''

''How about if you had the murder weapon? Can't you prove the bullets that killed Carla came from her gun?''

''Well, yes,'' said McKinley. ''That would certainly give us more to go on.''

I led Turner and McKinley over to Miss Caslon. ''Miss Caslon, please get Ellen Suttlan's gun and show it to the detectives.''

''Certainly.'' Miss Caslon walked back into Wayne Cameron's office.

''Whoa, wait just a minute there,'' said McKinley. He caught up with Miss Caslon. ''Don't touch anything.''

''You don't have to worry about that,'' said Miss Caslon. She opened the top drawer of Wayne Cameron's desk and pointed to the gun.

McKinley looked in the drawer. ''That's it? That's the gun?''

Miss Caslon nodded.

''That's not a gun,'' said McKinley. ''It's a cigarette lighter.''

29

Turner, McKinley, and the rest of the cops all got a good laugh out of the cigarette lighter. Even Johnny chuckled until he caught me glaring at him. I felt foolish enough without him making it worse.

Not long after the gun debacle, the customs agents took Ellen and Wayne away, the regular cops cleared out, and the partners went off to wherever partners go.

Sherry and Miss Caslon commiserated with me. "Don't feel badly," said Miss Caslon. "We all thought it was a gun."

"Yeah," said Sherry. "Anyone could have made the same goof."

Sure, I felt rotten about making a fool of myself, but I felt even rottener because, after finally tracking down the Lady in Pink, I still couldn't prove she'd killed Carla. Turner and McKinley would never pay attention to me now. That was too much to explain to Miss Caslon and Sherry, so I didn't even try. Instead, I introduced them to Johnny.

"Aren't you Tod Trueman?" asked Sherry. "I saw your pilot on TV last year."

While Johnny told Sherry all about the six new *Tod Trueman* episodes, Miss Caslon pulled me to the side. "If you have time," she said, "Mr. Duggins would like you to drop by his office. He wants to thank you in person.''

"Thank me for what?

I'd never seen all the way inside Mr. Duggins's office. When I opened the door, I heard voices.

"I'm sorry," I said. "I didn't know you were in conference. I'll come back."

"Come in, Miss Midnight. There's no one else here."

The voices came from a television, which also served as the only source of light in the dim room. Mr. Duggins sat in a reclining chair, totally engrossed by a video of an old *Perry Mason* show. When the actress on the stand finished her teary confession, Mr. Duggins flicked the television off. "Those were the days," he said.

He got out of his recliner and switched on the overhead lights. In the light I saw that what I had taken to be a massive desk in the center of the room was actually a regulation-size, slate-top pool table with thick elaborately carved legs.

"You wanted to see me?" I said.

"I wanted to thank you, Miss Midnight."

"I don't know what you mean."

"Now, Miss Midnight, you needn't be humble. Your special project uncovered the smuggling plot and exposed the miscreants before the authorities had a chance to do so. If the authorities had acted before you captured Ellen Suttlan and Wayne Cameron, it would have been very, very bad for the firm. Under my supervision, together with Alice Caslon and Sherry Ramone, you saved Bateman & Crews from utter ruin."

"I don't know what to say," I said.

"Naturally," said Mr. Duggins, "you and the others will be amply rewarded. Additionally, I'd like to offer you a full-time position with Bateman & Crews as special project coordinator."

"Thanks, Mr. Duggins, but I think I'll stick to millinery for a while."

"Millinery?" he said.

"It's a long story."

Outside, in Miss Caslon's alcove, Johnny and Miss Caslon waited for me.

Miss Caslon shook my hand. Her grip was surprisingly strong. "I'd like to thank you as well, Miss Midnight. If Mr. Duggins hadn't brought you in to straighten out this mess, it would have been a disaster for Bateman & Crews."

"I was only doing my job," I said, trying to keep a straight face.

"What was that all about?" asked Johnny.

"I'll tell you later."

Much as I wanted to get out of Bateman & Crews, I had one more stop to make on the way out—Ray Marshall's office. As I suspected, his office was empty, cleaned out, vacant. No sign of Ray anywhere.

"What exactly was his part in all this?" asked Johnny.

"I'm not sure."

Johnny drove me back to Midnight Millinery in Lemmy's car. It wasn't legal for him to be driving without a licensed driver in the car, but I didn't let it bother me.

"Want to come in?" I asked.

"No, thanks, I've got to get up to Lemmy's neighborhood and find a spot to park the car."

Chuck and Elizabeth were hard at work. Elizabeth pounded away on a little laptop computer; Chuck sat at the big computer. Thanks to Detective Turner, who had handed out my business card at the Sixth Precinct—the business card I didn't know I had, the business card Chuck and Elizabeth made behind my back—they'd taken in dozens of cop résumés. Apparently the cops at the Sixth were anxious about rumored cutbacks in the police force. I halfway suspected Chuck and Elizabeth had started those rumors themselves to drum up more business, but they denied it.

"You're not going to believe what happened," I said. I was right. After I told them, they didn't believe it.

"Do you expect us to believe that you, Brenda Midnight,

tackled Ellen Suttlan, now positively identified as the Lady in Pink, brought an international smuggling ring to justice, and saved one of the largest law firms in New York City from ruin?'' asked Chuck.

''It's true,'' I said. ''Except that Ellen Suttlan had on a bright blue suit, so it's no longer accurate to call her the Lady in Pink.''

''I believe you,'' said Elizabeth.

''Thanks.''

''What about your call to me this morning?'' asked Chuck. ''What kind of garbage was Ray Marshall feeding you.''

''It wasn't garbage. I'm pretty sure Ray knows that the hacker's calls came from Midnight Millinery. I think he was warning me. He said he could catch the hacker if he wanted to.''

''That's a crock,'' said Chuck. ''It doesn't make sense. If he could do it, then why didn't he?''

''He had another agenda at Bateman & Crews.''

''What?''

''I don't know. I'm not sure whose side he was on. I do know that I don't want to think about it anymore right now. All I want to do is go home and freshen up.''

''We understand,'' said Elizabeth. ''You've had a hard day. It must have been very stressful, with the Lady in Pink holding you at gunpoint like that.''

''Stressful? Yeah, sort of. Only''—I hated to admit this to them—''only it turns out the gun wasn't, well it wasn't exactly a gun, you know, at least not like a gun is a gun. Not like that.''

Like I knew he would, Chuck picked up on my floundering and pounced. ''What do you mean by 'not exactly a gun'?''

''Well, I thought it was a gun, so in my head it was a gun. It was shiny; it was metal. Sherry Ramone thought it was a gun; Miss Caslon thought it was a gun; even Wayne Cameron thought it was a gun. Ellen Suttlan certainly waved it around like it was a gun. She wanted us all to believe it was a gun.''

''Get to the point,'' said Chuck.

''If it wasn't a gun like a gun is a gun, what was it?'' asked Elizabeth.

I'd really hoped to sidestep the entire issue, but I could see they weren't going to let it die. ''Cigarette lighter,'' I said softly, looking down at the floor.

''You've got to be kidding,'' said Chuck. He slapped his hand on the table. ''Was this the same 'gun' the Lady in Pink used to rob Midnight Millinery?''

''Maybe. I don't know that much about guns. They all kind of look alike to me.''

''Well,'' said Elizabeth, ''the Lady in Pink couldn't very well have killed Carla with a cigarette lighter, could she?''

''That's what bothers me most of all,'' I said.

I took it easy the rest of the day. I played catch-the-chewy-toy with Jackhammer, nibbled on some graham crackers, listened to my favorite blues show on the radio, and finally drifted off to sleep at about ten o'clock.

Around midnight Johnny called. ''You know that torch singer Rita Renaldo?''

''You woke me up to ask me that?''

''Just answer.''

''Is she the one with waist-length red wavy hair, a pouty mouth, and cleavage? I think I've recently seen some posters of her dressed in a long green low-cut sequin sheath. Why?''

''That's Rita Renaldo all right. Those posters are for her sold-out show at the Paramount. When I drove back uptown today I couldn't get it out of my head how forlorn you'd looked when you saw the customs agents take Ellen Suttlan off to the hoosegow.''

''What's that got to do with Rita Renaldo?''

''I'm getting there, Brenda. Be patient. Rita Renaldo and I have something in common: our agent, Lemmy Crenshaw. By the time I got up to Lemmy's neighborhood, there were no more parking spaces. I circled the block dozens of times and was about to give up and take the car to a lot when I saw Lemmy getting out of a cab. His deal in Philadelphia turned sour, so he came home early.''

''Why are you telling me this?''

''I'm getting to the point. Lemmy jumped in the car with me and while we circled the block looking for a space I remembered about Rita Renaldo. One thing I've learned from hanging out at the precinct with Turner and McKinley is that they're both crazy about Rita Renaldo. They've got posters of her in their lockers; they know the words to all her songs. As a harmonizing duo, they sing along to her tapes. Because of the Lemmy connection, I can get tickets to Rita Renaldo's completely sold-out show at the Paramount, her first east coast appearance in over a decade, a show that Turner and McKinley couldn't get tickets for at any price. So I got Lemmy to comp me a couple of tickets and gave them to Turner and McKinley. That means Turner and McKinley owe me a big favor. You interested now?''

''I still don't know what you're getting at, but I'm interested.''

''I didn't like seeing you so depressed, so I made a deal with Turner and McKinley. I told them I'd give them tickets *and* backstage passes to see Rita Renaldo, but only if they arranged to question Ellen Suttlan about Carla's murder before she slips through a crack in the system.''

''Did they go for it?''

''You bet. Detective McKinley has a sister whose ex-husband's first wife's brother is a customs agent. The sister owes McKinley a favor, and her ex-husband owes her, and so on down the line until it was finally arranged that Turner and McKinley got to question Ellen Suttlan. I just talked to Turner.''

''Did he and McKinley get a confession out of her?''

''Unfortunately, no. Ellen Suttlan admitted to using the Trusts and Estates Department at Bateman & Crews as a cover for her smuggling operation; she ratted on Wayne Cameron; she admitted to stealing pearls from Snake Mezuna's mother; she even admitted to robbing Midnight Millinery at cigarette-lighter point. And she admitted going to Carla's apartment with the intention of getting Ashley's dress, but when she got there, Carla was already dead. She admitted she cut the pearls off Ashley's dress, or as many as she could under the circumstances, but she swore she didn't kill Carla.''

''Did Turner and McKinley believe her?''

''I'm sorry, Brenda, but until they have any evidence to the contrary, they believe her. They need a smoking gun. That cigarette lighter just doesn't cut it. They said they've got a new theory about the case.''

''What's that?''

''They wouldn't say.''

The worst part, the part that kept me from sleeping, was that even I didn't believe the Lady in Pink had killed Carla. Not anymore. I either had the right person with the wrong motive or the wrong person with the right motive. Either way I was confused. I forced myself to rethink everything with the Lady in Pink out of the equation.

Who else knew Carla had the pearls? Wayne Cameron? Miss Caslon? Mr. Duggins? The Bateman & Crews personnel director? Not that I was an expert, but I couldn't imagine any of them as the killer. Ray Marshall? No. He was up to something, but not murder.

Then again, maybe my first idea was right after all. Maybe someone was just trying to ruin Ashley's wedding. Whoever wanted that—Ashley or someone else—for whatever reason, by now the trail was cold enough to ice-skate on.

30

A red-hot scorcher of a New York day, the kind that sneaks up at the tail end of summer, when everybody least expects it, and bang—the whole city is in a bad mood. At nine o'clock in the morning the thermometer outside the window read ninety-five. The humidity had to be at least as high. Carla's eight-year-old window air conditioner coughed, sputtered, and protested, but managed to get the apartment down to about ninety.

Outside was worse. The sun beat down and bounced off cement and metal, searing my eyes. Air stuck in my throat and sandy grit stuck to my skin. The city stank of too much summer.

One foot on the sidewalk and Jackhammer yelped and put on his brakes. I tried to coax him to the fire hydrant, but he refused to budge. I took him upstairs and checked the bottom of his foot for blisters. It was fine. He felt better after I sprayed cool water on his back.

I was still trying to figure out what, if anything, to do with myself besides sip iced coffee through a straw, when Margo called.

"Brenda Midnight, you are hot, hot, hot," she said.

"Tell me about it," I said. "This one-two punch socking it to us at the end of summer is an insult."

"No, Brenda, I don't mean hot like the temperature. I mean hot like in hot item, like in your hats are flying out of Einstein's Revenge. Or rather, your hats would be flying out of here if I had any of them to sell. Everybody wants that hat in the window. How soon can you get me more?"

"I'm not sure." Big black velvet hats were the last things in the world I wanted to think about in the heat.

"Well," said Margo, "as many you can make, that's how many I can sell. So you'd better get cracking."

"I'll have to let you know if—"

"Not *if*, Brenda. I want to hear how many and when."

I didn't want to make the hats for Margo. It wasn't just because I was still recovering from yesterday's events at Bateman & Crews, or because I didn't want to work with steam and thick velvet on a sweltering hot day. The real issue was that my artistic integrity was at stake. I hadn't established Midnight Millinery to crank out the same hat over and over. In fact, I never made more than four of any one style and none of them were exactly alike. I'd keep the first prototype and then make two or three distinct variations to sell. How could I expect customers to pay a lot of money for a hat, wear it to some big affair, and then see the same hat parade by on six different heads?

Friends were always telling me I had no business sense, that I should learn from Henry Ford and set up a production line, charge less money for more hats, and end up making more money. Carla, of course, understood my feelings on the subject. I remember her telling me, "Brenda, if you're going to do that, you may as well get a job in a hot dog factory."

Unfortunately, the desire to maintain my artistic integrity often conflicted with my need to pay the bills. In the past I'd always resisted the temptation to go for the dough. But now the situation at Midnight Millinery was critical. I had no fall line to speak of, and while I'd been off wasting time at Bateman & Crews, Chuck and Elizabeth had turned the place into a résumé-typing service.

I called Johnny for advice. Not that he was any great arbiter of artistic truth, but he was a good friend who sometimes understood me.

I told him what Margo wanted me to do.

"For chrissakes, Brenda, you're making too big a deal about a few lousy hats. It's not like Margo wants you to knock off someone else's design. It's a hat you designed, a hat only you can make."

"I'd be knocking off my own design."

"That's one way of looking at it, I suppose—the pauper's way. If I were you, Brenda, I'd go ahead and make the hats. You'd better do something before Chuck and Elizabeth take over and you end up working full-time at Bateman & Crews."

"Chuck and Elizabeth promised to leave after one month."

"How are you going to throw them out if they're your only source of income?"

Johnny had made his point. "Okay," I said, "I'll make the hats."

I called Margo back and told her I'd get her some hats as soon as I could. "Would you mind if I twisted each brim into a slightly different shape?" I asked. "So they're not all exactly the same."

"Of course not," she said. "Twist away."

Even with that compromise, I felt I was selling out. But as long as I'd decided to make the hats, I figured I might as well plunge in and get it over with as soon as possible. At least the air conditioner over at Midnight Millinery worked better than Carla's. "Come on, Jackhammer," I said. "I'll carry you over the sidewalks."

No sooner were Jackhammer and I out the door than I ran into Ray Marshall waiting for me in front of the building.

"Ray," I said, surprised. I didn't expect to see him again.

"Sorry if I startled you," he said, " but I knew you'd be out sooner or later, and I wanted to explain in person." He was dressed casually, in bright green high-top sneakers, faded cutoffs, and a well-worn gray T-shirt.

"Explain what?" I asked.

"Why I had to leave Bateman & Crews before all the fireworks yesterday."

"Fireworks? What fireworks?"

"Come on, Brenda, don't act dumb. I'm playing straight with you; please do the same for me. I heard what you did yesterday and I've got to admit I'd grossly underestimated your abilities. Funny thing is we were both at Bateman & Crews to bring down the smugglers, only you were hired from the inside, and damned if you didn't beat me to the punch. Customs agents were in place, ready to act. You single-handedly stole their thunder."

I was still pretty confused about Ray's role in all this. I took a stab. "You're with customs, then?"

Ray laughed. "Hardly. I'm private. I used to be a computer consultant, but I hated all the hand holding. Clients called at all hours asking why their floppy had flopped. To make it interesting I became an investigator specializing in computer infiltration."

"You're telling me that all the while Bateman & Crews thought you were keeping their computers in order, you were snooping around to see what Ellen Suttlan and Wayne Cameron were up to?"

Ray nodded his head. "That's close enough."

"Well, then," I said, "if you're not with customs, who hired you?"

"A private citizen with a grudge against the firm and a direct line to customs. I'm sorry, I can't say more than that. I'll tell you one thing, though, my client is mighty disappointed that Bateman & Crews is in the clear. Your name is mud with him."

"Is my name mud with you too?"

"Hell no. As soon as things settle down a bit I'd like to see you again. You did a great job. You uncovered the truth. The firm-wide conspiracy my client wanted to dig up simply wasn't there. One thing, though, Brenda, a warning: The next time you need a little computer breaking and entering, don't go to amateurs."

I looked him straight in the eye. "Ray, I don't know what you're talking about."

Someday I'd tell Ray the really real reason I'd been at Bateman & Crews. But never in a million years, no matter where our relationship ended up, would he get me to admit I'd conspired with Chuck to hack into the Bateman & Crews computer.

I wasn't sure when Elizabeth had stopped wearing her solemn single braid, but she'd started letting her hair fall loose in soft waves around her face. "Damned steamy, isn't it?" she said when Jackhammer and I got to the shop.

"Like a blast furnace," I said. "I had to carry Jackhammer over here. He won't put his feet down on the hot cement."

"Can't say I blame him," said Chuck.

I told them about my encounter with Ray Marshall, which got Chuck all riled up.

"Bullshit," he said, sounding angrier than I'd ever heard him. "Ray Marshall is full of shit. There's no way he could have traced those calls back to us. I tell you, Brenda, I know what I'm doing."

"Then how'd he know it was us?" I asked. "He's warned me two times now."

"He didn't actually say he knew it was us, did he?"

"No. Not exactly."

"Like I said, Brenda, your new boyfriend is full of shit."

"He's not my new boyfriend."

"Then stop glowing when you talk about him."

"If I'm glowing at all, it's from the heat."

"What are you doing here anyway?" asked Chuck. "I thought you were going to stay home today and take it easy."

"I thought so too, but Margo called and talked me into making more hats like the one she put in her window."

"Isn't production work against the Brenda Midnight code of artistic integrity?"

"Sometimes I'm forced to bend the rules. I've got to

make money somehow. With no fall line, Einstein's Revenge is my only hope to sell any hats this season.''

"Don't worry about money," Chuck said. "Elizabeth and I are raking it in. You get your third for nothing, though you could help out every once in a while if you wanted.''

"I will not type résumés.''

"There's a lot more to it than that," said Elizabeth. "It's amazing what we can do with these computers. Before you know it we'll be a full-fledged graphic arts studio.''

"Before I know it, it will be the end of the month," I said. "Remember our deal. You guys promised to be out of here.''

They both ignored that. "We took in a thousand dollars yesterday," said Chuck.

"You're kidding.''

"Nope. Elizabeth, show her the figures.''

Elizabeth handed me a printout of the day-by-day income for the shop. I had to admit that the shop hadn't been busier since the old days when the previous tenant ran a numbers game from behind the candy counter.

"Impressive," I said, "but I don't want to talk about it now." I needed to do some hard thinking about my future. Meanwhile I needed to get going on the hats for Margo.

"In that case," said Elizabeth, "I'm going online. I have a tentative electronic rendezvous with Dude Bob Forty-three.''

"She's talking dirty to that creep again," said Chuck.

Elizabeth flipped open the lid of her tiny portable computer. A long wire connected it to the phone jack in the wall. "I'll have you know, the Dude and I do not talk dirty." She rolled her thumb over the trackball, tapped the keyboard a couple of times, and waited while terrible spitting and gurgling noises came out of the computer. Then she smiled and started typing fast on the dark gray keyboard. Every so often she'd pause, then type up another storm. For all I knew she probably *was* talking dirty to Dude Bob 43.

* * *

I dragged out the black velvet. There was enough for a dozen hats and enough of the chartreuse trim for even more. Twelve hats should be enough to keep Margo happy for a while.

Cutting through heavy velvet and buckram was a slow, painful process. I got big red dents in my scissoring fingers and a twinge of pain in my wrist.

Chuck looked concerned when he saw me rubbing my wrist. "Can't you cut that stuff some other way? Like with lasers or something?"

"No," I said. "I'm doing couture. I cut by hand. I do most of the stitching by hand. I don't use glue. I don't use prepackaged flowers or gewgaws. I may be making a dozen of the same hat, but I won't compromise quality."

"Well," said Chuck, "you're cruising for a big bruising, or at least a pinched nerve. Haven't you ever heard of repetitive stress or carpal tunnel syndrome?"

"I'm just making hats."

"I know what I'm talking about, Brenda. At least take a break and shake your hands every fifteen minutes or so." Chuck finally quit nagging me when his stupid résumé customers started to show up.

I tuned them out as much as possible until one guy kicked up a fuss and called Elizabeth an uptight old biddy and Chuck a carrot-topped freak. All three of them were yelling.

"Excuse me," I said. "What seems to be the problem?"

The red-faced customer glared at me. Throbbing veins popped out on his temples. "Who, may I ask, are you?" he asked in a nasty, surly voice.

"Brenda Midnight," I answered.

"Then that's *your* name in the window?"

"Yes," I said. "It's my shop."

"Then you instruct your idiot employees to fulfill your obligation and do as your sign in the window promises."

"What are you talking about?"

Elizabeth spoke up. "He wants me to forge NYU sta-

tionery for him and then use it to type up a letter of rec-
ommendation from one of the deans.''

''That's ridiculous,'' I said. ''We don't do that.''

''You can't refuse,'' the customer argued. ''The sign in
your window claims you do letterheads, does it not?''

''I guess,'' I said. I hadn't actually bothered to read it.

''And further,'' he went on, ''it says you do letters. Well,
I need a letterhead and I need a letter and I need them now.
I have an important interview in an hour.''

''I told him it wasn't legal,'' said Chuck.

''We design original letterheads,'' said Elizabeth. ''We
don't counterfeit existing ones.''

''They're right,'' I said. ''We are not going to break the
law.''

The customer walked over to me and slammed his briefcase on my worktable. His face got even redder and his
hands tightened into fists. ''Don't you go quoting the law
to me. I demand that you do this letterhead as you advertise.
If you don't''—he leaned closer to me and raised his
voice—''I'll sue you. I'll inform the authorities of your
deceptive advertising practices.'' He emphasized each syl-
lable by jabbing his forefinger in front of my face. That
was too much for Jackhammer. He roused himself from his
spot beneath the vanity and jumped into my lap. From there
he climbed up onto the worktable. Then, with a curled lip
worthy of Elvis, he snarled at the man.

The customer jumped back. ''Get that vicious rabid dog
away from me,'' he said. ''Call that thing off.''

''I will not,'' I said. ''Get out of my store.''

Still snarling and baring his teeth, Jackhammer walked
to the end of the worktable, leaned over the edge, and
yapped at the customer who was backing out of the store
using his briefcase as a shield.

Once he was gone, Chuck and Elizabeth applauded.

''That was great, Brenda,'' said Chuck. ''You really told
him a thing or two.''

''Jackhammer should get all the credit,'' I said. I moved
my chair around to the other side of the worktable so my

back faced the door. I didn't want to look at any more of their customers. "Let me know if someone wants a hat."

The hats began to take shape as my work progressed from cutting and sewing to steaming. Through whooshes of steam vapor, I vaguely heard the bells on the door jangle. A voice cut right through the steam, sending a chill up my spine.

"No, it isn't a good morning," the harsh voice snapped, "and, it's going to get a lot worse if you don't cooperate."

Steam iron in hand, I spun around to look. "Not you again," I said.

"Afraid so," she said. The Lady in Pink, still in yesterday's blue suit, pointed yet another gun at me.

31

When she saw the gun in Ellen Suttlan's right hand, Elizabeth gasped and threw her hands up over her head. Chuck giggled nervously. Even Jackhammer, who'd been in a feisty mood ever since scaring the irate customer away, slunk over to his pile of fabric and buried his head.

"Give me a break," I said. "You can't possibly expect me to believe that this time you've got a real gun. What are you doing out of jail anyway? You're supposed to be in the federal lockup downtown."

"Does that mean I can put my hands down?" asked Elizabeth.

"Yes, Elizabeth," I said. "Do whatever you want."

Elizabeth put her hands in her lap. "Thank goodness. My arms were starting to hurt."

Ellen whirled around and aimed the gun at a spot in the center of Elizabeth's forehead.

"This time, I assure you, the gun *is* for real."

Elizabeth looked at me, then at Ellen; then she put her hands back up in the air. Chuck stopped laughing and stuck his hands up too.

While Chuck and Elizabeth kept Ellen distracted, quietly as possible I reached my hand into the drawer of my worktable and felt around. There were the obvious items. The wooden spools of thread, number five needles, scissors, razor blades, lengths of blocking cord. Also, over the years

I'd adapted a lot of objects, never intended for such use, as tools for making hats. For instance, to protect my eyeballs, I kept a collection of wine corks to jam over the wire's pointed end while wiring up a brim. So there were corks scattered throughout the drawer. I had a rubber plate scraper, though under the pressure of the moment, I couldn't remember what on earth it was for. Finally I found what I'd been feeling for—the old-fashioned metal curling rod that I'd bought at the flea market with the intention of using it to curl ribbon. It didn't really curl ribbon, but I'd kept it around anyway, figuring that someday, if my hair straightened out, I might need it. Or, someday, if face-to-face with a small fake gun for the third time, I might need a bigger fake gun.

I made sure both my hands carefully concealed most of the curling rod and hoped that the part Ellen would see would look enough like the barrel of a gun. Then, curling rod in hand, I stood up and leveled it at Ellen. "Drop your gun," I snarled. "Or whatever it is."

Ellen pointed her cigarette lighter at me.

"Drop your gun," she said.

"Drop yours," I said.

Chuck and Elizabeth watched in amazement. Jackhammer climbed out from under his fabric and watched in amazement. Part of me stood outside myself and watched in amazement. As we all watched in amazement, Ellen Suttlan carefully set her cigarette lighter down on the floor.

"Get it, Chuck," I said.

He picked it up, laughed, tossed it in the air, caught it on its way down, and spun it around his finger cowboy style. "Anyone need a light?" he asked, laughing hysterically with his finger poised on the trigger.

I froze when I saw the trigger. The lighter Ellen Suttlan had used yesterday hadn't had a trigger. That lighter had been a plain tube-shaped metal lighter, no more dangerous than the curling rod I'd just fooled her with. But the lighter in Chuck's hand was a different story. I could see the whole thing and it was actually shaped like a gun. "Chuck, no," I yelled, but it was too late.

Chuck pulled the trigger and the fake gun fired a real live bullet into one of the floorboards. Chuck stopped laughing. "Oh shit," he said. "It is real."

Jackhammer raced around the store growling and barking. The color drained out of Elizabeth's face. Chuck, who had no color in his face to start with, turned an ill-looking green.

"I told you it was real," said Ellen.

"Be careful, Chuck," I said, "and bring Ellen's gun over here." I put her gun in the drawer next to my curling iron.

"Now tell me," I said, acting a whole lot calmer than I felt, "who let you out of jail?"

"Somebody sprung me."

"Who?"

"I've got a good lawyer, not one of those wimps at Bateman & Crews. A few words with him and the feds pulled me out of the cage, handed me my belongings, and said 'skedaddle.' I'm out. I came here first thing to get the rest of the pearls. If you just hand them over to me, I promise to be out of your hair for good."

"You mean the pearls you stole from Snake Mezuna's mother, lost due to Wayne Cameron's ineptitude, and later cut off Ashley Millard's wedding dress while my friend Carla lay dead on top of it?"

"Yeah, those pearls. I'm sorry about your friend, by the way, but I didn't kill her."

"You're just damned lucky I believe you," I said. "You didn't happen to see who did kill her, did you? Like someone running out of the apartment?"

"Look," said Ellen, "when there's a fresh dead body in an apartment it's hard to notice much else. The door was wide open when I got there and your friend was dead on top of the dress. I'm thinking somebody already called the cops and any second they're gonna come charging in, so I hurried. I must have dropped a few pearls on my way out.

I didn't care so much because, at the time, I had no idea
that the old lady was Snake's mother. Now things are completely different. Thanks to some lousy rat over in France,
Snake found out who I am and he's after me. Sooner or
later—probably sooner—Snake is going to find me and it'll
be curtains. I thought if I could round up all the pearls and
give them back to the old bat, maybe I can patch things up
with Snake.''

"So you didn't see anything that morning."

"The only thing I remember besides wanting to get the
hell out of there fast was your call coming through."

"My call?"

"It came over your friend's answering machine. You
asked where she got that lace with the 'beautiful beads'
that she'd given you. That's how I knew you had some of
the pearls too. I looked up your name in her address book,
came right over, and robbed you."

I shuddered to think of my voice floating around the
room where Carla had just died.

"Come to think of it," she said, "I did see one other
thing."

"What?" I asked.

Before she could answer, the bells on the door jangled,
startling us all. For a moment there was dead silence as we
all comprehended the vision in the doorway.

Chuck was the first to speak. "Here comes trouble."

I had never seen a picture of Snake Mezuna, nor had he
been described to me. Still, I knew him when I saw him.
So did everyone else. Jackhammer slunk across the floor,
then leaped into my lap and buried his head in the bend of
my elbow. Everyone stared, transfixed by the vision of evil.

Snake Mezuna slammed the door hard enough that the
glass rattled, threw the deadbolt, and turned over the OPEN
sign. None of us had any doubt at all that the gun in his
sinewy, long-fingered hand was for real. He aimed it at
Ellen and she screamed.

"Shut up." His raspy high-pitched voice mixed a little bit of Texas with a little bit of hell.

Ellen shut up. Once her mouth closed, her lower lip began to quiver.

Tall and lean, Snake Mezuna had tiny black eyes that sank deep into a narrow, pale smooth-as-an-egg face. Despite the steamy weather, he wore a fringed brown leather jacket over a white T-shirt and narrow deep blue tie. A scraggly burned-out dark blond ponytail stuck out from under a battered tan cowboy hat and hung halfway down his back. The hat needed a good steam-cleaning and reblock job.

"In case any of you gets any ideas, I want you all to watch this very carefully." Slowly, he took aim at my collection of wooden hat blocks on a shelf far against the back wall. "Third one from the left, second row down."

"Not that one," I said without thinking. I should have kept my mouth shut.

He brought the gun around until it pointed at me instead of the hat block. The muscles around his eyes tightened. He squinted at me for what seemed like forever. "Why not 'that one'?" asked Snake.

"Because that one's an antique. Very rare. Nobody makes hat blocks like that anymore. See, there used to be this old guy, had a dusty wood shop in the garment center and turned out the . . ."

Snake obviously didn't give a hoot. He shot the block, dead center. Then he turned around and, with his back to the blocks, shot every one of them in the row, left to right, in the center of their foreheads.

Snake smiled. "That was a demonstration. I hope it got my point across. Now, here's what's going to happen. First I'm gonna lecture. The topic of my lecture today is a hundred and one reasons why you shouldn't steal from an old lady. After the lecture, if I'm still in the mood, I'm gonna shoot—maybe just her"—he pointed the gun at Ellen, whose lip still quivered—"or maybe, if it suits me, all of you."

Snake had exaggerated. He didn't really have 101 different reasons why you shouldn't steal from an old lady. What he had was 101 ways of saying what boiled down to the same thing: "because it pisses me off." He paced back and forth, leather fringe flapping, muscles taut, a bundle of stored energy waiting to explode. He punctuated key points with a thrust of his gun.

He went on and on and on and finally asked, "Are there any questions?"

Amazingly enough, Ellen raised her hand meekly. Her voice cracked. "I . . . I . . . I have one."

"Shoot," he said.

Under the circumstances, I felt that was a poorly chosen word.

"What about if I return all the pearls to your mother?"

Snake sneered. "I don't give a shit about the pearls. My mother doesn't give a shit about the pearls. I replaced those pearls a long time ago. But I do give a shit about some bitch who messes with my mother. For that, you must pay."

"Look," said Ellen a little louder this time, "your mother's not the saint you think she is. How do you think I got those pearls in the first place? Do you think I ripped them off her neck like a chain snatcher on the subway? No way. Your mother was running a con job on me. She used the pearls as bait. The old switcheroo. I didn't steal the pearls from your mother. All I did was outsmart her."

For a minute Snake said nothing. Then he sighed and shook his head. "Aw, Jesus, don't tell me Ma's running that same old scam again. I told her a million times—Ma, you're too old, you make mistakes. . . ." His voice trailed off.

Ellen let out a nervous giggle. "What's a little scam between friends?"

"Nothing," said Snake, "but you and my Ma ain't exactly what I'd call friends."

I was sure he was going to shoot her right then and there. I put my hands over Jackhammer's ears and closed my eyes. But the next thing I heard wasn't gunfire, it was banging on the door.

I opened my eyes and looked. Standing outside, gesturing wildly, was this morning's irate customer. With him was a policeman.

32

Jackhammer jumped out of my lap, zoomed over to the door, and went completely nuts. Five pounds of rage. He scratched at the door, he barked, he growled, he snarled, he sprung up and down twisting his body, thrashing this way and that.

The cop banged on the glass and yelled, "Open up. We've got a complaint about a vicious attack dog in this store."

Snake stood there, nostrils flaring, his mouth turned down into a mighty frown, but he didn't say anything, or move, or in any way acknowledge the turmoil at the door. I didn't know what to do. Afraid to approach Snake, I caught Chuck's eye. He shrugged his shoulders and shook his head. Elizabeth did the same. Finally, I had no choice. I walked over to Snake and looked him straight in the beady eyes. "What should I do?"

He glared at me, shook his head, and said, "I goddamned don't know."

The cop banged on the door again. "Come on, I can see you people in there. Open up."

"I have to do something," I said.

Still no answer from Snake.

"Well," said Chuck, "if nobody else is going to do anything, I'll tell the cop we can't open up because it's a hostage situation." He took a tentative step toward the door.

"No." Snake's voice whipped through the air, stopping

Chuck in midstride. "Stay right where you are. This is *not* a hostage situation. Absolutely *not* a hostage situation. I don't *do* hostage situations."

"Okay, okay," said Chuck. "Sorry I brought it up. It seemed like a hostage situation to me, but as long as you say it's absolutely not a hostage situation, I guess I'll be moseying on home about now." Again he took a step toward the door.

Again Snake didn't like that. "No," he said, this time louder and nastier.

Chuck stopped. "I knew it was a hostage situation. It was a hostage situation from the get-go. This really sucks."

"I think he's right, Mr. Mezuna, sir," said Elizabeth. "If you won't allow us to leave, then we're hostages. Unless maybe we're prisoners. I know it's a fine line, but . . ."

Snake pondered that thought for a moment. He looked up at the ceiling, then down at the floor. Finally he sighed. "All right, what *do* we do now?"

"Don't give me this 'we' bit," I said. "You can't shove the responsibility on us. This is your trip, all the way. Remember, you're the stone-cold killer, you're the one who took *us* hostage, or prisoner, or something. You figure it out. I've got enough problems."

My biggest problem right then was Ellen Suttlan. She'd been slowly edging toward me. I didn't know what she had in mind, but I was afraid she was after her gun in my drawer. If I'd thought it would do any good, I'd have pulled the gun on Snake. But, given his demonstrated expertise in that area, it seemed really dumb to point a gun at him. Fortunately, Snake hadn't noticed her barely perceptible movement.

"Brenda's right," said Elizabeth. "Much as we'd like to help you out, it's your decision."

"Look," said Snake, "I'm a hitman, that's all. One, two, bang, bang, and I'm out of there. Hostages are too messy for me. Besides, if anyone I know finds out, I'll be a laughingstock."

"Then you should have thought of that before you came blasting in here," said Chuck.

No matter what their profession, when professional people stepped out of their professional roles and acted out of pure unbridled passion, they very often screwed up. If Snake had been less interested in teaching right and wrong—which he clearly was not qualified to teach—he would have skipped his lengthy 101 reasons why you shouldn't steal from an old lady lecture. He could have easily gone bang bang, blown Ellen away, and been long gone before the cop came to the door with the irate customer.

All of our hemming and hawing about the situation became irrelevant when the cop finally caught a glimpse of Snake's gun, recognized a hostage situation when he saw one, and radioed for help.

"Aw crap," said Snake. We all stared out the door and watched the hostage team gather outside. "This is just great, exactly what I needed to make my day."

Elizabeth offered him her ergonomic chair and helped him adjust it. Later she told me she'd hoped he'd fall asleep, but her plan backfired. If anything, his fascination with all the controls kept his mind engaged.

For a while we all stood around and watched Snake. When it didn't seem like he was going to do anything right away, besides mumble curse words to himself, I asked if he'd mind if I went back to steaming my hats. "I've got an impossible deadline to meet."

"I don't give a pissy toad's belly what you do."

Good, I thought. I liked to use my time efficiently. This way, if I ended up living through the day, I'd have some hats for Margo. And if I didn't live through the day? Well, at least working calmed me down a little.

A couple of the hat blocks Snake had shot holes in had nice curved crowns that I used for pressing open seams. Fortunately, the bullet holes didn't seem to make any difference, though the reminder was a little unsettling.

The sound of the whooshing steam had a lulling effect on all of us. Even Jackhammer gave up his guard position at the door, curled up in his fabric bed, and went to sleep. Chuck and Elizabeth turned through the pages of a graphic arts magazine. Ellen Suttlan stopped edging toward me. She must have taken a moment to think about it and concluded, as I had, that Snake pretty much outclassed us in the shooting department. She sat at the vanity and looked at herself in the mirror.

The jangling phone broke the mood.

"It's probably the hostage negotiator," said Chuck. "Want me to get it?"

"Go ahead if you want," said Snake, "but I'm not talking to nobody."

Chuck grabbed the phone. "Midnight Millinery and Computer Graphics Services." He looked at me out of the corner of his eye to catch my reaction. "Yes," he said into the receiver, "we do résumés. No, I can't promise you one-day turnaround for today. We're booked solid." He hung up the phone.

"Shit, man," he said to Snake, "you're losing us business."

Snake didn't seem to care. In fact, he was looking rather glum. When the phone rang again he nodded at Chuck to pick up the phone. Chuck held the receiver out to Snake. "It's the hostage negotiator. He wants you."

"Did he ask for me by name?" asked Snake.

"No," said Chuck. "He asked for the guy in the cowboy hat with the gun."

"At least something's going right. If this ever gets out, that Snake Mezuna is holed up with a bunch of whimpering hostages in a hat store in the middle of Greenwich freaking Village, I'm finished, done, washed up."

"Do you want to take the call?" asked Chuck.

"No. You tell that hostage negotiator to go take a hike."

The phone rang every so often after that, but no one answered.

We might have been relatively calm inside, but outside

the hubbub on the street intensified. Once the TV and radio news crews made the scene, joining the cops and hostage team, it was pandemonium. If I bent down far enough, I could see sharpshooters on the roofs across the street.

We probably would have gone on like this far into the night if Johnny hadn't run out of half-and-half for his coffee, which he needed to drink in order to concentrate on the new *Tod Trueman* script. He had to know it by tomorrow because that's when Lemmy said they'd be filming episode number one.

On his way to the deli Johnny saw the commotion on West Fourth Street. Thinking it was a movie shoot, he stopped by to network. Johnny was a firm believer in the old actor's proverb: You never know who you're going to run into or when they might be casting. But what Johnny saw was not a movie shoot. He saw complete and utter chaos centered on Midnight Millinery. He saw hostage negotiators at a loss for what to do when no one would talk to them. Johnny pushed his way through the crowd. When he looked through the window, he saw me in there steaming my hats. And he saw Snake Mezuna and Snake Mezuna's gun. And then Johnny became Tod Trueman, one-man urban rescue team.

Johnny knew how I'd illegally subleased my basement space to Pete's Café next door to use for their wine cellar. He also knew how we'd illegally broken through the basement wall so they could get to their wine without having to go through the metal flap in the floor of Midnight Millinery, and he knew what the two landlords involved and the city agencies would say if they knew about the illegal sublet or the illegal passage in the cellar wall. It didn't take much to talk Pete into letting Johnny into his cellar. From there, Johnny made his way through restaurant supplies, through the small passageway, and into the wine cellar, where he found the narrow stairway that lead to the metal flap in the floor of Midnight Millinery.

*   *   *

I can't remember ever being more surprised than when I saw Johnny erupt from that metal flap in the floor about six feet away from my blocking table. "You're surrounded," he said, looking every bit the sexy, suave leading man. "Drop your gun," he snarled dramatically at Snake, "lie down, and spread 'em."

Snake looked at Johnny. Then he looked out the window at the sharpshooters and the hostage negotiation team. Then he looked at his gun. Then he didn't look at anything, because while he was doing all that looking I sneaked up behind him and bonked him on the head with one of the hat blocks.

33

"I'm telling you," said Johnny, "no casting director in his right mind would pick a guy like Snake Mezuna to play a hitman." He banged his fist on the bar so hard the bartender turned around to make sure everything was all right.

"Why not?" asked Elizabeth. "He certainly had me convinced. I didn't doubt for a minute that he was a vicious hitman, quite capable of blowing all of us away."

I agreed. "He looked pretty scary to me too, especially around his cold beady eyes. I knew exactly who he was the instant he stormed through the doorway."

"Me too," said Chuck. "I could tell that dude was gonna be a serious problem."

"That's the point," said Johnny. "A hitman is supposed to blend into the woodwork, not stick out like a sore thumb. At six and a half feet it's impossible for Snake not to be noticed. The cowboy hat and fringed jacket don't help much either."

"Yet," I said, "supposedly he's been very successful in his career. Say what you like about his looks, apparently he does disappear in the crowd."

"Shhh," said Chuck, putting his forefinger to his lips, "the news is on."

Johnny jumped up off his bar stool. "Be right back. I've got to call Lemmy. He's going to flip out when he sees this."

217

The cops detained us long after they carted a dazed Snake Mezuna away from Midnight Millinery. We told the story dozens of times, in many different configurations— singly, two at a time, three at a time, all together. When the police were done with us we had to go through it all again for the FBI, then for the media. And when the media were done with us, we headed straight to Angie's, minus Ellen Suttlan, who'd sneaked off without thanking us for saving her pathetic life or telling me what she'd been about to say when Snake showed up.

"I don't want to watch the news," said Elizabeth. "I haven't watched the news since the mid-sixties and I'm not about to start now."

"Forget your politics, Elizabeth. This time it's us on the news. Don't you want to see yourself?" asked Chuck.

"I was on the news plenty back then. Besides the war, which was international, and civil rights, which was national, there wasn't much else going on. No crime like today. So the local news always managed to squeeze me in somewhere. I always looked like hell too. I shudder to think about it."

"You won't look like hell now," I said. "Ever since you let your hair out of that braid, you've been ravishing."

"I'm also thirty years older."

"Doesn't matter. Watch the TV and you'll see."

Johnny hurried back to the bar. "Lemmy turned on his tube. Did I miss anything?"

"No pictures yet, just the teaser and a commercial," I said. "It's coming on any second."

We turned our heads and focused on the TV mounted at the end of the bar. The screen filled with a photo of a younger hatless Snake Mezuna silhouetted against a graphic of a gun and target. The news anchor read, "Today in Greenwich Village, notorious hitman Winkley 'Snake' Mezuna . . ."

Chuck cracked up, coming close to spitting gin-and-tonic all over the bar. "*Winkley*. What kind of name is Winkley for chrissakes? No wonder . . ."

Johnny pointed. "Look, that's us now."

Interspersed with the lowdown on Snake's murderous career were shots of Turner and McKinley stuffing a subdued Snake into a cop car, and bits of Chuck, Elizabeth, and me with microphones stuck in our faces, gesturing wildly with our hands, excitedly telling the story of Snake's capture. Johnny stood off to the side, less breathless, less excited, more professional. When he spoke into the microphone it was with a calm deep voice that put the news guy to shame. "I couldn't have done it without Brenda Midnight," he said. "We make a good team."

With that, the Snake story was over. In the blink of a screen a reporter with blond hair moussed into a windswept shape was standing in front of a hospital somewhere in the Bronx. Behind her, flashing lights and ambulances.

"Oh, Johnny, that was such a sweet thing to say," said Elizabeth.

Johnny put his arm around my shoulder and squeezed. "It was the truth. Brenda and I *do* make a good team. Together we succeeded in capturing Snake. Cops and governments and secret agents all over the world have been trying to do just that for decades. This is fantastic publicity for *Tod Trueman*. Lemmy must be doing flip-flops in front of his tube."

"The Midnight Millinery and Computer Graphics store did okay too," said Chuck. "This is like free advertising. People will be flocking to the door."

"It's not the kind of advertising I want," I said. "Unfortunately the kind of people who'd flock to the door to see where I bonked Snake Mezuna over the head will scare off all my hat customers."

"I've got it," said Chuck excitedly. "We'll sell them hats you've blocked on *the* block, the block that knocked Snake out."

I buried my head in my hands.

"Do you think this story will go national?" asked Elizabeth.

"At least," said Johnny. "The capture of Snake Mezuna is an international story."

Elizabeth smiled. "In that case, I've got to let Dude Bob Forty-three know."

I guess Elizabeth liked the way she looked on TV this time around.

As we left Angie's, Chuck doubled over and laughed hysterically, "Winkley. I still can't get over that name."

I had to go down to Einstein's Revenge to give Margo the hats I'd finished. Johnny wouldn't let me walk down there alone. "Every creep in the world is out on a steamy night like tonight."

After hanging out with Snake Mezuna all day, the streets didn't seem all that dangerous to me, but I let him come along with Jackhammer and me anyway.

"You were great today, Johnny. You probably saved all our lives. It was a brave act."

Johnny stopped walking and took my hands in his. "I'd do it again in an instant, Brenda. When I saw you in there with Snake, I went berserk. I had to get you out of there. I was afraid the cops would bungle it. I really meant what I said before, Brenda. We make a good team; I couldn't have done it without you."

I started to walk again, but he held my hand tighter. "This whole thing has me thinking again, Brenda. You know, about you and me. Maybe we've made too big a deal out of a silly rug. I'm thinking maybe I should get rid of the damned thing."

I wasn't ready to discuss relationship-type things, so I pretended I hadn't picked up on Johnny's mile-wide opening.

"My god, you're famous. Both of you." Margo took the hats out of the hatbox, shook them loose from the tissue paper, and placed them carefully on her countertop. "After watching the news, I sure didn't expect to see you tonight. How on earth did you make three hats and capture that creepy Snake Mezuna guy in the same day? From the way you sounded this morning, I didn't think you were even going to make any hats.''

"I worked while he was holding us hostage. It was a great way to pass the time.''

"You're kidding. You really worked when your life was in peril?''

"She sure did,'' said Johnny. "The first thing I saw when I peeped through the flap in the floor was Brenda with her steam iron.''

Margo put on one of the hats and posed in the mirror. "Snake Mezuna Hostage Hats. Oh my god, I feel a theme coming on. Brenda, this is so exciting. We've got a gold mine here. I'm going to have to change the window, get you in here on a Saturday for a personal appearance. You will come, won't you? You too, Johnny. This is going to be so great, I can't stand it.''

"I don't know, Margo, it's kind of . . .''

Margo put up her hand to shush me. "I won't take no for an answer. We can start the promo tomorrow night at the opening.''

"What opening?''

"Just the most important opening of the season. Gil Davison's opening at the Millard Gallery. You didn't forget, did you?''

"I don't know, Margo. I'm not exactly popular with the Millards these days. Besides, I hate Gil Davison's art.''

"Forget the art; this is hype. Come on. You've got to go. If nothing else, it'll be a goof. Besides drumming up business for your hats, it will be your chance to see Gil Davison together with Ashley Millard, the almost married couple of the moment. Not to mention the almost unmarried couple of the moment, Walker and Simone Millard.''

"Really? Are they getting a divorce?''

"No, but they may as well be. So, what do you say, Brenda? You'll be down here anyway bringing me more hats. We'll go to the opening together.''

"Okay. I'll go." It would be kind of fun to see Gil Davison and the Millards in action.

Johnny didn't have much to say on the way home. I didn't want to risk saying anything for fear it would bring up the subject of our relationship, so we walked along in silence. Even at midnight the air was as hot and smelly as the inside of an exhaust pipe. Jackhammer trotted along beside us, occasionally stopping to sniff a garbage bag. Off to the west heat flashes filled the dark sky.

"Looks like a big storm coming," I said.

"I hope so," said Johnny. "Anything to break this heat."

There must have been twenty calls on the answering machine from people I hadn't heard from in years. They all said pretty much the same thing: ". . . way to go Brenda . . . I didn't know you had it in you . . . fabulous use for a hat block . . . if that great-looking Johnny isn't seeing anyone, give him my number . . ."

The last message was from Ray. "You're amazing, Brenda. Snake Mezuna. Almost single-handedly. If I had any idea that Snake . . . Anyway, how about dinner tomorrow to celebrate? Call back as late as you want. I'll be up most of the night."

I called him back. "I'd love to go to dinner, but I promised to go to an opening in Soho."

"That's okay. I'll meet you at the opening and we'll go from there. Until then, Brenda, please think about something. If you ever decide to give up millinery and go into this stuff full-time, we would make a damn fine team, you and I."

First Johnny, now Ray. Funny, I'd never considered myself part of any team.

I wanted to do one last thing before going to sleep. I gathered up the handful of pearls I'd found, opened the window, and tossed them up into the air. They shimmered for an

instant on their way to the ground in a distant flash of
lightning. I stayed there for a long time with my head out
the window, marveling at the New York buzz, the vibration
that never goes away, not even in the middle of the night.

Around three o'clock in the morning the telephone rang.
"Look, I figure I owe you this much. . . ."
  "Who . . . ?"
  "Ellen Suttlan. I'm on a cellular phone on my way to
the airport, on my way out of this burg forever. Since you
saved my life, the least I can do is finish up what I started
to say yesterday. I did see something else that morning.
The man who lives next door to your friend had his door
open a crack. He slammed it shut when I caught his eye."
    The connection broke. Ellen either hung up or went into
a tunnel.

I dragged myself out of bed, threw on a robe, and went
next door to ring Randolph's bell. When he didn't answer
I pounded on the door. "Vile lying yuppie scum." Still no
answer, so I went home, called him, and let his phone ring
for an hour, but the son of a bitch wouldn't answer.

34

Sometime in the very early morning, the storm I'd predicted finally hit. I watched out the window as the wind tore leaves from the trees. A box of Styrofoam packing peanuts crashed against razor wire, ripped open, and let loose thousands of white puffs. Swept up in the violent wind, they soared up, then down, falling in drifts like snow.

Later, when Jackhammer and I got outside, the storm had blown off to the east, leaving fresh, dry, cool air in its wake. The majestic gingko tree in front of the building had snapped in two. Its branches lay across the sidewalk. Garbage on the street had been thoroughly soaked and pummeled into papier-mâché—no longer recognizable as yesterday's newspaper or last week's cereal box—and left as sludge against the side of buildings.

Elizabeth was out walking Penelope the chow. To keep the dogs apart we stayed on opposite sides of the street and yelled to each other. "Did you hear that storm last night?" she asked.

"A doozie," I said, "but it's nothing compared to the storm that's going to hit when I find our despicable neighbor Randolph. Do you know where he is? I can't get him to open his door or pick up his phone."

"He's probably sleeping at his new place already."

"What new place?"

"Didn't you hear? Randolph bought a two-bedroom in

the East Seventies. I guess his ship finally came in."

"Damn him. Ellen Suttlan called me late last night and said she saw him peeping out his door the morning Carla was killed. If he saw her, he must have seen something else. As soon as I get ahold of that pond scum, I intend to get the truth out of him."

"I'll ask around the building," said Elizabeth. "Someone is bound to know his new address."

Jackhammer finally noticed Penelope and glared at her from across the street. Penelope growled. Jackhammer snarled back and yanked at his leash. He was amazingly strong for such a little squirt. I picked up the ferocious five-pounder and carried him inside.

Elizabeth was still off somewhere with Penelope, and Chuck hadn't come in yet, so for the first time in a long time I had Midnight Millinery all to myself. Jackhammer reorganized his scattered pile of fabric. I cleaned up squashed coffee cups, sticky snack cake wrappers, and smelly cigarette butts left by the authorities, the press, and whoever else had been in the place yesterday.

So much had happened since Carla had been murdered. I'd been led this way and that, on one wild goose chase after another, never even coming close to nabbing the killer. I'd failed Carla in a big way, as an investigator and as a friend. I was feeling pretty down in the dumps when Chuck showed up around ten o'clock. "That was some cool storm, wasn't it? You should see the East Village. All the crap in the street is all blown to one side and kind of all stuck together."

"It's the same here."

"Only here there was a lot less crap on the street to begin with. Over there, we've got mountains of gooey gunk."

He helped me finish cleaning up the mess inside the shop. When we dragged the garbage bag outside to the curb, Chuck looked up and down the block. He shook his head. "I don't get it. I figured we'd be mobbed today with people wanting to see the Snake-bopping site."

"Thank goodness," I said. "I've got to make a bunch more hats for Margo, so I'm glad we're not mobbed."

"Brenda, you've got no business sense."

I was sick of hearing that. However, I didn't bother defending myself. I had too many hats to make.

A little later Elizabeth came in dragging a branch of the fallen gingko tree behind her. "I thought we could use it in the window display. You could hang your hats on it."

"Hmmm," I said. It was a terrible idea but I didn't want to hurt her feelings.

"I had to bring it in off the street. It's been in front of the building for fifty or sixty years, ever since it was erected. I can't stand to see it ground up and turned into landfill."

"We all gotta go sometime," said Chuck.

"Speaking of going, did you find out where Randolph moved to?" I asked.

"No, not yet. The doorman says the super knows, but the super is gone for a couple of days because his daughter in Cleveland had a baby girl—seven pounds eight ounces."

I worked on the hats all day. Chuck and Elizabeth had a few customers but from what I could tell, none of them had any idea what had gone on in the store yesterday. At least not before Chuck told them. When he did they couldn't wait to get out of the place. I think Chuck is the one with the lousy business sense.

When I'd made five hats I decided to pack it in and go home. "Gil Davison's opening at the Millard Gallery is tonight if you guys want to come."

Chuck liked the idea. "Free wine. Artistic girls in short skirts. You can count on me. What do you say, Elizabeth? It's a happening thing."

"It's going to have to happen without me, I'm afraid," said Elizabeth. "I've got a cyberdate with Dude Bob Forty-three."

"So make it for a little later. You can type at Mr. Forty-three anytime."

''No. I hate openings. I gave up art because I hate openings.''

''I thought you gave up art to protest the Vietnam War,'' said Chuck.

''The Vietnam War, the commercialization of Christmas, the subway fare. It was a lot of things.''

''You also gave up the news, but you watched it last night.''

''Last night was an extraordinary circumstance. But I'll tell you what: If you promise not to nag me, I'll think about it.''

''Good, it's all settled, then,'' said Chuck. ''Afterwards we can all go out and grab something to eat.''

''Not me,'' I said. ''Ray is meeting me there and taking me to dinner.''

''Him again?'' said Chuck. ''I thought he was out of the picture. What about Johnny?''

''I don't know, what about him?''

I gave Randolph's door a couple of bangs on my way in. Still no answer. ''Wait'll I get hold of you,'' I said.

Ray had already seen my long black dress. He'd seen my short black dress too, though not for very long because that date had ended early when his beeper beeped him away. For a moment I considered the radical idea of wearing a red dress to a downtown opening, but I'd already decided to wear my red hat and the two reds would look hideous together. I ended up in the short black dress.

I was adjusting the red hat, getting the perfect over-the-eye tilt, when the doorman buzzed and said Chuck was on his way up.

''I just came by for a second,'' he said. ''Elizabeth said she'd go to the opening if I dressed decent. I thought if you loaned me one of those ties Carla's students made, that might be decent enough.''

''Sure. I'm glad Elizabeth decided to go.''

Chuck climbed up on the ladder and pulled down the box of ties.

Seeing the box made me feel rotten all over again. "I can't believe I haven't even gotten around to returning these to Carla's students. It's bad enough I can't find her killer. You'd think I could at least get it together to return a few ties."

Chuck held one up to his neck and looked in the mirror. "I like this one. It'll work with jeans."

"It's yours," I said.

Chuck looked at the piece of paper safety-pinned to the back of the tie. "What's this?"

"Nothing. You can give it to me," I said. "It's the name of the student who made the tie and the grade that they received."

Chuck opened the safety pin. "Will you get a load of this," he said.

"What?"

"This here's a B-plus tie. Walker Millard's B-plus tie."

I grabbed the paper out of Chuck's hand. "Let me see that." Sure enough, it said Walker Millard.

"Weird, huh," said Chuck.

"In a way, it makes a lot of sense," I said. "It explains how Carla got the Millard job in the first place. If Walker was one of her students, naturally he'd think of her to do his daughter's wedding dress."

"Well, if you want, you can return Walker Millard's tie tonight after I'm done with it. Oh, and before I forget, Johnny came by the shop looking for you. Elizabeth and I talked him into going to the opening tonight too."

"Goddammit, Chuck. You knew Ray was going to be there."

"You know, Brenda, it completely slipped my mind."

35

I smelled at least fifteen different designer perfumes clashing and competing for air space in the jam-packed lobby. Dozens of thin, trendy, black-clad people with sucked-in cheeks and lots of attitude waited for the single creaky elevator to arrive. There were several art galleries in the building, and it felt like every single one of them was having an opening.

One look at the crowd and Margo made a beeline for the staircase. "Let's hoof it," she said. "That old elevator gets stuck half the time anyway."

Even the stairs were crowded as people went from floor to floor, checking out all the openings. The Millard Gallery was on the sixth floor. A couple of hundred people milled about sipping jug wine from plastic cups. Every so often, a laugh cut through the background murmur of conversation.

Margo's eyes darted from one fashionably dressed person to another. Everyone was in black. If there was any constant in New York, anything at all to depend on, it was that year after year, decade after decade, black was in, the epitome of the in. This was especially true below Fourteenth Street. In other parts of the country, people wear all sorts of different colors, but everyone looks like everyone else. In New York, everyone wears black, yet no one looks like anyone else.

The longer Margo looked, the bigger her smile. There

were short black full dresses, long black tight dresses, tight short black dresses, black ties worn with black T-shirts, black jackets, black jeans, black tights, black socks, skin-tight black stretch pants, and black pants wide enough for two people to climb into and still have room to jitterbug.

Margo held out her arms as if to embrace the whole roomful of people. "Look at this, Brenda. It's a virtual sea of black apparel. It's going to be a fabulous season for Einstein's Revenge. I've ordered the blackest blacks. Everything is right on target. Absolute dead center. It's going to be my best year yet. I'm positively giddy. I think I'll go head in the direction of the bar. Want anything?"

"No thanks."

I inched my way slowly through the crowd, looking for Ray while keeping my eye out for the Millards. I spotted Walker Millard in the back near the offices, leaning up against a column with his arms folded. He surveyed the whole room, paying special attention to the females. Simone Millard, dressed in layers of black chiffon, floated through the crowd, stopping briefly here and there to brush cheeks and mingle with anyone who mattered. I kept away from her. I hadn't seen her since that day in Carla's apartment when she and Ashley had demanded their deposit back.

Gil Davison held court in the center of the room. He had on paint-splattered overalls that looked like he'd splattered them specially for the occasion. A gaggle of art groupies surrounded him and stared trancelike, captivated by his bullspiel. I moved a little closer so I could hear him. "These eight works," he said, gesturing grandly at the art, "are my finest achievement to date, the culmination of years of total immersion into . . ."

I drifted by Gil and his admirers and did something that almost never happens at openings—I actually looked at the art. I didn't glance at it. I didn't pretend to look at it. I studied it carefully and concluded that Gil's new work was an even bigger joke than his old work. Priced about the same as a two-bedroom condo in a decent part of town, three of the eight large assemblages had red dots by their names to show they'd already been sold. Curious, I found the price list. Make that two bedrooms on a high floor with a view and a fireplace.

I picked up on a conversation behind me. "... juxtaposition and subsequent linking of diverse images, the artist has forged a viable subtext ..." I turned around and looked to see if maybe the speaker was joking. But no, he had a straight face.

It had all been done before. It had all been done better before.

I took note of another voice behind me. "Don't you just love Gil's new work?" I turned around to say that I thought it stank, and found myself looking straight at the artist's wife-to-be, Ashley Millard. She also wore black. "Oh, it's you," she said, not sounding any too pleased to see me. Maybe I should have returned their deposit. She gave me a searing look of contempt, then hurried off to greet a new batch of potential buyers who had just pried themselves out of the elevator.

"What's her problem?" asked Chuck.

"Boy, am I glad to see you," I said. "That was Ashley Millard. As to her problem, I don't know. I guess she'd rather I weren't here. I'm not sure why. There's got to be more bugging her than a two-thousand-dollar deposit. Maybe she's still pissed at Carla for getting killed and ruining her wedding, which would imply that she did want to marry Gil Davison after all, which would in turn, mean, that someone else wanted to ruin her wedding. I believed that for a while too, until I decided that motive was wrong. Actually I'm not sure what I know anymore."

"You want to run through that again?" asked Chuck.

"Nope. How do you like the opening?"

"Party's okay. The art sucks."

"Where's Elizabeth?"

"She's getting drinks. Here she comes now."

Elizabeth squeezed through the crowd holding two glasses of wine over her head. She handed one to Chuck.

"Just what I expected," she said. "Hype here, hype there, hype everywhere I go. But, you know, the weird thing is, I'm kind of enjoying myself. It makes me remember the reasons I gave all this up. Plus I can tell Dude Bob Forty-three all about the sophisticated opening I attended."

"So where's Ray, anyway?" asked Chuck. "I can't wait to meet the man who says he can expose the hacker. The man who makes your heart flutter."

"Please, Chuck, when you meet him, don't embarrass me."

"You know I'd never embarrass you. In case you care, your 'just good friend' Johnny is over by the bar talking to Margo."

I did care; I wanted to avoid him. I didn't want him to see me with Ray. But things didn't work out that way. Johnny, being lots taller than me, saw Ray before I did and showed him where I was. So, with Johnny looking on, I introduced Ray to Chuck and Elizabeth and Margo and then stood there embarrassed until enough time had passed and enough small talk had been exchanged for me to lead Ray off to the side.

"I'm starved," I said. "Let's get out of here."

"Sure," said Ray.

With a quick wave to the gang we left, using the same staircase Margo and I had used on our way in. We'd gone about two flights down when I heard Elizabeth call my name.

"Brenda, wait. You won't believe who's here."

I shouted up the stairs, "Who?"

"Randolph."

I grabbed Ray's hand and ran back up the stairs to where Elizabeth stood.

"Where? Just point that bastard out to me."

"He was arguing with a woman," said Elizabeth.

"Funny," I said, "how that doesn't surprise me."

"There she is now." Elizabeth pointed at the woman who'd been arguing with Randolph.

I was amazed. "Don't you know who that is?"

"No."

"That's Simone Millard."

Unfortunately, Randolph was long gone.

Some milliners carefully, painstakingly plan out their new designs. They make dozens of sketches on paper, then draft a perfect pattern and try it out first in muslin or cheap felt before committing themselves to the final material. I can't work that way. I commit to the material early on. I rarely have anything more than a half-baked idea before I dive in and start hacking away. It keeps the design spontaneous. It also makes for a scary time in the process when I get completely confused, thinking the design has failed and that I've destroyed the fabric. When things get to that stage, in total desperation, I shake things up. To take a fresh look at the problem, I rip the hat or try it on backward or upside down. I look at the design as pure form, not as a hat. Then, a tiny change, a slight tilt of the brim, the tightening of a bow, and in one exhilarating moment everything clicks into place and I have a new hat design.

That's the only way I know to describe how I felt when Elizabeth pointed to Simone Millard. All my confused and misguided theories evaporated, and I knew. I knew who killed Carla and I knew why. And I knew it had nothing to do with ruining Ashley's wedding or the Lady in Pink or Snake Mezuna's mother's pearls.

36

I had to act quickly, before the opening ended and everyone got kicked out of the gallery. I grabbed Johnny and sent Ray and Elizabeth off to find Margo and Chuck.

"What's the matter?" asked Johnny. "You look . . ."

I interrupted. "Are we still on Turner and McKinley's good side?"

"Best friends. We not only gave them Rita Renaldo tickets, but Snake Mezuna as well. That made the whole precinct look good. Plus they still feel bad about botching the investigation of Carla's murder. They're not really such bad guys."

"Well, they've got a chance to make amends now. Call and tell them to get down here fast."

"Why? What's going on?"

"No time to explain."

"I'll have to tell them something."

"Tell them to dress nice. It's a trendy crowd."

The next half hour seemed to take forever. Every cell in my body was on red alert. Everyone seemed concerned that I was acting weird, but I was too nervous to explain.

"Just stick around," I said. "You'll see soon enough."

It wasn't soon enough for me. I paced. I hyperventilated. I worried that the cops wouldn't show. Finally, the elevator doors banged open and out stepped Turner and McKinley, in nicely fitting custom-made suits. Except for the way they scoped out the room, they didn't look like cops at all.

Turner spoke first. "What's this all about?"

I didn't want to beat around the bush. I pointed across the room. "Arrest that woman."

"Just for the hell of it?" asked McKinley.

"No," I said. "Arrest her for the murder of Carla Haley."

"I'm afraid it's not that easy," said Turner. "We can't arrest someone just on your say-so. What kind of proof do you have? What kind of evidence?"

I had a lot of explaining to do and no time to do it. I figured Turner and McKinley weren't going to give me too many chances to get this right, Rita Renaldo tickets or not.

Ever since Carla had been murdered, I'd done a lot of things that were quite out of character for me. I'd lied, sanctioned a felonious electronic break-in, tackled a smuggler with my bare hands, and knocked out a hitman with a hat block. Again I was up against a wall. Again, out of sheer desperation, I had to do something I wouldn't normally do.

What I did was so disgusting and so totally tacky that if not for Chuck and Elizabeth and Margo and Johnny and Ray and Turner and McKinley watching, I never would have believed it was me. First, with apologies to Elizabeth, I loosened Chuck's tie and pulled it off over his head. Then I took out my compact and freshened my lipstick. Then, when the time was right, I walked across the gallery right up to Walker Millard, planted a big kiss on his left cheek, slipped the tie over his head, tightened it, and said, "You left this at my place, dear," which I'm proud to say, wasn't a lie, even if it was a bit misleading. Of course I made sure Simone was watching and within earshot because she was the one I wanted to mislead.

It worked. With layers of black chiffon rippling behind her, Simone marched over and slapped Walker on the right cheek. Hard. "Bastard."

She said it loud enough to attract the attention of everyone in the gallery. Conversations stopped in midsentence.

Everyone pushed and shoved trying to get closer to the action, except Ashley, who shrank away from the crowd and endured the indignity of hearing her parents air their dirty laundry in public by staring down at her expensive patent leather pumps.

Rubbing his slapped cheek, a very confused and surprised Walker Millard looked at me, then at Simone, then at the tie, then back at me. "Who are you? Where did you get this tie?"

Simpering flirtatiously I said, "Don't you remember? You left it at my place."

"Impossible. I don't even know who you are. I left that tie at Carla Haley's."

"Aha!" said Simone. "So, finally you admit to your Tuesday-night tryst with that Carla Haley whore. You play me for a fool, but I've known about that for a long time." She lunged at his neck.

Walker pushed her hands away. "Affair? You've got to be kidding." Walker Millard laughed. First a nervous titter, then finally an all-out guffaw.

Simone raged. "How can you laugh? Do you really get such a kick out of humiliating me? That's exactly what your whore did when . . ."

Simone didn't finish her thought. I can hardly blame her, with everyone in the gallery listening to every word. I looked around and made sure Turner and McKinley were close by. They were not only close by but they were moving closer, taking big strides toward us, hands reaching for their guns.

"When what, Simone?" I said. "Go ahead and finish your sentence, Simone. Tell your husband how you went to Carla Haley's apartment that morning. Tell him how you confronted Carla, accused her of having an affair with your husband. You say she laughed? Was she still laughing when you pointed your gun at her? Still laughing when you pulled the trigger? Still laughing when she died on top of your daughter's wedding dress?"

Walker Millard wasn't laughing anymore. "My god,

Simone. I was not having an affair with Carla Haley. Carla Haley was teaching me how to sew. You killed my sewing instructor.''

I don't remember much about what happened next. It must have been pretty confusing because everyone remembered something different. Elizabeth remembered the part where Simone slapped Walker again, leaving a bright red mark on his other cheek. Chuck remembered the look on Gil Davison's face when he realized he was no longer the center of attention and maybe never would be again, since the only gallery that would show his stuff seemed to be going to hell in a handbasket. Margo remembered Simone's struggle with McKinley and that her dress ripped and all of Soho found out that she wore mismatched underwear. Johnny remembered seeing Walker Millard try to sneak out the back and how he forcefully detained him with another of those Tod Trueman holds. Ray remembered how Ashley burst into tears and no one paid any attention.

All I remember was the look on Simone's face. That was when I knew that finally, after all this time, I'd hit the nail right smack on its ugly head.

Johnny talked Turner and McKinley into letting him come along as an observer to learn more about the post-arrest process. Margo went to Leo D's to meet her sleazy boyfriend, Marc, and start spreading the gossip. Ray and I decided we should do dinner some other time, but Elizabeth invited Chuck and Ray and me back to her apartment to sample her latest batch of cookie experiments.

Ray and I walked along, not saying much of anything. The night was cool enough that I shivered and Ray put his jacket over my shoulders.

Chuck and Elizabeth, following close behind, chattered the whole way home about men and women and sewing.

"Lots of men sew," said Elizabeth.

"Not any men that I know," said Chuck. "Men that I know play guitars or take apart computers."

"I don't care what you say," said Elizabeth. "I know it for a fact. One of my ex-husbands made his own shirts."

"You're kidding."

"Nope. He was damned good with a needle and thread."

"If men really do sew like you say, they try awfully hard to keep it a secret," said Chuck.

"How sad," said Elizabeth. "If Walker Millard hadn't been ashamed of taking sewing lessons, if he'd only told Simone what he was really doing on Tuesday nights, Carla would be alive today."

I was glad it was dark. I was glad Ray wasn't talkative. I didn't want anyone to see me cry.

Chuck bit into the lumpy cookie. "Cool. It tastes like pesto."

"They're chocolate chip basil," said Elizabeth. "Do you like them?"

"Yum," said Ray.

"Interesting," I said.

"I can't taste the chocolate," said Chuck.

"It's very subtle," said Elizabeth.

We all chewed on cookies for a few minutes, without a word being said. Finally Chuck broke the silence.

"Brenda, you're not going to keep us in suspense forever, are you? How'd you know it was Simone?"

I really didn't want to go into it, but I knew they'd never let it rest. I took a deep breath, sat back in my chair, and began. "Now that I do know, I see that I should have known a lot sooner. My biggest mistake was believing Randolph when he said he hadn't seen or heard anything the morning Carla was killed. He said he'd been listening to a Whitney Houston tape cranked up loud through headphones. A really lame story, but I went for it. Everything started to fall into place when Ellen Suttlan told me Randolph had seen her that morning. I knew he must have seen the murderer and must have lied about it. Why would he lie about it? Blackmail. That's how he could afford that new two-bedroom apartment on the Upper East Side.

"Then there was the tie. When Chuck saw Walker Millard's name pinned to the tie, I knew Walker had been one of Carla's students. So, you've got nosy Randolph watching everything all the time, and Walker Millard visiting Carla every Tuesday night for months, and a detective hired by Simone Millard to follow Walker Millard everywhere he went. So the detective reports to Simone that her husband sees Carla for a couple of hours every Tuesday; Simone confronts Carla and kills her. Randolph hears the shot and sees Simone leaving. She's enough of a celebrity that he recognizes her, sees an opportunity, and blackmails her. When Elizabeth told me she'd seen Randolph and Simone arguing at the opening, I knew."

"What about Ellen Suttlan, the Lady in Pink, or whoever she is?" asked Elizabeth.

"All she ever wanted were the pearls. Like she said, she found Carla dead, cut as many of the pearls off the dress as she could, and got the hell out of there. She was busy robbing me when Elizabeth and Jackhammer discovered Carla's body."

Much later, after we'd finished our cookies, after Ray had walked me across the hall and kissed me good night on my doorstep, when it was just Jackhammer and me, I finally let loose with the tears. It started with a single tear that rolled slowly down my cheek. By the time it reached my chin I couldn't hold back. I sobbed, I keened, I wailed. Just as it seemed I'd never stop, I did.

I think the worst part of all was that Carla's death had been trivialized. She'd been killed for a stupid reason, a misunderstanding, all because a man was afraid to admit he sewed.

Maybe that wasn't the worst part. Maybe the worst part was that solving the murder didn't bring Carla back.

Jackhammer and I stayed up most of the night. I emptied out Carla's closets and drawers, put all her things in the center of the room. Little by little I dragged my things out of the plastic garbage bags and put them into Carla's closets and drawers. Then I put Carla's things into the bags. When there was nothing left but the floppy-brimmed straw hat I'd made for her, I looked at it for a long time. Then finally, I dropped the hat in the bag, closed it up, and shoved it into the corner.

37

Early the next morning Johnny called. His call didn't wake me up because I hadn't been able to sleep.

"Turner and McKinley located Randolph and brought him in. He tried to lie and squirm his way out, but, with a little good cop–bad cop action, they managed to persuade him to come clean. He confirms everything you suspected."

"Then they've got a good case against Simone."

"Yes, but that's not all," said Johnny. "It gets even better. When we searched Simone's apartment we found a gun that matches the caliber of the gun used to kill Carla. It's too soon for the test results, but you and I both know, even Turner and McKinley know, that it'll turn out to be the murder weapon. Simone will be going to prison for a long time."

"That's good."

"You must feel great now that this is all over."

"Yeah, I guess so," I said, and hung up.

I didn't feel great and I didn't know if I'd ever feel great again. At a loss for what to do, I put a couple of graham crackers in my pocket and walked Jackhammer over toward the Hudson River. I sat down on a stoop in front of an abandoned building on West Street. While Jackhammer rolled around on a dusty patch of ground, kicked up his feet, and had a real fun time, I stared out over the water at

New Jersey and munched on graham crackers.

When I got home I called Carla's sister Bernice in South Carolina.

"Don't tell me you're calling about some problem with that apartment," she said, "because if you are, you can forget it. I washed my hands of that mess."

"No, Bernice, it's nothing like that. I just thought you'd like to know that the cops arrested Carla's killer. It was all a mistake. . . ."

"Nothing to do with drugs or prostitution?"

"No nothing like that."

Bernice sighed. "Thank goodness. Now Carla can rest."

Elizabeth pounded on my door. "Guess what? I just got the best news in the whole wide world."

"Yeah, what's that?" It was going to take a lot to cheer me up.

"Jackhammer's owner called to tell me he's getting married."

"So, congratulations. What's the big deal? If his bride wants a Brenda Midnight wedding veil the answer is no, absolutely not."

"The good news is that his bride's got asthma," said Elizabeth.

"That sounds like great news."

"She's allergic to everything under the sun."

"The news just keeps getting better. What are you driving at, Elizabeth?"

"She's allergic to everything under the sun, including dogs. That means she's allergic to Jackhammer. That means if you want the little guy, he's yours."

"You're right, Elizabeth. That is the best news in the whole world." I jumped up and down. I hugged Elizabeth. I hugged Jackhammer. I felt good.

Over the next several weeks I made dozens of hats for Margo, each one slightly different. She sold them as fast as I could make them. Each time I brought her more she handed me a big check and pleaded with me to do a guest appearance at Einstein's Revenge with Johnny. I didn't want to and Johnny was too busy being Tod Trueman. Margo told me that the Millard Gallery had closed, Walker had moved to California, and Ashley was suing someone over something and had broken her engagement to Gil Davison. Or was it Gil who broke it off? Either way, Gil was an artist without a gallery. .

There were weeks that I made more money selling hats than Chuck and Elizabeth made with their computers. They were still at Midnight Millinery because Chuck convinced me that, statistically speaking, a one-month trial was bogus, so I extended their trial stay to three months.

One week there was a lot of excitement because after Dude Bob 43 saw the nationally broadcast news story of the capture of Snake Mezuna, he came to New York to meet Elizabeth face-to-face. He's not a cyberpervert at all. He's a handsome soft-eyed gentleman in a tweed jacket. It was love at first sight until one night, over a very romantic dinner at a charming French restaurant, Elizabeth told Dude Bob 43 that she'd given up art in the mid-sixties to protest the Vietnam War. Dude Bob 43 had done three tours of Vietnam and was damned proud of it. He called her a peacenik and stormed out of the restaurant. She called him a fascist warmonger and ran out after him. They ended up falling into each other's arms. Now she calls him her little hawk, and he calls her his little dove. They continue their romance and the Vietnam debate online.

As far as romantic dinners go, Ray and I finally got around to scheduling ours. He'd been out of town for a while on a new assignment he couldn't tell me about, and I'd been real busy with the hats, so I hadn't seen nearly as much of him as I'd have liked. In fact, I hadn't seen him at all, although we spoke on the phone every day or so. But the day finally came, the reservations were made, and I was excited.

Jackhammer and I got to Midnight Millinery bright and early.

"You sure look chipper today," said Chuck. "What gives?"

"Date with Ray. We're finally having our long-delayed romantic dinner."

"Oh." Chuck still hadn't warmed to the idea of Ray.

"Take my advice and don't bring up politics," said Elizabeth.

For the next few hours I focused totally on the hats. When I finished, Chuck was gone.

"Where's Chuck?"

"He had to go help a friend move or something," said Elizabeth.

"Will you be okay by yourself? I'd like to get out of here. I want to take a little extra time to get ready for Ray."

"You go right ahead. I'll be fine."

Ray took me to a wonderful, romantic, intimate restaurant, tucked away on an improbable deserted street in Tribeca. Everything about it was perfect, the decor, the food, the service, the wine, so when Ray asked me back to his apartment for coffee afterward, I quickly agreed. A perfect end to a perfect evening.

We sat close to each other in the cab and looked out the window at the twinkling lights of the city. "I can't wait for you to see my place," Ray said. "I've been fixing it up. I got something today. . . . Well, you'll see for yourself soon enough."

He lived in a newly renovated six-story building off Seventh Avenue in Chelsea. As we passed through the sparkling clean lobby, I caught our reflection in a beveled mirror. I thought we looked good together. Carla would have called us a cute couple.

He unlocked the door and opened it with a flourish, standing back so I could go in first. While I stood in the foyer he switched on the overhead light. There, right smack in the middle of his sparsely furnished living room was Johnny's orange-and-yellow shag rug.

I gasped.

"Like it?" he asked. "Your friend Chuck called today and mentioned that a friend of his was going to throw this rug out. He'd remembered my mentioning that I didn't have much furniture and asked me if I wanted it. I think it's just what the room needed to give it a homey touch. What do you think?"

What I thought was that I had to get out of there.

As I reached for the phone to call Chuck and tell him what a lowdown creep I thought he was, it rang. I let the answering machine pick up.

"Brenda, this is Robin of Robin's Early Bird Temps. I apologize for calling you so late at night, but a fabulous job just came in for tomorrow. It's for the partner of another big law firm. Of course, as soon as they mentioned law I thought of you."

I picked up the phone before she hung up. "Sorry, Robin. I'm back in the millinery business. Full-time."

Murder Is on the Menu at the Hillside Manor Inn

Bed-and-Breakfast Mysteries by
MARY DAHEIM
featuring Judith McMonigle

BANTAM OF THE OPERA
76934-4/ $5.99 US/ $7.99 Can

JUST DESSERTS
76295-1/ $5.99 US/ $7.99 Can

FOWL PREY
76296-X/ $5.50 US/ $7.50 Can

HOLY TERRORS
76297-8/ $5.99 US/ $7.99 Can

DUNE TO DEATH
76933-6/ $5.99 US/ $7.99 Can

A FIT OF TEMPERA
77490-9/ $5.99 US/ $7.99 Can

MAJOR VICES
77491-7/ $5.99 US/ $7.99 Can

MURDER, MY SUITE
77877-7/ $5.99 US/ $7.99 Can

AUNTIE MAYHEM
77878-5/ $5.50 US/ $7.50 Can

NUTTY AS A FRUITCAKE
77879-3/ $5.99 US/ $7.99 Can

SEPTEMBER MOURN
78518-8/ $5.99 US/ $7.99 Can

Buy these books at your local bookstore or use this coupon for ordering:

Mail to: Avon Books, Dept BP, Box 767, Rte 2, Dresden, TN 38225   G
Please send me the book(s) I have checked above.
❏ My check or money order—no cash or CODs please—for $_____ is enclosed (please
add $1.50 per order to cover postage and handling—Canadian residents add 7% GST). U.S.
residents make checks payable to Avon Books; Canada residents make checks payable to
Hearst Book Group of Canada.
❏ Charge my VISA/MC Acct#_____ Exp Date_____
Minimum credit card order is two books or $7.50 (please add postage and handling
charge of $1.50 per order—Canadian residents add 7% GST). For faster service, call
1-800-762-0779. Prices and numbers are subject to change without notice. Please allow six to
eight weeks for delivery.
Name_____
Address_____
City_____ State/Zip_____
Telephone No._____   DAH 0597

JILL CHURCHILL

"JANE JEFFREY IS IRRESISTIBLE!"
Alfred Hitchcock's Mystery Magazine

Delightful Mysteries Featuring
Suburban Mom Jane Jeffry

GRIME AND PUNISHMENT
76400-8/$5.99 US/$7.99 CAN

A FAREWELL TO YARNS
76399-0/$5.99 US/$7.99 CAN

A QUICHE BEFORE DYING
76932-8/$5.50 US/$7.50 CAN

THE CLASS MENAGERIE
77380-5/$5.99 US/$7.99 CAN

A KNIFE TO REMEMBER
77381-3/$5.99 US/$7.99 CAN

FROM HERE TO PATERNITY
77715-0/$5.99 US/$7.99 CAN

SILENCE OF THE HAMS
77716-9/$5.99 US/$7.99 CAN

Buy these books at your local bookstore or use this coupon for ordering:

Mail to: Avon Books, Dept BP, Box 767, Rte 2, Dresden, TN 38225   F
Please send me the book(s) I have checked above.
❏ My check or money order—no cash or CODs please—for $_____is enclosed (please
add $1.50 per order to cover postage and handling—Canadian residents add 7% GST).
❏ Charge my VISA/MC Acct#_____Exp Date_____
Minimum credit card order is two books or $7.50 (please add postage and handling
charge of $1.50 per order—Canadian residents add 7% GST). For faster service, call
1-800-762-0779. Prices and numbers are subject to change without notice. Please allow six to
eight weeks for delivery.

Name_____
Address_____
City_____State/Zip_____
Telephone No._____   CHU 1196